DUMPED,
Act🗑ALLY

ALSO BY NICK SPALDING

Dry Hard

Checking Out

Mad Love

Bricking It

Fat Chance

Buzzing Easter Bunnies

Blue Christmas Balls

Love . . . Series

Love . . . From Both Sides

Love . . . And Sleepless Nights

Love . . . Under Different Skies

Love . . . Among the Stars

Life . . . Series

Life . . . On a High

Life . . . With No Breaks

Cornerstone Series

The Cornerstone

Wordsmith

NICK SPALDING

DUMPED, ACTUALLY

LAKE UNION
PUBLISHING

Published by Lake Union Publishing, Seattle

www.apub.com

Amazon, the Amazon logo, and Lake Union Publishing are trademarks of Amazon.com, Inc., or its affiliates.

ISBN-13: 9781542041324
ISBN-10: 1542041325

Cover design by Ghost Design

Printed in the United States of America

I'd like to dedicate this book to all of the women who have ever dumped me. You made me a better person, a better husband and a better writer.

. . . ha!

CHAPTERS

CHAPTER ONE

MAN PROPOSES, WOMAN DISPOSES

'Will you marry me?'

I look up into Samantha's eyes, and see tears of sublime happiness forming in them.

Behind us, the jazz band has stopped playing, on cue, awaiting her answer. The crowd that have formed around us hold their breath, expectant looks writ large across their faces.

The sun bathes the entire plaza in its warm and comforting light, and there's a happy breeze teasing Samantha's blonde hair, which frames the smile that she has on her face exquisitely. It's like something out of the best romantic comedy you've ever seen – only it's real and it's happening to *me*.

'Yes, Ollie,' she says breathlessly. 'Of course I'll marry you!'

A cheer goes up from the crowd, the band start to play the wedding march and I embrace my new fiancée, spinning her around, as we both laugh and cry with the joy that fills our hearts.

It's the perfect moment, in the perfect day.

I couldn't be happier.

Roll credits.

***

'Lauren, don't wipe bogies on that man's leg.'

My glorious daydream is instantly shattered as I look down to see a pudgy finger covered in green-and-brown jelly coming ever closer to my jeans.

With a mild cry of revulsion, I step back out of range of the snot-covered digit.

'Ow! Ollie!' Samantha exclaims from beside me in the queue. 'You stepped on my foot!'

'Sorry, sweetheart!' I cry, giving the bogey-wielding child a dark look.

The mother, well aware of the horror her offspring is about to inflict on my brand-new skinny jeans, pulls Lauren away, with an apologetic expression on her face.

Luckily for all concerned, the queue starts to move forward again, and Lauren and her snotty finger are taken well out of my personal space. I pity the poor person that Lauren eventually attaches that slimy mess to. It looks like the kind of thing that will take several hot washes to get out, and possibly several bars of anti-bacterial soap if it gets near the skin.

Speaking of hot – the sweat running down my face is testament to the unseasonable weather we're currently experiencing in the long queue for entry into Thorn Manor, the country's newest and most exciting theme park.

I gaze again at my girlfriend, who seems to have got over my moment of clumsiness and looks eager and excited about the day ahead.

Samantha's love of theme parks is absolutely adorable. We've spent many long and happy days visiting the best of the bunch around the UK, trying out the rides, eating far too much junk food and probably spending way too long in queues like this one.

This is Thorn Manor's opening day, and it is *gleaming* with corporate freshness. Like a brand-new toy still in its box, desperate to be played with for the first time.

What better way to celebrate Samantha's twenty-ninth birthday than a day spent here?

And what better place could there be for me to get down on bended knee and ask her to marry me?

It's just *perfect*.

When I managed to score tickets to Thorn Manor's opening day, I knew that it was just too good an opportunity to pass up. The serendipity of it opening on Samantha's birthday was the kind of thing that could make you believe that there actually was a God, and that He had an innate sense of good timing.

I couldn't have scripted it better if I'd tried.

It took me weeks to work out the best way to propose, and several more weeks to get everything in place for it. The management of the theme park were more than happy to help out, I'm pleased to say. They leapt at the chance to have a marriage proposal happen on their grand opening. The positive PR will be magnificent for them.

Letting Samantha and me be among the first to try out their new rollercoaster, 'The Blitzer', was extremely kind of them as well. As was allowing the band I've hired to be waiting for us at the end of the ride, after we get off it.

It's all been timed down to the minute.

The Blitzer's first loop around the track will happen at midday. It will slow to a halt in front of the ride's broad plaza three minutes later. When Samantha and I get off the coaster, the band will start to play everybody's favourite piano power ballad from a few years ago, 'All of Me', which is Samantha's absolute favourite.

Then I will take the 24-carat-gold diamond ring from the top pocket of the waistcoat the trumpet player is wearing and get down on one knee to ask Samantha to be my wife.

It will be wonderful.

It will be epic.

It will be *perfect*.

It had better be, anyway – the amount of money and time I've spent arranging all of this would make you sick. My credit card bill and the bags under my eyes are both gigantic, and unlikely to fade any time soon.

Never mind, it'll all be worth it once I hear her say yes!

And I am absolutely positive she *will* say yes. We've been together long enough that I know how she feels about me. After all this time, I know Samantha very well, and I'm sure that she's as ready to take this next step in our relationship as I am. Our love for one another is very strong. She is most definitely 'the one'. I have no doubt about it whatsoever.

'Bloody hell, it's *boiling*,' Samantha says with a gasp, pulling her vest top away from her midriff.

'Don't worry, sweetheart,' I tell her, 'we'll be in soon. We're nearly at the front of the queue.'

'God, I hope so. I could really do with a drink.'

I give her a smile. 'The first thing we'll do is go and find the nearest concession stand, and I'll buy you a raspberry smoothie.'

That's Samantha's favourite. She loves them.

She gives me a big smile back. 'Thanks, Ollie. You're too good to me.'

'Hey . . . it's your birthday!' I reply – as if that really makes any difference. I'd do anything for Samantha, whatever the day. That's how much I adore her.

She laughs and lightly touches the Pandora necklace I gave to her earlier this morning, before we set off for our day out. It was slightly more expensive than the jazz band, but not by much.

The Light Touch Quartet are one of the most popular touring contemporary jazz acts out there, and getting them here today has been quite the effort. Their agent, an extremely awkward individual called Barret Bartholomew – who I'm sure was drunk every time I spoke to him – kept trying to raise their fee. I know damn well that he ended up rinsing me out like a wet rag, but what choice did I have? You only get to propose marriage once, and I wasn't going to skimp on the details. Especially not on the soundtrack.

The Light Touch Quartet should be hidden away somewhere in Thorn Manor's shiny recesses, ready to come out and play their part just after the clock strikes twelve. I've had a text message from Amy, the Thorn Manor PR manager, to tell me they're in place, so all is going according to plan.

My heart rate speeds up a little as I again begin to contemplate the events that are about to unfold. It's ten minutes past ten now, so in just two hours I will be engaged to the most wonderful woman in the world. I can't believe my luck.

'Lauren! Don't be so disgusting!'

I look down to see Lauren the bogey girl wiping her finger across my kneecap.

'Eurgh!' I cry with revulsion as she leaves a smear of glistening nose production on my jeans.

'I'm so sorry!' the mother says, producing a packet of baby wipes from her purse. 'Let me get that off for you.' She thrusts her daughter out of the way and bends down to attack my kneecap with the baby wipe. All this does is make my knee a bit damp and smear the bogey around a bit more, but I thank her for her efforts anyway.

'It really is very kind of you to try to get it off,' I tell her, attempting to sound entirely unbothered. Inside, though, I could almost scream. I do *not* want to ask Samantha to marry me with a snot-covered knee. It's not something that is part of my perfect little daydream, God damn it. At no point in the past few weeks and months have I dreamed of getting engaged with the excavations of a six-year-old's olfactory orifice upon my person!

'That's gross,' Samantha points out as Lauren is once again dragged far away by her mother. 'What a horrible little shit.'

I shrug my shoulders and smile. 'Ah, these things happen,' I tell her, repressing my frustration for all I'm worth. This is Samantha's special day – in more ways than one – and I don't want it ruined by bogies. She doesn't need to see how I'm feeling. Better to just pretend it doesn't bother me in the slightest.

Samantha gives me a strange little look. 'You shouldn't let people get away with that kind of crap, Ollie,' she says as we finally get to the front of the queue, and the ticket kiosk.

I shrug again. 'Why let these silly little things get to you?' I wrap an arm around her shoulders. 'Come on, we're nearly in. Let's forget about Lauren and her snotty finger. We're here to have a great time!'

Samantha smiles, but there's an incredulous look on her face that makes me wince a little, for reasons I'm not too sure about, to be honest.

But never mind . . .

Here we are, in Thorn Manor!

The girl in the kiosk waves us through when I show her our pre-booked tickets, and we walk into a broad and gleaming forecourt, rammed full of excited and enthusiastic members of the public, all keen to try out the plethora of new rides and attractions on offer.

Samantha skips happily up to a large map in the dead centre of the forecourt. 'What shall we do first, Ollie?! There's Mount Terror, that looks good . . . Or Star Warriors – that's the light-gun game I told you about. Ooh! What about Mega Rapids? That'd cool us down!'

I smile indulgently. I love seeing her this happy. 'We'll go wherever you want, darling,' I tell her, sliding one arm around her waist. I then look down at my smeared jean leg. 'Just let me go to a toilet first to get this off, eh?'

Samantha nods and laughs. I don't think I've seen her this giddy in a long time. 'Yeah, yeah, that's cool. You go do that, and I'll get us both a drink.'

'Great.'

We make our way through the milling crowd to a concession stand on the left-hand side of the expansive forecourt. Behind this building are the toilets, so I hand over ten pounds to Samantha, and ask her to get me a Diet Coke, before making my way into the toilet to try to remove little Lauren's nose production from my jeans.

It's while I'm doing this in front of one of the shiny new sinks that my phone goes off. I answer and it's Amy, the park's PR manager.

'Hi Ollie! Just wanted to call to let you know everything is in place for later, as we planned. I've got the band holed up at the back of the visitor's centre, just by The Blitzer.'

'Thanks, Amy! Has the trumpeter got the ring in his waistcoat, like I asked?'

'Er . . . yes, kind of.'

'Kind of?' My heart skips a beat. Everything *has* to be perfect today. Nothing must go wrong!

'Yeah. It's in his pocket, but I wouldn't really call it a waistcoat.'

'What do you mean?'

'It just looks a little too small to be a waistcoat, and the way it connects to his—'

The door to the toilet bangs open suddenly, and a large, irate, red-faced father bursts through it, accompanied by two small, screaming boys.

I have to shout down the phone now to be heard over their cater-wauling. 'Just tell me he's got the ring, Amy!'

'Yes, yes! He's got it. Horst seems like a very nice man. All of the band do. I'm sure everything will go well!'

'Great!'

'It's certainly going to be quite the show when they start up! Everyone will notice!'

'I'm sure they will!'

The irate father is now pushing both boys into a cubicle, ordering them to take a piss as quickly as possible, so they can get to Minecart Mayhem before the queue gets too big.

'I never would have thought somebody like Samantha would like that kind of music!' Amy continues.

'Yes, it's not really the kind of music you'd expect someone as young as her to like, but she's a very special lady!' I reply, moving myself away from the screaming boys.

'Yeah . . . she must be. Well, I guess I'll see you after the show's over, Ollie. Good luck!'

'Thanks, Amy. Speak to you later.'

I pocket the phone with relief and look down at my now slightly damp – but also clean – kneecap. It'll dry out in no time in the heat.

Time to get back out there and have some fun!

I exit the toilet, leaving the irate father to bully the urine out of his sons, and rejoin Samantha, who hands me a large Diet Coke, of which I gratefully take a swig.

'Thanks for bringing me here today, Ollie,' she says with a smile.

'My absolute pleasure, sweetheart. This is your birthday, and I want it to be a special day for you.'

'Thanks! Shall we go get started then? I want to get at least three rides in before we hit The Blitzer at midday!'

'No problem!'

We take off in the direction of Mount Terror, weaving our way through a load more irate fathers and mothers as we do so. There's a small part of me that wants exactly what they've got, though – small children to share this kind of experience with. Maybe after Samantha and I are married that could be the next thing on the list. I grew up with parents who loved each other as much as Samantha and I do, and I can't wait to give my own child the same upbringing I had. I want to be the kind of parent who smothers their child with love – just like Mum and Dad did for me.

This thought puts a large and contented smile on my face as we join the line for Mount Terror.

As we do, I look at my watch again, which says half past ten.

Not long now, Ollie . . . Not long now!

But before I get the chance to pop the question, it's time to experience a few hair-raising rides at this brand-new theme park.

If I'm being brutally honest, I'm not really much of a fan of this kind of thing myself. I'd prefer a nice walk in the country, or a day at the beach, but Samantha is something of an adrenaline junkie, and I'm more than happy to suffer my way through being jolted and jerked around a few metal tracks to make her happy. My experience of rollercoasters has increased exponentially since I met Samantha. I'd never been on one before I met her, but now I've been through more loop-the-loops than a Red Arrow. That's what I love about her. She's introduced me to things I would never have done alone.

The only ride I'm really not looking forward to at all is The Blitzer itself. I catch sight of its gigantic silver, looping track as we make our way towards Mount Terror. It's apparently the highest single inverted-loop rollercoaster in the northern hemisphere – and boy does it look it. My stomach does a tiny flip as I stare up at the top of the loop, which looks like it's a good two miles in the air.

Still, it's only three minutes of my life, and straight after it I get to the thing I *am* looking forward to, so I'll grit my teeth and put up with it. Samantha will no doubt have the time of her life on the damned ride, and that's what's important.

By the time we get off Minecart Mayhem, it's ten to twelve and time to go join the queue for The Blitzer. The first ride on the rollercoaster is only open to those like us who managed to score special tickets. Everyone else will have to wait until we've had our turn. It cost me another hundred quid to secure the first ride – in another shining example of Ollie Sweet being royally rinsed of his cash. But you really can't put a price on a moment like this, can you? I've been dreaming of this proposal for so long, there's no amount I wouldn't have spent to achieve it.

An area of the plaza in front of The Blitzer's entrance has been sectioned off with ropes and poles, forming the queue line, and a temporary booth sits right in front of it. As we approach this, I notice that a small stage has been constructed within the sectioned-off area, and my heart rate increases. That must be for the band.

'What do you think that's for?' Samantha asks, pointing at the small, low stage.

'No idea.' I shrug. 'Probably something to do with The Blitzer's first outing.'

Samantha nods. Ha! She has no idea!

In no time at all, we are both stood with a crowd of about forty people outside the ride's entrance. The Blitzer has a wintry theme, so everything is coloured in icy blue, white and silver. It's rather like standing at the North Pole, if it had been created by children full of imagination and E-numbers.

Amy emerges from the entrance with an excited look on her face. She is joined by two middle-aged men, both dressed in expensive suits, and even more expensive hairpieces. These must be Jacob and Silvester Marleston, the owners of Thorn Manor.

Amy welcomes all of us to the new ride and promises it will be the greatest experience of our lives. I think she might be overstating things a bit there, but she is in PR, so I'll let her off just this once.

She gives a little speech thanking the Marleston brothers for constructing the park. They both smile the smiles of men with seven figures in their bank account. Amy then thanks all of us for being here.

As she does this, a park photographer is skipping around the crowd, snapping away merrily to record this most prestigious of moments. I've already arranged for him to also take photos of my most prestigious moment, which will follow the three minutes of high-speed mayhem I'm about to endure.

With her speech done, Amy lets us into the entrance to the ride. The small crowd whoops and hollers with excitement as we go in. Samantha's voice is one of the loudest of all.

We all walk through an atrium covered in fake snow and plastic ice, before emerging on to the broad platform, with the rollercoaster cars parked next to it. I'm slightly taken aback when I notice that the cars don't have a bottom, and are instead suspended from the track that hangs overhead.

'Er . . . how are we supposed to sit in that?' I ask Samantha. It's becoming apparent to me that in all of my excitement about arranging today, I didn't really pay that much attention to what kind of ride The Blitzer is.

'We don't sit in it, Ollie!' she replies with excitement. 'You hang from those harnesses, which have a full one-eighty-degree range of parabolic movement.'

Well, I may not have read up much about The Blitzer, but my girlfriend clearly has.

'Oh . . . great,' I say, starting to go a little white. I was prepared for a fast ride around in a little rollercoaster car with my feet planted firmly on the floor and my hands gripping a metal bar for dear life. I'm not prepared for 180 degrees of hanging parabolic movement – whatever the hell that is.

Too late to turn back now, though. I have a marriage proposal to get to.

Samantha immediately makes a beeline for the front carriage of the three-car coaster. We don't get the front row, because that's been commandeered by two teenagers, but we do get the next row back, so it'll pretty much be a front-row seat for this experience in extreme parabolics.

I have to stand on tiptoes to get myself into the strange stand-up harness, with my genitals resting on a thin padded rest that protrudes from the back of the moulded plastic. A rather overweight young man in a Blitzer T-shirt and khaki shorts bellows at all of us through a microphone to be careful as the safety bars are lowered from above. I press myself back into the padded harness as a large U-shaped bar descends, tightly bracing my shoulders and midriff once it's in place.

This feels less like I'm about to enjoy a thrill ride, and more like I'm about to undergo a battery of scientific medical examinations for something very unpleasant.

Samantha grins broadly at me, her eyes out on stalks. I try to return her enthusiastic expression, but only manage to look like I'm experiencing bowel problems.

I can't see my own face, but I'm pretty sure I've gone as white as the Joker.

Suddenly a booming voice fills the entire area.

'It's time to blitz!' the deep, manly voice tells us. 'Are you ready?'

I'm not sure, manly voice. I'm not sure *at all*.

'Blitzing in three . . . two . . . one . . . go!'

And with that, the rollercoaster flies into motion with stomach-churning speed.

Aaaargh!

This isn't how rollercoasters are supposed to start! You're supposed to do the chugga-chugga bit first! A nice slow motion up the track to the top, before descending the other side!

Where's the chugga-chugga?! I needed the chugga-chugga to prepare myself!

Instead, we're shot forward at what feels like the speed of sound. My whole body is forced back into the harness as we rapidly approach that hellish-looking loop I spied earlier from the safety of the park's walkways.

I can already feel my gorge rising as we hurtle towards the sharp incline.

Don't be sick, you idiot! You can't propose marriage with half-digested porridge drying on your shirt!

The Blitzer's car hits the incline at roughly Mach 10, and immediately hurtles skyward.

From beside me I hear Samantha scream with delight. In front, the two teenagers have their arms held out and are screaming as well. In fact, everyone is screaming. Except me. Out loud, anyway. My internal scream meter is off the charts, though – largely trying to convince my stomach to behave itself as we continue to climb skywards.

Just think about the proposal, just think about the proposal, I keep chanting to myself in some sort of safety mantra as we reach that godawful-looking loop.

Now I'm up close to the damn thing, I can see that the loop twists around itself as it reaches its zenith.

Which the car hits almost as soon as I've realised what's going to happen. I am jerked to the left as the rollercoaster starts to enter the twisty section of track.

It's at this point I truly begin to understand what 180 degrees of hanging parabolic movement is.

Absolutely horrendous, as it turns out.

The harness starts to swing around wildly, and I'm thrown in what feels like all directions at once. This forces a noise from my throat that I have never heard before, and will probably never hear again.

'*Mfmurglehoon!*' I cry, incomprehensibly.

There's every chance that in my kinetic terror, I've inadvertently begun speaking in a strange and alien language. I can only assume that '*Mfmurglehoon*' is alien speak for, 'My kidneys are about to merge forcibly with my rectum. May I have a little cry?'

We're mercifully through the twisting, turning, inverted loop in a few seconds. Sadly, we're now heading back down again, and the speed is building once more to ridiculous levels.

I look down – and down – to see that we're now descending towards the ground in a kamikaze run that can only end in our swift and violent deaths.

Luckily, the track takes a sharp turn as we're a mere twenty feet from impact. Unluckily, this forces my stomach into my ankles.

'*Hurmooblegah!*' I cry, my impressive command of alien gibberish now extending to two complete phrases. This one means, 'Ah, it appears my pre-frontal cortex has flown out of my nose. Could you pop it back in again, please?'

All coherent thought leaves me as we power back towards the large building that houses The Blitzer's platform, and the waiting second round of riders.

I'm now no longer white like the Joker; I have gone the green of the Incredible Hulk, jumping effortlessly from one comic book brand to another in my sheer terror.

I feel Samantha's hand grasp mine as we start to slow towards the cavernous building in front of us. This instantly makes me feel a little better.

As we move from harsh sunlight into cool darkness, I start to feel a bit more human still – especially as the rollercoaster is now slowing to a manageable level.

'Are you okay?' Samantha asks me.

'Yeah!' I lie. 'That was quite something!'

The something being the worst something that's ever happened to me.

'It was fucking great!' she cries with excitement. 'Can we do it again later?'

I don't want to nod. I really don't. Nothing would give me greater pleasure than to never see The Blitzer again as long as I live. But this is Samantha's birthday, so if I have to take one more ride on this hellish contraption, then so be it. Besides, I'll be engaged to be married if we do ride it for the second time, so it won't be all bad.

This thought immediately reminds me of what I'm really here for today, and I stiffen up a little.

'Oh, it's okay, Ollie! You're fine! It's over!' Samantha says, feeling my hand tighten on hers.

'Yeah, yeah! I know!' I tell her, knowing full well that it's just getting started.

The rollercoaster cars swing around gently at the far end of the building and return to the platform from which we began. I am immeasurably happy to feel the safety bar rise, releasing me from its death grip. As I lower myself to the floor, I feel my legs start to buckle, and have to take a second to steady myself.

I feel decidedly sick to my stomach as we alight the ride on the opposite platform, allowing the next bunch of excited theme-park goers to have their turn. I wonder if any of them will learn how to speak alien as well. Maybe we could get together afterwards and discuss matters of intergalactic importance.

Samantha jumps off the ride like she's been given a new lease of life. I hobble off like someone's just told me my lease is up at the end of the month.

I take a few deep breaths, partly because I'm glad to be alive, and partly to prepare myself for what's coming next.

If Amy and the Thorn Manor staff have their timing right, then when we emerge from the ride's exit, the jazz band will start playing the song, filling the plaza with its sweet melody. I will then walk Samantha to the front of the stage, take the ring from Horst the trumpeter – and do the deed. Then that fantasy I had in my head while waiting in the queue will come true, and I'll have my romantic happy ending, before the credits roll.

That's if I can get out there without either fainting or throwing up.

'You sure you're okay, Ollie?' Samantha asks, putting her arm around my waist.

I wave a hand. 'Yeah, I'm fine, honestly. Just a bit dizzy. I'll be okay in a second. Let's get outside so I can get a breath of fresh air.'

That might actually do me some good. It's like a sauna in The Blitzer building, thanks to all the sweaty bodies and hot coaster equipment.

Much like a train station, the exit to the coaster is over a walkway that extends above the track, and back out through the plastic ice and snow. By the time we're over the walkway, I feel much better, though my legs still don't want to work properly.

I'm straining my ears now to hear the beginning of 'All of Me' – but am disturbed to find I can't hear anything. The agreement was that the band will start up as the riders stream out of the building. Why aren't they playing?

With my eyes shielded from the sun, and my anxiety levels sky-rocketing, Samantha and I emerge from The Blitzer's exit.

The second we do, I hear a loud voice from my immediate left, where the stage area is being momentarily blocked by bodies.

'*Eins! Zwei! Drei! Vier!*' it screams.

OOMPAH   OOMPAH   OOMPAH   OOMPAH   OOMPAH OOMPAH OOMPAH-PAH!

What the hell??

OOMPAH   OOMPAH   OOMPAH   OOMPAH   OOMPAH OOMPAH OOMPAH-PAH!

The crowd instantly parts, as if driven back by the cacophonous noise erupting from the stage. As they do, I see the band for the first time, and go into full panic mode.

In front of me are four portly gentlemen in green lederhosen, white shirts and peaked caps with feathers stuck in the bands. One is holding a tuba, one an accordion, the third a trombone and the fourth – the portliest of the four – is slightly out in front and blowing on a trumpet like his life depends on it. All of them are bouncing up and down on the spot in time with the rapid rhythm.

OOMPAH OOMPAH OOMPAH OOMPAH OOMPAH OOMPAH OOMPAH-PAH!

'*All of me loves all of you!*' the trumpeter starts to sing. '*All of me loves all of you! All of me loves all of you! All of me! All of you!*'

'*Oi!*' the rest of the band sing together.

OOMPAH OOMPAH OOMPAH OOMPAH OOMPAH OOMPAH OOMPAH-PAH!

'Bloody hell!' Samantha cries, wincing at the high-pitched trumpet. 'What is this??'

I look at her in dismay. I wish I knew myself.

OOMPAH OOMPAH OOMPAH OOMPAH OOMPAH OOMPAH OOMPAH-PAH!

'*All of me loves all of you! All of me loves bits of you! Bits of me loves most of you! Parts of me! Most of you!*'

'*Oi!*'

Is he trying to sing 'All of Me'?

Those aren't even the right lyrics! They're not even *close*!

OOMPAH OOMPAH OOMPAH OOMPAH OOMPAH OOMPAH OOMPAH-PAH!

I glance over to the right of the jigging four-part monstrosity, to see PR girl Amy standing off to one side with a mixed expression of horror and disbelief. Her expression is mirrored on the faces of pretty much everyone in the nonplussed crowd. Even those people excited to be having their go on the second outing of The Blitzer are completely frozen to the spot, such is the bizarre nature of what's going on in front of them.

OOMPAH OOMPAH OOMPAH OOMPAH OOMPAH OOMPAH OOMPAH-PAH!

'*Some of me loves all of you! All of me loves parts of you! Chunks of me love lumps of you! Lumps of me! Chunks of you!*'

'*Oi!*'

I have to put a stop to this! I have to put a stop to this *now*!

On legs that are now incredibly shaky, I stumble over to the stage and throw my hands up.

'Stop! For the love of all that's holy, please stop!'

OOMPAH OOMPAH OOMPAH OOMPAH OOMPAH OOMPAH OOMPAH-PAH!

'God, stop! Please, STOP!'

OOMPAH OOMPAH OOMPAH OOMP—

The band clatters to a halt instantly. If nothing else, they have some musical discipline about them.

The red-faced trumpeter looks down at me with concern. 'Iz everyzing alright, Mister Oliver Sveet?'

I blink a couple of times – mostly due to the accent, if I'm being honest. I have to confess to being slightly stunned that the Germanic voice this man is speaking with matches the lederhosen so absolutely. There's a beauty to its ridiculous perfection that part of me almost admires.

'Who the *hell are you*?' I ask him. 'Where are The Light Touch Quartet? I was promised contemporary jazz!'

The man contrives to look deeply apologetic. 'Ah. I zought you vould have been informed by Mister Barret Barzolemew?'

'Informed of what?!' I rage.

'Ze Light Qvartet are zadly unable to be here today, on account of zome light food poisoning. Mister Barret Barzolemew zought we vould be a good replacement. My name is Horst, and ve are The Oompah Troompahs.' He beams at me as he says this and waggles his trumpet.

I'm truly gobsmacked. 'He thought replacing contemporary jazz with whatever the hell you lot are was *a good idea*??'

Horst looks slightly offended. 'Ve are ze most popular Bavarian oompah band in ze zouth of England, I vill have you know.' He puffs out his chest. 'Ve are much respected!'

As if to underline this point, the trombonist gives me a short, sharp note on his instrument. It's like some kind of audible exclamation mark – and it's very annoying.

'But I ordered contemporary jazz! It's my girlfriend's favourite!'

Speaking of whom . . .

'Ollie? What the hell is going on? Have you got something to do with this?'

I spin around. 'Ah . . . er . . . ah . . . yes! This was all supposed . . . supposed to be for you!'

Samantha looks amazed. And not in a good way. 'You hired an oompah band for my birthday?'

I shake my head vigorously. 'No! No! They were supposed to be contemporary jazz! They were supposed to be playing "All of Me"!'

'Ve vere!' Horst objects.

'No, you bloody weren't!' I argue. '*Chunks of me love lumps of you?!*'

Again, the apologetic look is back. 'Ah . . . vell, ve are not very familiar vith ze zong, so ve busked it a little.' He pinches his finger and thumb together.

'A *little?*'

'Ollie!' Samantha says. 'Can you please explain what's going on here? Everyone *is looking at us.*'

She's not wrong. The crowd are all hanging on my every word. They must think this is a bit of street theatre laid on by the theme park. I can even see that Jacob and Silvester Marleston have joined the throng, standing next to poor old Amy, who looks like she wants the ground to swallow her up.

I have to try to salvage this before it all goes completely south.

'I . . . I arranged all this for us, Samantha!' I tell my girlfriend. 'Not just for your birthday . . . but for something even more special!'

'What? What's so special?'

I go wide-eyed. This is the moment.

Not quite the moment I wanted – I will be demanding my money back from Barret bloody Bartholomew the first chance I get – but it is *the moment*, nonetheless.

I look back at Horst the trumpeter. 'Please tell me you at least have the thing that Amy gave to you?' I ask him.

He beams at me. 'Of course!' Horst then dips a pudgy hand into his lederhosen and pulls out the ring box that contains a couple of thousand pounds of my hard-earned cash, in the shape of an engagement ring.

As he bends down and hands it to me, several things happen at once. First, my legs turn completely to rubber. Second, my hands start to shake. Third, I hear Samantha gasp. Fourth, the trombonist emits a long, low, drawn-out note from his instrument that earns him a dark look from both me and Horst.

But then I turn back to my beloved, and everything else just melts away into the background.

Samantha's hands shoot up to her mouth as she realises what's going on. Her eyes start to bulge a little.

I slowly begin to lower myself on to bended knee.

Sadly, those rubbery legs are still not up to snuff, and I tip forward with my knee buckling, managing to squarely headbutt one of the cream-coloured flagstones beneath my feet.

'Ow! Bloody hell!' I wail, pulling myself back to upright, with one hand going to my forehead. That's going to leave a nasty bruise.

'Ollie! Are you okay?' Samantha asks, momentarily forgetting her shock at what's going on.

'I will be,' I reply, trying my best to go back on to bended knee.

It's not going to work, though. I'm just too shaky, for a multitude of reasons. I'm just going to have to settle for doing this on both knees. This makes me look less like a proposing boyfriend and more like someone expecting to be beheaded for treason, but there's not a damn thing I can do about it.

I gaze up into Samantha's eyes, and gingerly raise the ring box, opening it as I do. When the lid pops open, she gets her first look at the 24-carat shiner that I spent a month's wages on. Her mouth drops open, and her eyes go even wider.

Around us, the crowd issue a collective intake of breath. From one corner of my eye, I see my best friend Lauren with her finger stuck right up her nose again, staring at me with what I hope is amazement.

This is it.

This is *the moment*.

My life since I met Samantha has been building to this.

Time to ride the rollercoaster.

'Samantha, I love you,' I say, voice trembling. 'And I want to spend the rest of my life with you. Will you . . . Will you marry me?'

Samantha looks down at me, tears in her eyes. The sun bathes her in a warm, happy light as she takes a deep breath, steels herself and opens her mouth to speak.

My heart skips.

This is where the rest of my life begins.

'No.'

My jaw drops open and starts to twitch up and down a little. Suddenly, my tongue feels very fat. 'Whaa?' I manage to say.

'*No*, Ollie,' Samantha repeats, shaking her head, and backing away from me. 'I don't want to marry you.'

The crowd, who have been on the legendary tenterhooks this entire time, issue a collective *ooooooh* noise.

My jaw wobbles a couple more times. I'm starting to resemble a ventriloquist's dummy – but one who has most definitely lost his ventriloquist somewhere unpleasant.

'Bu . . . bu . . . bu . . .' I say.

Samantha looks around at everyone watching us. Her face is flaming red. 'Get up, Ollie! For God's sake, get up!'

'Bu . . . bu . . . bu . . .' I repeat.

Her hands fly to her head in the time-honoured expression of overwhelming stress. 'Oh God, Ollie! Why are you doing this?! It's ridiculous!'

'Bu . . . bu . . . bu . . .' I say yet again.

She starts to shake her head. 'What's wrong with you? Why did you *do this*? On my *birthday!*'

'Bu . . . bu . . . bu . . .'

Her head shakes even harder. 'I can't . . . I can't do this, Ollie! I just can't. I've been worried about me and you for a while now . . . And this? This just shows me what—' Samantha looks skywards in apparent exasperation. 'Jesus Christ!' She looks back down; this time her face is resolute. 'I've been thinking about having a talk with you, Ollie. But I didn't want to do it like this!'

'Bu . . . bu . . . bu . . .'

Her face crumples into a mixture of anguish and frustration. 'I don't think . . . I don't think we should . . . should see each other any more. It's just not working for me. And this' – she waves her hand around, taking in the crowd, the oompah band and the rollercoaster – 'this just shows me why we shouldn't stay together. It's all just too . . . too *strange*.'

'Bu . . . bu . . . bu . . .'

Samantha backs away from me even further, so she's now at the edge of the crowd – all of whom are watching probably the most memorable thing they're going to experience today, even if they take multiple rides on the sodding Blitzer.

'I'm leaving now, Ollie,' she tells me. 'I'm really sorry, but I think it's best we don't see each other again.' The crowd then parts to allow Samantha to disappear into it . . . and to disappear from my life.

'Bu . . . bu . . . bu . . . but I love you,' I say, to no one in particular.

From the crowd, Lauren moves forward, slowly walking over to where I am still knelt in utter defeat.

My brain is simply not allowing me to process what's just happened. All I can do is stare at the flagstones and continue to let my jaw twitch up and down with the horror of it all.

Lauren approaches and looks down at me with what I think is the deepest sympathy a small child can muster. I look up into her innocent little eyes, trying to find some kind of answer in them.

How can this have happened?

How could Samantha do this to me? After all we've been through? After all this time?

Lauren steps forward, as if to give me a hug. It's the sweetest thing I think I've ever experienced. A moment of pure kindness in a sea of cruel horrors.

I smile at her weakly and lift my head.

As I do she raises one tiny hand . . .

. . . and wipes a massive green bogey right down the centre of my nose.

'Lauren!' her mother screams with horror.

The crowd, who up until now have seemed deeply sympathetic to my plight, can't let this moment of high comedy go without a robust group chuckle.

The trombonist in Horst's band – a man who has so far displayed a remarkable ability to punctuate moments with just the right note on his instrument – gives us all a loud and tremulous *waaaa-waaaa-waaaaaaaaaaaaaaaaaaa.*

So, this is how it ends.

Not with a bang, but with a bum note.

My world has just utterly collapsed around me.

Time and space have become abstract concepts.

Existence has fallen into a void from which it will never escape.

I have become one with nothingness.

All I am now is a smeared bogey, and a single, pathetic trombone note.

Single.

I'm single again.

. . . and I've lost her. I've lost Samantha. I've lost . . . *the one.*

Oh, the horror.

The unbending, unwavering, unadulterated *horror.*

Roll credits.

CHAPTER TWO

We Were Going to Ride an Elephant

We were, you know.

A big, happy, grey elephant, with massive flapping ears and a trunk you could pull a tree out of the ground with.

From almost the first time we met, Samantha and I both knew we wanted to visit India together, and ride an elephant by a jungle waterhole. There would be someone playing a sitar close by, of course. How could there not be? One of the first romantic movies we watched together was *Monsoon Wedding*, and I think the fascination stemmed from there.

This attraction to the country was one of the first things we bonded over.

Very soon, the idea of going on holiday to India together was firmly placed in both our minds. It was just a matter of raising the cash we'd have needed to take the trip.

Of course, it was my intention for India to be the place we went on our honeymoon, but—

. . . oh Christ, here come the tears again.

There have been a lot of tears in the past two weeks, and I would have a lot of trouble trying to describe that fortnight to you.

I've moved through it like a ship with no captain.

I remember calling work to let them know I needed some time off. My boss, Erica, didn't sound happy about it, which made me wince, but I managed to convince her I'd come down with food poisoning. It wouldn't have mattered if she hadn't believed me, though. There was no way I could face work. I'd have quit before going in. How the hell are you supposed to write an ongoing men's lifestyle feature for a bloody website when your own life has turned into a living nightmare?

I also called my parents.

I told them about what had happened with Samantha and received exactly the same kind of response I have had from them after every one of my other break-ups. Complete disbelief that something like it could have happened to me . . . *again*.

You see, my parents are, for the lack of a better phrase, the perfect couple. Their love for each other only seems to grow stronger every day, and I've never seen them argue.

Literally, *never*. Not even once.

This is an impossibility right up there with time travel – and yet if I could invent a time machine and trace their relationship right back to its roots when they were both eighteen, I bet I wouldn't be able to find any indication that they'd ever had a serious, proper argument in their entire lives together. Dad doesn't complain when Mum nicks his pudding, even when she doesn't order any herself. He asks for two spoons, so she can have some of it with him. *That's* how happy they are with each other.

Because of the success of their relationship, my mum and dad have a hard time understanding what I'm feeling, bless them. They try, of course. Lots of moral support and fulsome affection. But they have absolutely no idea what I'm going through, so their advice tends to drop into cliché within five seconds flat – and tends to be nautically themed, thanks to their love of going on pleasure cruises.

'Plenty more fish in the sea.'

'Worse things happen at sea.'
. . . and so on, and so forth.

Mind you, I guess they're right. I'm sure being eaten by a great white shark *is* worse than getting summarily dumped in front of a hundred theme park visitors, with a green smear of childish snot stuck to your nose – but I could have really done without them making the observation to me, if I'm honest. Still, I love them for trying. It's much appreciated.

For a moment, I considered picking up the phone and calling Brett, my best friend from university. He helped me through the break-up with Yukio – which up until now was the worst one I've ever had to endure. Yukio was the love of my life throughout the three years of university, and when she dumped me to move back to Tokyo, I could have slit my wrists with a Ginsu knife. Luckily, Brett kept all sharp implements out of my grasp, and got me drunk enough to get through the four or five months it took to start feeling like an adequate human being once again.

But I haven't spoken to Brett in a very long time. Life kind of got in the way. He has no idea who Samantha is, let alone any knowledge of my recent break-up. On Facebook, it looks like he's had a baby and is enjoying the first few months of fatherhood, so who am I to bring him down with my problems? Also, I think I'd feel incredibly uncomfortable if I talked to him now, given how I've acted over the years.

I don't really have any other friends I can turn to. Samantha had become the central pillar of my social life and, now she's gone, I feel all at sea, with no islands to swim to.

Every time I've lost at the game of love, I've cursed myself for not staying in better contact with my friends, and yet every time I start a new relationship I do exactly the same thing. I remember they used to have a nickname for me whenever I found love again – *Invisible Ollie*. Alright, not the punchiest of nicknames, but you can't fault them for accuracy.

You don't get to do that kind of thing over and over again without losing contact with those friends almost permanently. I'm certainly not close enough to anyone to seek comfort from them for my problems now. I'm sure it'd come across as totally out of order, anyway. Invisible Ollie only ever pops up again when he's been dumped – that was what they thought then, and it's what they'd think now.

You see, I don't do things by half measures, me. When I fall in love, it becomes all-encompassing. I throw myself into my relationships 100 per cent, and that sadly has an effect on the other connections I have in my life.

I have to confess, I often put my romances ahead of my friendships. It's not something I do consciously, but it always happens all the same. When I'm head over heels in love, I also tend to get my head stuffed up my *arse* when it comes to my friends.

All of this leaves me sat at home in front of the television alone, watching the evening news unfold before my reddened eyeballs.

This is half an hour of unmitigated horror, of course, and is doing nothing for my current mood. There are only so many reports about famine, war, poverty and politics you can watch before wanting to shove a fork into those reddened eyeballs, making them even redder, for very different reasons.

What really finishes me off is when they go over to their Asia correspondent for a story about poachers killing elephants in India for their ivory. I just can't take that. Not now. Possibly not ever.

I turn the channel, to find that Sky Movies is showing *Notting Hill*, one of my favourite movies. In other circumstances I would happily watch it . . . but the idea of sitting through a romantic comedy right now fills me with more horror than the elephant poaching.

I flick the television off, and ponder my next move.

It's six thirty on a balmy, cloudy, summer's day. Perhaps it would be a good idea for me to go out for a walk.

I've done a lot of this in the past two weeks. When you feel cast adrift and miserable, it's very hard to concentrate on anything, and mindlessly trolling around the local streets is about the only way of passing the time that you can come up with.

I could do with getting out for some fresh air to clear my head today, that's for certain. Not only am I still in deep, deep mourning for the loss of my relationship, I also know that I have to go into work for the first time since the break-up tomorrow, and that's going to be a cold slice of awfulness in and of itself.

Not only will I have to explain away my absence without actually telling anyone what's happened to me, I'll also have to contend with the febrile atmosphere at the website's office as well.

I've loved working for Actual Life for the past six years.

It's been my dream job – working at an exciting lifestyle website . . . like the one Actual Life *used* to be, anyway.

But since the takeover happened six months ago, it's been a fast slide down into the mire of corporate-takeover shenanigans and painful cutbacks. Samantha was frankly the only thing keeping me from getting extremely depressed about the whole situation, and now she's gone there's nothing to prevent that from happening. God knows what's occurred at work over the two weeks I've been absent. But I'll find out tomorrow, I'm sure.

I was planning on writing a lovely long article about my successful dream proposal to surprise everyone at the website with – but I obviously won't be able to do that now, will I? In fact, I had a great idea for an extended feature about spectacular wedding proposals in general, with mine as the centrepiece – one I'll have no chance to do.

With that idea firmly thrown out of the window, I'll need to think of something else, which isn't going to be easy, considering my state of mind.

I might have to dust off that story about mocktails I've been avoiding, largely because I'm not the biggest fan of cocktails – alcohol-free or otherwise.

But now even I'm getting sick of hearing me talk about how horrible everything is, so let's get up and go for a soothing walk around the park, shall we?

It takes me about ten minutes to amble through the streets to the broad expanse of publicly owned green space, which has actually gone a rather sickly shade of yellow thanks to the lack of rain recently.

I immediately decide that this was a terrible place to come when I start to spot happy couples walking along arm in arm all around me. Whatever pleasure I may have thought I could get from this little sojourn is extinguished as I pass my third cheerful couple, playing with their equally cheerful little dog.

Right after this, I am almost struck dumb with misery when a hugely expensive grey Aston Martin passes me on the road just outside the park with a number plate that reads 'DB SAM'.

Seriously. I kid you not.

DB SAM.

Dumped By Sam.

Of course, it doesn't actually mean that. It's an Aston Martin DB 8, and the penis in the huge black sunglasses sitting in the driver's seat is probably called Samuel . . . But at the same time it absolutely DOES mean that. I'm 100 per cent sure of it.

I came out for a stroll through the park, but it's quite clear that the universe is trolling *me* this evening – the infinitely wide *bastard*.

I actually stop there on the pavement and look down at my shoes with a leaden sigh.

When I begin walking again, it's not in the direction of my one-bedroom flat. Instead I head towards the town centre. I am not really conscious of why I'm heading in this direction, at least not at first. The shops are a good half an hour's walk away, and I really should be going home, as I have an early start tomorrow – and yet, here I am, trudging along the pavement in the direction of Aldi and H&M, for reasons which escape my conscious mind for the moment.

But then it comes into view.

The thing my subconscious has been guiding me towards ever since I saw that bloody number plate.

The multi-storey car park squats like an ugly grey eyesore at the edge of the town centre. Butted up against the aforementioned Aldi, it is usually full to bursting with the vehicles of enthusiastic and unenthusiastic shoppers alike. From it, you can easily make your way along the main high street and into The Spire – the new shopping mall somebody thought would look really good plonked next to the five-hundred-year-old church, which was quite happy for half a millennium without a Starbucks parked beside it, thank you very much.

At this time of the evening, the multi-storey is largely empty, as most of the shops have closed for the day. I see a few people wandering around Aldi looking for bargain meat, though. I myself often wander around Aldi looking for bargain meat. It's what you do when you're in Aldi. You look for bargain meat, and those knock-off Oreo cookies that taste exactly the same, but cost half as much.

Samantha and I shopped in Aldi three days before she dumped me. We bought a big shoulder of lamb for five quid, and two packets of Moreos.

Oh good grief, I don't want to start crying outside Aldi. People might think I missed out on the bargain meat, and throw a load of cut-price bacon at my head in pity.

I duck into the multi-storey to get out of the eyeline of those who might pelt me with sympathetic pig products, and trudge over to the stairs.

The car park has a total of six levels, and actually has rather an impressive view from up the top. It might be nice to go have a look at it, given that the late evening sun has broken through the clouds and is lighting up the sky with a very pleasant red glow.

At least, this is the reason I give myself for going up to the top of the car park. I try to ignore the fact that the locals call one corner of the top floor 'Street Pizza Central' because in the last ten years a handful of people have ended their lives by jumping off it.

Look, I don't think I'm actually *suicidal*. Not really.

Okay, I'm in a dark place right now, and I can't see a way out, but that doesn't mean I want to end it all with the sweet embrace of death.

But being in a dark place means you have dark thoughts, and sometimes those dark thoughts lead you to places where those dark thoughts can come to the surface. It's like probing a rotten tooth with your tongue. You don't want to do it, but you just can't help yourself.

Does it make you feel any better if I tell you that this isn't the first time I've been up here in the past two weeks?

I've actually made the slow walk up these steps a total of four times now – one visit for every one of my failed adult relationships. And not once on any of these occasions have I jumped off. Not once.

And I see no reason why that should change today.

But I have very dark thoughts, you see.

The top level of the multi-storey is completely empty when I arrive, just a tiny bit out of breath. This is fairly typical. I've only seen a maximum of one or two cars up here in the evening before, at the absolute most.

With hands plunged deeply into my pockets, I amble with my head down over to one of the edges of the concrete building, not paying attention to my surroundings until I lean against the wall and look out.

That pink sun really is quite lovely. And in other circumstances it would put something of a smile on my face.

Not today, though. No smiles for Oliver Sweet today.

My brain returns to mull over the question that has dominated my thoughts for the past couple of weeks.

How could she?

How *could* she?

You know how bad it is when a song gets stuck in your head for days? Well, that's nothing to having a simple three-word question lodged in there like a cancerous tumour.

At least you get to hum a little tune when you're stuck with an earworm song.

Repeating the same rancid question over and over in your head is enough to drive anyone mad.

. . . or up to the top of a car park – where they have no intention of jumping, of course. *None whatsoever.*

How could she?

How could she *do it?*

How could she throw away everything we had together?

After all of that *time?*

I thought we had a bond. I thought she loved me as much as I loved her. I thought it was finally *right.* I thought it was . . . *meant to be.* I thought she was the one!

The evening's pink glow is blurred by a sudden flurry of unwanted tears.

Why does this keep *happening* to me?

I'm a pretty good bloke . . . I think.

I've never lied or cheated. I've never been anything but respectful. I've always tried to be kind. I'm a *good* man. I really am. I don't brush up too badly when you stick me in nice clothes. I have a decent chin. Somebody once told me I looked a little like a young Keanu Reeves, and that felt just fine. My penis is perfectly adequate. In fact, I'd go so far as to say it can look quite impressive when it's nice and warm, and I haven't masturbated in a while. I've never had any complaints in the bedroom. I've not been told I'm a sex god either, but we'll take that one on the chin and move on, safe in the knowledge that performance-wise I'm a good seven or eight at least.

So, why does this keep happening to me?

The pink sunlight has no answers for me. Nor do the people coming out of Aldi laden down with lamb joints and Moreos.

I lean out over the concrete wall, looking straight down at the pavement far below. I'm struck by a momentary wave of vertigo, but force myself to keep looking.

I am not suicidal at all. Not at all.

But I can also feel the weight distribution in my body starting to tip forward a little. If I were to – oh, I don't know – lift one leg up slightly, it might continue that process even more. I do this, just curious to see if I'm right or not.

Yes. Look at that. My entire body weight has shifted forward, and I'm now leaning quite far out over the wall. Not enough to risk falling, you understand. Not at all. For that to become anywhere near a reality, I'd have to take my hands out of my pockets, and place them on the wall. If I did this and *pushed* a little, then that would probably start to make this situation quite precarious. Even *dangerous*, you might say.

I take my hands out of my pockets and put them on the wall. Gently, I push away, in the direction of the pink sunlight.

Oh *my*.

Oh my, oh my . . .

Now my heart is racing. The one leg still on the ground is trembling.

How could she?

How could she?

HOW. COULD. SHE?

Now I'm in real danger of falling forward. The only thing stopping me is the clear and certain knowledge that I did not come up here to commit suicide. I have never come up here to commit suicide, and I will *never* come up here to commit suicide. Not at all.

A little more . . .

A little more . . .

A little less . . .

A little more . . .

'Fuck about, chief. If you're going to do it, do it, otherwise move over, will you?'

An involuntary scream bursts from my lips and, just for a split second, I *am* falling.

This is it. This is where it all ends.

And then my subconscious mind decides that it's had quite enough of this bullshit and takes over. It makes my hands grasp the concrete wall as tightly as possible, and thrusts both of my legs backwards. This arrests the tipping motion enough to pull me away from the brink, and I stumble back from the wall, all the blood draining from my face.

'Oh my God!' I wail.

'Pfft. He's got nothing to do with it, mate.'

I look over to my right to see that sat on the wall about ten feet away from me is a tall, skinny man dressed in a white vest, with the England football team logo embroidered on it, and a pair of what look like women's shorts, so garishly patterned with brightly coloured flowers that it hurts my eyes to look at them. He's also wearing a rather worn pair of black flip-flops.

The man is incredibly pale, and has a haunted look in his eyes that makes his entire face seem somehow sunken in on itself.

'Who—' I start to say, still feeling incredibly discombobulated.

The man sniffs, wipes his nose with one long, almost emaciated forearm and rolls his eyes. 'Someone who's bloody fed up of watching you dry hump that wall, pal.'

'I wasn't going to jump!' I spit out. For some reason I feel the intense need to convince this complete stranger of that. Just in case he's reaching for his phone to have the men with white coats come over and take me somewhere padded.

He rolls his eyes again. Given how sunken his face is, this gesture is amplified almost to the point of caricature. 'No. You weren't,' he agrees. 'You looked like you were doing the bloody hokey-cokey, chief. Somebody who looks like they're doing the hokey-cokey is not someone who is one hundred per cent committed to the idea of ending their life – if you don't mind me saying.'

I don't quite know what to reply to that. The idea of a suicidal hokey-cokey is something I can't get my head around at all. How would it go?

You put your whole soul in, your whole soul out . . .

'Who are you?' I ask the man, feeling my body and mind starting to calm down a little from their brush with the infinite.

The man sticks out a hand. 'Derek Wimslow. Though my mates call me Wimsy.' His face darkens. 'The pricks. You might as well call me it too, though. Everybody has for years, no matter how much I ask them not to. Why should the last person I ever speak to break the habit?'

'The last person you ever speak to?'

He nods. 'Oh yes. Unlike you, buddy, I'm *definitely* going to kill myself this evening. I was just waiting for you to stop shagging the wall first.'

I blink a couple of times. For the first time, I really acknowledge the fact that Wimsy here is sat on the wall I was leaning against (and not shagging), with his legs dangling out over the drop. My stomach lurches.

'Don't do it!' I say, moving towards him slightly.

He holds up the hand that he'd proffered for me to shake. 'Don't come any closer, mate! I'm quite happy to wait for you to piss off, but if you force me to do it, I will with you watching!'

'No! No! Don't do that!' I cry.

He gives me a disbelieving look. 'Why not? You were obviously thinking the same bloody thing!'

'No, I wasn't!'

'Oh . . . you usually spend your evenings rubbing your goolies up and down against a car park wall, do you?'

Again, I have no answer to this. Possibly because this is the first time I've heard someone use the term 'goolies' in reference to testicles for about twenty years.

'Why are you going to jump?' I ask Wimsy. For some reason it's very important to keep this man talking. If I can do that, maybe I can persuade him not to go through with it.

Dabbling with the sweet embrace of non-existence is something I seem to have no problem doing myself, but I'll be buggered if I'm going to stand by and watch somebody else top themselves.

'Why do you care?' Wimsy asks with a sneer.

'Because . . . Because . . .'

Why *do* I care?

'Because . . . if someone's going to do something that drastic, I want to know why!'

Wimsy squints at me. 'You really want to know why I'm here?'

I don't. Not really. I have a whole heap of my own problems, without wanting to hear about – and possibly take on – anybody else's . . . but I can't just let this man join the other inhabitants of Street Pizza Central, can I?

'Yes, I do.'

He sniffs. 'Why should I tell a total bloody stranger about myself?'

I think for a second. 'You tell me yours and I'll tell you mine?' I venture, hoping this will be a good enough deal for him.

Wimsy thinks for a moment, and then swings his legs around so he's sitting towards me, instead of with his legs dangling over the edge. This makes my heart rate slow considerably. If I can keep him talking, I might be able to get through this without watching him hit the concrete at terminal velocity.

All thoughts of initiating my own demise have fled from my head at this point. My sorry, sorry situation has been temporarily forgotten as I try to stop this man from doing something I'd most definitely regret.

'Alright,' he says, scratching his chin. 'But don't you come any closer than where you are, pal.'

I hold up my hands. 'No, no. I won't.'

Wimsy nods and then thinks for a second before speaking. 'My dog died,' he says matter-of-factly.

I don't actually come out and say, *Is that it?*, but you can see from the expression on his face that he knows I'm thinking it.

'No, that's not *it*,' Wimsy says, rolling his eyes. 'Though some people love their dogs enough to kill themselves, you know. Don't be so judgemental.'

Oh great. Now I'm getting lectures about morality from a man about to break the ultimate taboo.

'My dog died, because I had to move into a rental flat. He fell off the balcony.' Wimsy's lip trembles. 'One minute I can see the little fella barking happily away at a passing pigeon. The next, he's leaping into the air to catch it, and . . .' He trails off for a moment. When he looks at me, that haunted look in his eyes has grown even darker. 'I never knew a bichon frise could fucking jump like that, did I? What with them stubby little legs of his. But up he went, like a bloody kangaroo, and over that balcony with a last little yelp.' Wimsy wipes a tear from one eye. 'He was nowhere near that fucking pigeon either, the silly little sod.'

Don't laugh, Oliver.

If you laugh, Wimsy will tip himself backwards over that wall before you know it.

'It was seeing him do that earlier that gave me the idea to come up here tonight. If it's good enough for Mr Sparkles, then it's good enough for me!'

Seriously. *Do. Not. Laugh.*

'I was only in the flat because I had to move out of the house I'd been paying the mortgage on for fifteen years,' Wimsy carries on. 'My wife, Penny, cheated on me, you see. With our accountant.' He looks utterly dismayed. 'Have you ever heard of someone having an affair with their bloody *accountant*?' Wimsy wipes another tear away. 'His name is *Reginald*. He's fifty-four. He's *balding*, for fuck's sake!' He grits his teeth momentarily. 'But there he was, pumping up and down on my Penny in our bed.' Wimsy then gives me an amazed look. 'He had a tattoo on his arse. It said, *I got the long one in Phuket, 1997*. What do you reckon the long one is, chief?'

I shake my head slowly back and forth. 'I have truly no idea,' I say in a hushed tone.

'No, me neither.' Wimsy trails off again, as if marshalling his thoughts. There can't be more to this, can there? 'She cheated on me with him because I lost my business. I was a graphic designer. One of the best.' Wimsy actually looks proud as he says this. It's a marked change of expression from what I'm used to. 'Everything was going fine until that bloody mistake.'

'Mistake?'

'Yeah. I took a contract from a water-bottling company, who had just signed a deal with a Chinese distributor to sell their water over there. They wanted a new logo that would appeal to Chinese people, so I did one that had a lot of Chinese lettering on it.' Wimsy suddenly looks absolutely horrified. 'How was I supposed to know what those letters meant?? I asked a fella on the internet to send me the Chinese for *the water of life*. That sounds good, doesn't it?? That sounds about right?'

'Yes!' I nod my head up and down vigorously. It seems incredibly important to agree with Wimsy right now.

'How was I supposed to know the bastard was having me on?' Wimsy balls his fists. 'But out the proofs went . . . to all the people in the water company, and their Chinese partners. And you know what the Chinese letters actually said?'

'No,' I reply, knowing that something truly horrendous is coming.

'*You have big piss in your mouth*. That's what it said.' Wimsy looks so utterly crestfallen, I want to give him a nice long hug, but I know if I step forward, he'll be gone. 'They all saw it. The Chinese were mortally offended, of course. The water company lost the contract, and they made sure that everyone knew what I'd done to them. Work dried up almost immediately. I was bankrupt in six months. I only hired the bloody accountant to help me out of the mire, and he ends up sticking the long one to my Penny!'

This is the saddest story I've ever heard. I'm on the verge of crying for this poor, poor man.

Also, trying not to laugh is taking every ounce of my willpower. It's very confusing.

'Aren't you going to ask about the shorts?' Wimsy says, pointing at his knee. I'd temporarily forgotten about the garish shorts he's wearing in all the excitement about pigeon-chasing dogs and Phuketian long ones.

'What about them?'

'They're Penny's. Somehow, I accidentally took them when she kicked me out of the house with all my other clothes. So . . . ask me why I'm wearing them. Go on!'

'Why are you wearing them?'

'These are the only sodding clothes I've got left. The rental flat I'm in got burgled last week. They took everything. The TV, my iPad. And for some reason, all of my sodding clothes, except this stupid vest and these bloody flowery shorts!' He grasps at them in sheer frustration. 'The only reason Mr Sparkles went for that pigeon was because he was so hungry!' Wimsy gives me one final look of suffering that is bordering on insanity. 'They stole his fucking dog food! What kind of burglar steals *dog food*?'

'One who owns a dog?' It's out before I can stop it. Damn my treacherous mouth.

'That's what the copper said. I didn't think he was funny, either.' Wimsy looks down. I've never seen a more dejected-looking individual in my life. And with good reason. Have you ever heard such a tale of disaster in your life?

When he looks up again, I can see the unfairness and bad luck of it all etched into the very pores of his skin.

'So, that's my story. That's why I'm up here. What about you, then? What reason have you got to contemplate jumping? It must be bad. Look at all the stuff I've been through. It takes all of that to force a man to end it all, doesn't it? So . . . come on, chief. Spill the beans like you agreed. Why are you up here, ready to jump?'

'I . . . I . . . I got dumped.'

Wimsy's eyes narrow. 'You what?'

'I . . . got dumped. My girlfriend dumped me.'

He blinks rapidly a few times. 'You . . . got dumped.'

'Yes.'

'And that's it, is it?'

'Er . . . yes.'

'That's the reason you're going to kill yourself?'

'It was in front of a Bavarian oompah band,' I add, trying to justify myself a little.

'A what?'

'You know . . . Bavarian oompah.' I mime a trombone. '*Oompah, oompah, oompah-pah* . . . like that.'

One corner of Wimsy's mouth curls up. 'How does that go again?'

I mime the trombone once more, putting a little more effort into it. '*Oompah, oompah, oompah-pah*,' I repeat, this time adding the little bobbing motion in my knees.

For a few moments, Wimsy just stares at me as I continue to bob up and down. And then, with absolutely no warning, he lets out the loudest and heartiest laugh imaginable, throwing his head back as he does so. I stop bobbing up and down instantly. A man chuckling that uncontrollably is in danger of losing his balance.

'Why are you laughing?' I ask, a little offended. I didn't laugh at Mr Sparkles, did I? Or the Phuketian long one. He could show my misfortune the same kind of courtesy.

Wimsy looks at me in amazement. 'Why am I laughing?'

'Yes . . . why?!'

He wipes a tear away from his eye. 'My life has fallen apart completely, and you're actually up here contemplating chucking yourself off, just because some lass gave you the heave-ho.'

I am incensed by his lack of sympathy. 'It was in front of *hundreds* of people,' I say, trying to further justify my position. 'One of them wiped a bogey down my nose.'

'B . . . *bogey?*'

'Yes! Right down my poor bloody nose.' I point to the protuberance in question, by way of underlining the gravity of the situation.

Wimsy is clearly unable to grasp this particular gravity, as he starts to wail with laughter again, putting him ever closer to losing a fight with the *other* kind of gravity.

'Oh God,' he exclaims, slapping his thigh. 'You are too much, pal. Just too much!'

'My heart is broken!' I shout at him, trying to make him see the seriousness of it all.

'Oh, I'm sure it is, mate. I got dumped by a girl once when I was a kid. It was horrible.'

'We were going to ride an elephant!' I blurt out, some uncertainty now creeping into my voice. I'm keenly aware at this stage that my sad story of heartbreak and loss doesn't really stack up to what Wimsy's just told me about his own life. I'm in the depths of depression right now, but that doesn't mean I've lost *all* perspective, thank God.

Wimsy stares at me. 'You were what?'

'Going to ride an elephant. A big, happy one with a curly trunk.' I say this in a deflated voice, knowing full well that I sound just a little bit ridiculous.

'Really? What would that trunk have looked like?'

For a moment, I distractedly start to wave my right arm around in front of my nose – then I realise Wimsy is taking the piss, and stop. The damage is already done, though. Wimsy goes off into another gale of laughter that sends him even closer to tipping over the edge.

I take a small step closer to him. He may have mortally offended me by not taking my pain and misery seriously, but I'll be damned if I'm going to let him fall off this car park.

Saving Wimsy's life has now become inextricably tied up with my own pathetic existence. Thanks to my run-in with this poor bastard, I am no longer feeling even *slightly* suicidal. His tale of extreme woe has brought me up sharp, and has thankfully knocked some sense into me.

Yes, I am as miserable as sin because I've lost the love of my life, but Wimsy here has instantly proved to me that things could be so, so much *worse*.

I feel like I owe him quite a lot for doing that. Stopping him from killing himself would be a good way to repay him.

'Stay back!' he roars, getting the crazed laughing under a bit more control.

'I don't want you to fall!'

'I don't care what you want!' he snaps. 'I came up here to end this sad little life of mine, and instead I have to get into a conversation with a walking comedy sketch.' He looks skyward and bares his teeth. 'I can't even commit suicide properly!'

'Then don't! Don't kill yourself, Wimsy!'

'But I want to!'

'But you shouldn't!'

'Why? Why the fuck shouldn't I?'

Oh good grief . . . why shouldn't he?

'Because . . . Because . . . Because Mr Sparkles wouldn't want you to!'

He looks incredulous at this, and with good reason. 'Mr Sparkles?' 'Yes! He was a good dog, I'm sure! I bet he loved you! I bet he wouldn't want you to kill yourself!' This is a horrible, horrible gambit to take, but I'm committed now. 'He'd . . . He'd want you to go on! He'd want you to live! He'd want you to . . . to . . . get another Mr Sparkles!'

Wimsy looks at me with pure hate in his eyes. I don't think I've helped matters. 'Mr Sparkles jumped off a twelfth-storey balcony to catch a pigeon that was a hundred feet away. Mr Sparkles was a *moron*.' His eyes narrow. 'And do you know who called him Mr Sparkles in the first place?'

Oh God.

'Yeah. That's right,' Wimsy hisses, nodding slowly. 'It was bloody Penny!'

And with that, Wimsy tips himself backwards off the ledge.

I act on instinct, leaping forward and grabbing at Wimsy's flailing legs as they fly up into the air. By some stroke of pure luck, I manage to get a firm grasp around both of them. As I do, though, his left heel kicks me in the face.

Both of Wimsy's flip-flops have flown skyward. One describes an arc out over the drop, while the other flies directly up for a few feet, before falling back . . . and landing perfectly on top of my head.

'Let me go!' he screams, dangling over the precipice and squirming for all he's worth.

'No!' I scream back, tasting blood as it streams from my nose. The flip-flop wobbles on my head, but does not come off. This is due to the fact that I'm rigid with a combination of fear and determination to not let this suicidal fool go. I can't look down at him as I might lose my grip if I do, so I stare right out in front of me at that beautiful sunset, the cords standing out on my neck with the strain of holding up a fully grown man.

'Fucking let me go!'

'No, Wimsy! You have to *live!*'

'I don't want to live!'

'You must, Wimsy! Life goes on!'

'No, it doesn't!'

'Yes! Yes, it does! No matter what happens to you, you have to keep going! No matter how much it hurts! Things can get better! Things *will* get better!'

I'm not sure whether I'm talking to Wimsy now, or myself.

'Oh, bugger off, mate! Just let me go!'

Wimsy bucks his hips, trying to free himself from my death clutch.

'No, Wimsy! I can't! I can't let you go!' Samantha's face flashes through my mind as I say this, for some reason.

Wimsy struggles for a few more seconds, but I still have a good enough hold on him to stop him from getting away from me. My arms are really starting to burn with pain now. If I can't get him back up here soon, I'm going to let him go through sheer exhaustion.

And then all the fight goes out of him, and I'm holding on to a dead weight.

'Oh, fucking hell,' he wails, arms dangling. 'You're a total *bastard*, chief.'

'Maybe! But I'm right, though, aren't I?! This isn't the right thing to do! Neither of us should be up here! Neither of us should be even *thinking* about doing this!' I grunt with effort as Wimsy's dead weight gets even heavier. I *have* to convince him to climb back up. 'Please don't lose hope, Wimsy! Please, *please* don't. Because *I* don't want to . . . and if you fall, I just might.'

'Oh . . . fuck me,' he says, with heavy resignation in his voice. 'Why did I have to bump into you this evening?'

'Luck?' I venture, feeling my grip really beginning to slip on Wimsy's rather hairy shins.

He chuckles at this. There's still a crazed edge to his laughter. 'Why?' he sighs, shaking his head. 'Why? Why? WHY?' He doesn't seem to be addressing me now, but some unknown third party. I can't say I blame him. Wimsy has been dealt an extremely bad hand in life, and I can understand him wanting a few words with the dealer.

'Why?! Why?! WHY?!' he screams a few more times, looking up at me as he does so. 'Why?! Why?! Wh—'

He stops, staring at me.

'Why have you got a flip-flop on your head?' he asks in astonishment.

I stare off into the distance for a moment. I have no idea why I have a flip-flop on my head. There are many things about my life I don't have an answer for, but this is currently the strangest of them.

I certainly don't know what I came up here to this car park for. Not really.

Maybe it was to seek some solace. Maybe it was to seek some answers. Maybe it was to flirt with something that would stop the questions.

I just don't know.

I wasn't planning on having a nosebleed with a flip-flop on my head, though. That's for sure as cobblers.

For some reason, this makes me laugh. I haven't laughed since Thorn Manor. It feels quite alien.

Wimsy also starts to laugh again, though this time it's a cleaner sound. Gone is that edge of insanity.

So, for a few moments, we laugh together. Him dangling over the edge, and me holding on to him for dear life.

'Oh God,' he eventually says, looking down for a second at the gulf of space between him and the concrete below. 'Oh fuck, I've gone and bottled it now,' he adds tremulously. 'You'd better pull me up.'

That's easier said than done. Almost all of the strength is gone from my arms.

I solve the precarious situation by folding Wimsy's lower legs over the car park wall with one arm, while leaning over to grab his England vest with the other. As I do this, he pushes away from the wall with his hands, pivoting his body upwards.

I feel something give in my bicep as I yank him to safety. I'm going to be on the ibuprofen for the next few days, without a doubt.

As Wimsy returns to an upright sitting position, the whole front of the vest rips, destroying his one remaining piece of clothing that isn't floral.

I succeed in pulling him off the wall completely, and we both collapse next to each other on the car park floor, breathing heavily. Above us, the pink sky is darkening to red as the sun dips lower. Thankfully, my nose appears to have stopped bleeding, though it still feels very tender.

'Well, what do we do now?' Wimsy asks after a few moments, staring up at the colourful sky overhead.

'I have no idea,' I say, truthfully.

I may have moved away from the idea of ending it all, but I still feel like my life is over. I'm still lonely and heartbroken.

All I know now is that chucking myself off a car park is no bloody solution. There must be something more constructive I can do to get over this. What that is, though, I really do have *no idea*.

Wimsy looks at me. 'Pint?'

I stare back at him for a second. This man is clearly in need of some serious psychiatric help, and I'm not sure alcohol is the best way for him to—

'Yeah, alright,' I reply.

Wimsy sniffs. 'What's your name?'

'Oliver . . . Ollie, if you like.'

'Alright, Ollie. Let's go get pissed.' Wimsy gets to his feet and looks out over the drop that he so nearly just succumbed to.

I also get to my feet, and look at the tattered remains of his vest. 'I've got a T-shirt you can have,' I tell him.

Wimsy nods and flashes me a quick grin. 'Thanks very much.'

It's not much, but I guess it's a start.

With something of a relieved sigh, I head back towards the stairs leading down from here, with my new friend Wimsy at my side. I won't feel completely comfortable until we're on the ground floor, though.

As we walk off in the direction of my flat so I can get him some clothing, I once again think about how I owe Wimsy a debt of gratitude for showing me some much-needed perspective.

Okay, I feel no better about what's happened to me, but at least I can appreciate that it could be so much *worse*.

And there's a small part of me that actually feels quite proud of what I've done here tonight. I managed to stop a man from killing himself. That actually sounds quite . . . *heroic* when you get right down to it, doesn't it?

I wonder if Samantha would take me back if she knew how heroic I'd been tonight?

Oh good grief.

I really am in a bad place.

But there are worse places I could be.

At the bottom of that car park with my shin bones poking out of the top of my head, for instance.

CHAPTER THREE

BACK TO ACTUAL LIFE

Never mind, though. At least I still have a job.

For now, anyway . . .

Things are hanging by a thread at the website I work for, and there have already been redundancies, so I probably shouldn't turn up for work so dishevelled and with a hangover, after spending the evening drowning my sorrows with my new pal Wimsy.

However, that is exactly what I am doing today, so let's hope no one's observant enough to noti—

'Wow. You look like you've been dragged through a hedge back-wards' – a familiar and amused voice says as I shuffle over to my desk – 'just after someone's thrown a brewery over you.'

I turn and affect what I hope is a sheepish grin. This actually makes both my head and my face hurt, which should give you some idea of the state I'm in today. 'Morning, Erica.'

'Good morning, Ollie. Nice to have you back at work after your obviously much-needed period of absence.' Erica Hilton has an almost supernatural capacity to lace her words with so much sarcasm you can practically taste it. 'I do hope the time you have spent convalescing from your – what was it? – *food poisoning* has helped you. It's amazing how much the after-effects of such a serious complaint can mimic a roaring hangover, isn't it?' Her voice is now filled with as much amusement as sarcasm. The pointed look she's giving me is hard to miss as well. You could probably see it from orbit.

'Ah, yeah. Feeling . . . much better now,' I tell her.

In point of fact, I don't feel any better, of course. One heavy drinking session with a man whose life is a bigger disaster zone than yours is not going to get you over being dumped in front of hundreds of people by the person you thought you'd spend the rest of your life with.

I woke up this morning with that same sharp ache in my chest, much as I had the previous day. It was just accompanied now by a throbbing headache and a tongue comprised of eighty-five per cent shagpile carpet.

'Really?' Erica replies. 'Because you don't look it, Ollie.' Oh dear, she sounds genuinely concerned about me. That can't be good. 'Why don't you come into my office for a quick chat before you start work? I can make you some coffee. I hear that's a very good cure for a hang— I mean, *food poisoning.*'

I start to protest, but then I am out of coffee at home at the moment, and Erica does have one of those lovely bean-to-cup machines in her office, so . . .

'Okay. The vast sea of emails can wait for at least ten minutes.'

Erica makes a face. 'Probably. Though there's one you really need to look at, which I don't think you're going to like one bit.'

Oh joy. It sounds like I have some work-related anxieties to add to my relationship problems.

You don't have relationship problems, you idiot. You're not in a relationship.

With a heavy sigh (which is something I am so well practised at these days, I could probably win a medal for it) I follow Erica towards her office for what I feel might not be the most pleasant of chats.

As I do, I nod to my fellow writers and the website designer, who share the open-plan office space with me. Most of them look as miserable as I do. Things are not happy here at the Actual Life offices these days. Not by a long shot.

Erica busies herself making us both a coffee, while I contemplate the inside of my eyelids for a minute.

'Here, drink that,' she tells me, plonking the coffee down in front of me and returning to the other side of the desk with her own cup.

Once sat, she regards me with a mixture of curiosity and sympathy. Erica Hilton's green eyes are just as expressive as her voice. She can convey oceans of intent with a simple look. It's always been quite disconcerting. Marry that with red hair that inexplicably seems to change hue depending on her mood, and she's a formidable person to be around.

I've maintained a very good working relationship with Erica since I started at Actual Life six years ago. That was when she hadn't been bought out yet, and owned the website outright. Back then it was still growing, and I was only the fourth staff member she'd hired. I got the job thanks to a speculative feature I'd written about why it's okay for men to enjoy watching romantic comedies. Erica read it, loved my style and tone, and offered me the job straight away.

I'd like to think I contributed to the website's huge rise in popularity over the first three years. I equally hope I've done nothing to hasten the decline it's undergone in the last two.

The decline seems to have started right around the time that arsehole from ForeTech bought Actual Life to add to his portfolio of online companies. I've met Benedict Montifore a grand total of three times, and after each occasion I've wanted to hose myself down with holy water.

I'm willing to bet the vital parts of my anatomy that aren't currently pickled in alcohol that the email Erica mentioned outside will be from him.

I take a sip of the coffee and rub my face, trying my best not to look Erica in her eyes.

'What's going on with you, Ollie?' she asks gently.

'What do you mean? I've had food poisoning.'

She gives me a look of derision. 'Pull the other one, Mr Sweet, it's got several bells on.'

'What do you mean?'

Erica leans forward. 'What I mean is that you called me two weeks ago to deliver a garbled message about having eaten some bad quinoa – which makes very little sense, by the way – and you sounded incredibly upset, rather than sick. I can tell the difference, you know.'

'You can?'

'Yes. Years of being a journalist talking to all sorts of people gives you a good ear for that kind of thing.' She cocks her head slightly to one side in a questioning manner. 'What's really going on with you, Ollie?'

Oh hell. I guess I'd better come clean. I don't like lying to Erica. I never have before, and it makes me very uncomfortable to do so now. She may only be six years older than me, but I look up to her a great deal as something of a mentor, and I'd hate to break her trust by continuing the charade of my quinoa-related food poisoning.

'It's Samantha,' I tell her in a dull voice.

'What about her?' Erica's eyes go wide. 'Nothing's happened to her, has it?'

'Nothing's happened to her, don't worry.' My lip wobbles a bit.

Traitorous lip! Why must you wobble in the presence of our boss?! Why can you not stay firm and rigid? Damn you, bottom lip! Damn you, and all that you stand for!

'What happened, Ollie?' Erica presses, as gently as possible.

'She . . . she dumped me. I asked her to marry me on her birthday, and she dumped me.' I hate how pathetic I sound, but I can't help it. Erica is the first person – other than a suicidal bloke in flip-flops – I've talked to about this face to face, and it's incredibly hard.

'Oh, Ollie. That's terrible,' Erica sympathises.

'Yeah. You could say that. I'm sorry I took so much time off.'

She waves a hand. 'Don't worry about it. When Chris left me, I could barely function for a month. Actual Life nearly never got going because of his awful timing. What happened with Samantha? You seemed so happy.'

I go on to tell Erica all about the hideous day at Thorn Manor, including the oompah band. I then fill her in about the following two weeks, and my run-in with Wimsy. I finish my sorry little tale by confessing that I have no idea how to get over the heartbreak. Not this time around.

Though I have to admit that I feel a tiny bit better at the end of it. Spilling my guts to someone I've always trusted is quite therapeutic. I say this to Erica.

'That's great. Glad I can be of a little help.' She sits back and puffs out her cheeks. 'Christ, though . . . that all sounds horrible, Ollie. I'm so sorry.'

God bless her, she didn't even laugh at the oompah band.

'Thanks. It's been a miserable time for me.'

'I bet.' Erica thinks for a moment. 'Well, what I'm certainly not going to do is tell you that there are plenty more fish in the sea, or that there's another girl out there for you somewhere. People tried to tell me the same thing after Chris left, and I could have clawed their eyeballs out.'

I give her a brief smile. 'Thanks. I don't think it would do me much good at the moment.'

'No, I'm sure it wouldn't.'

'I have to think of *something* to get me over this, though,' I tell her. 'I feel like I'm in a slow-motion car crash at the moment. If I wallow in self-pity for much longer, I'll start to rot from the inside out.' I chew on a fingernail. 'Quite how I do that, I have no idea.'

'Hmmm,' Erica says thoughtfully, drumming her nails on the desk. She then narrows her eyes a little, and smiles. 'Why don't you write about it?'

'What?'

She leans forward again, this time with a lot more animation. '*Write about it*, Ollie! You said talking to me felt therapeutic . . . Maybe getting it all out there to our subscribers will make you feel even better!'

'Oh God, I couldn't do that!' I reply instantly, feeling my guts roll over.

'Why? You're one of our best writers. I knew that the minute I read "I Have a Rom-Com . . . And I'm Not Ashamed to Watch It". And that feature you did last month about that weird restaurant, Control, Alt, Del-Eat, still makes me giggle every time I read it.'

'Please. Don't remind me. I can still taste the grasshopper,' I reply with a grin.

Then I remember that I'd taken Samantha along to the place to help me review it, and the grin disappears instantly.

'A feature about dealing with, and getting over, heartbreak would be *wonderful* for you, Ollie,' Erica continues. She's dropped into career-journalist mode now, unfortunately. If my boss has a flaw, it's that her worldview tends to be driven by her commitment to her work. That's what made her an award-winning foreign-affairs reporter in the first place, and what drove her to start Actual Life when the constant travel became too much. 'It would be incredibly popular, as well. Everyone has been dumped at one time or another. Reading about your heartache could help other people with theirs!'

'I don't think I'm up to something like that.'

'You could ask them for advice!' she carries on, not listening. 'I bet our subscribers would love that! An interactive feature, where you talk about what happened with Samantha, and ask for ways to cope with the heartbreak! It'd be *fantastic*!'

I shake my head. 'I can't, Erica, I really can't. It's just too raw for me right now.'

For a second, she looks like she's about to protest, but seeing the look of pain in my eyes brings her up short. 'Okay, Ollie. I understand,' she says, a little deflated.

It's a solid idea for a feature, of that there is no doubt. A lifestyle website trades on that kind of subject matter all the time . . . but I just don't think I can manage it – any more than I could manage that article about great marriage proposals, albeit for very different reasons. All I want to do is go back to my desk and finish up that article I've been writing about retro cinemas, start that next feature about the bloody mocktails, and completely forget about my destroyed love life for a few hours at least.

'What was the email you mentioned?' I say, trying to change the subject.

Erica rolls her eyes. 'He's at it again.'

She doesn't need to say who. We both know who she's referring to.

'What is it this time?' I say, dreading the response.

In just the past five months, ForeTech has reduced our staff of twelve down to eight, cut our expenses budget by half, reduced our server space by even more, and forced us on to a cheaper web-design software package that only does about a quarter of the useful stuff the old one did.

My ongoing romance with Samantha was the only thing keeping a smile on my face in that time, and now she's gone the situation at work seems even worse.

'He's decided to issue an ultimatum about subscriber numbers,' Erica says, her expression darkening. Her red hair has definitely gone a shade darker too. This should be impossible, but it has, nonetheless.

'What kind of ultimatum?'

'He says if we don't get them back above thirty thousand by the end of the month, he's shutting Actual Life down.'

I let out a gasp. 'Can he do that? Can he really do that?'

Erica shrugs. 'Maybe? Probably? Who knows?'

'But you're on the board of directors! Can't you vote any move like that down? I thought that was the reason you agreed to join ForeTech's board when you sold the site!'

'It was. But Benedict knows how to sweet-talk the others. He probably wouldn't have let his company go public if he couldn't. And if they decide to vote in favour of liquidating Actual Life, then there's not much I can do about it on my own.'

'Oh God.'

'Yes. My thoughts exactly. I'm going to try to work on them myself in the next few weeks, and convince them to block any move Benedict makes to shut us down, but I don't hold out much hope of it working.'

Erica looks decidedly miserable at the prospect of this. And who can blame her? Selling to ForeTech seemed like a good idea two years ago. It certainly brought more cash into the company to begin with. But, slowly and surely, Montifore has bled us dry – especially in the last few months. The bastard has made a fortune buying, selling and upgrading web-based companies. When he discovered that Actual Life was never going to be the profit-making powerhouse he thought he could turn it into, everything went sour. And now we all pretty much hang by a thread . . .

Erica bangs a hand on her desk, bringing me out of this unpleasant train of thought. 'Well, we're not going to keep the site running by sitting here talking about it. Do you feel up to working?'

'Of course I do!'

I'm not sure I really do feel that way, but a bit of positivity probably wouldn't go amiss, for multiple reasons.

'Great. Can you get that cinema feature done by this afternoon?'

'Sure can, boss!' I spring out of my seat with a display of enthusiasm that only goes skin deep. I feel decidedly guilty about not writing the article about my break-up that Erica suggested, so I have to compensate.

Erica smiles. 'Okay, then.' She gives me another sympathetic look. 'It'll get better, Ollie. Honestly.'

Damn you, bottom lip! Damn you to Hades and back!

'Thanks. I hope . . . hope you're right.'

Before my boss can see me get too emotional, I scuttle out of her office and over to my desk – where many, many emails await, along with an incomplete article I really must get finished.

This is probably for the best. A bit of hard work will keep my mind off Samantha for a while. I glance up at the clock on the wall, which says 9.15.

Samantha will be at the garden centre now. She'll be out doing the stocktake, after the morning delivery, as always.

Damn you, brain! You can join the bottom lip on its way down to hell!

***

I ignore all of the emails, deciding instead to concentrate on the piece I was writing two weeks ago about the flurry of retro cinemas that have opened across the country. I try to keep the back end of the feature as light-hearted as the first thousand words, but it's very hard to do so. I just about manage to crank the damn thing out, and then mail it over to Erica for her to have a look through. It reads to me like something written by two completely different people (which in a way, of course, *it is*) but I'm hoping she'll approve it.

Then come the emails.

Oh Lord, the *emails*.

It takes me a good two hours to get through them all. A lot are about setting up meetings and visits for future articles I plan on writing.

In most of my replies, I make profuse apologies for not being in touch in the past few weeks. Then I start on the dull admin emails that clog up my inbox like fat, lazy toads on an electronic log. Quite how a feature writer on a website can build up so many admin-related emails in such a short space of time is beyond me, but it's happened and there's nothing I can do about it, other than wade through them all until I see daylight out of the other side.

I leave Benedict Montifore's email until last. This is probably a mistake, but I can't bear to read it until after lunch, after I've had another coffee and a chicken salad roll. I figure raising my blood-sugar levels will help me cope with it.

I couldn't be more wrong.

The tone of the email is *ghastly*. Gone is the smooth-talking businessman of the past. Now, Benedict is showing his true colours, and his words are brusque, cold and extremely hostile.

Erica summed the damn thing up pretty well this morning. Benedict does want to liquidate Actual Life as quickly as possible. He says his motivation for doing this is '*the dramatic drop-off in subscriber numbers in the past six months*'. I unconsciously scrunch a sheet of A4 paper into a tight ball in my hand as I read this. The subscriber numbers wouldn't have plummeted in the first place had he not cut our staff and resources to the bone!

I'm actually livid by the time I get to the bottom of the email.

This is not a mental state I am accustomed to. I've never been a person who is quick to anger, but this single piece of electronic communication has made me madder than a rabid badger.

I should send him a reply.

I really, really should.

I should send him a long and heartfelt response to this rude and destructive email, detailing how poorly I think he's run the website since he bought it, and reminding him that he's playing with the lives of eight human beings!

Yes!

That's what I should do!

. . . I don't, of course. If I'm not a person quick to anger, I'm certainly not a person who's good at confrontation – even in digital form. Besides, I need this job to last as long as possible. My landlord is putting my rent up next month, and I haven't finished paying off the TV yet.

So, instead of replying to Benedict bloody Montifore, I open up a fresh new document in Microsoft Word and start to write about mocktails for men.

I adamantly try not to think about that other article – the one about the spectacular proposals. The glorious feature that a version of Ollie Sweet in another universe is happily tucking into, having had *his* marriage proposal accepted by the love of his life. The utter bastard.

No. It's mocktails for me. Whether I like it or not.

The first thing I need to do for this is think of a title.

'Mocktails for Men' is too boring.

'Mocking Masculinity'?

Too negative.

'One Man and His Softie'?

Too cheesy.

'Dry Hard'?

Nope. Been done.

Hmmm . . .

'Dumped Actually'.

What?

'Dumped Actually'. That's a good title for the story.

Eh? That's got nothing to do with mocktails!

No. It's for the feature about splitting up with Samantha. The one Erica asked you to write.

I'm not doing that.

No? You think a dull as ditchwater story about boring cocktails will help keep this website afloat, do you?

I don't know.

Yes, you do. It won't. But 'Dumped Actually' . . . Now that has potential.

No, it doesn't.

Yes, it does. And you know it. It'd be huge. The subscribers would love it. It'd bring in new readers. Because Erica's right . . . everyone has been dumped before. And everyone has stories to share.

I can't. I just can't.

Yes, you can. And you should. You need this job, remember?

I need to get on with my life.

Oh yeah. You're really doing that, aren't you? Nearly chucking yourself off a car park and crying into your breakfast cereal every morning.

Leave me alone.

I can't. I'm your brain. And your brain is right.

No.

'Dumped Actually', Ollie. It's called 'Dumped Actually'. It's a great title, isn't it?

No.

Yes. A clever play on Love Actually. *It'll go down a storm. You should use it.*

No.

Yes.

No!

Yes!

I don't want to!

Yes, you bloody well DO!

I jump out of my chair, startling the others in the office out of their collective misery.

'Sorry!' I say to them, instantly feeling embarrassed.

To escape public scrutiny, I hurry back over to Erica's office and throw the door open.

'"Dumped Actually",' I say, almost breathlessly.

'What?' she replies in shock, lifting her head from her laptop screen.

'"Dumped Actually". That's what I could call the feature about Samantha leaving me.' I think for a second. 'No. Not just about that. A feature about all the women who have dumped me over the years. It can't just be about one person.' For some reason, making that decision has made me feel better about writing the story. Writing about *all* of the relationships I've had somehow diffuses the impact of Samantha's loss. Just a little, anyway.

'I thought you couldn't bring yourself to do it?' Erica says.

I roll my eyes. 'Yes, well. I'm heartbroken and alone. But I'm a *journalist* who's heartbroken and alone. And I know as well as you do that it'd make a great article.'

Erica beams. 'It would.'

This is the main problem with being a journalist. You're always on the lookout for the next great feature idea, no matter where it comes from. And for some reason, people seem to absolutely *love* it when you write about personal stuff. That's why I was going to do the feature about marriage proposals . . . if mine had gone the way I wanted.

The window into another person's life is often a must-read.

And, to be honest, that's especially true when that window actually looks on to something *traumatic*. That's just human nature, I guess – the desire to read about how other people's lives are *worse* than yours is often greater than to read about other people's successes.

And it's the nature of a journalist like me to satiate that desire, no matter how painful it might be.

'And I want to do something to keep that git Montifore off our backs,' I add. 'A story about how men are drinking mojitos with no rum in them is *not* going to do it.'

'Agreed.'

'I'll need some time, though. It's going to be . . . difficult.'

'Take as much as you need.'

I nod my head. 'Right, then. "Dumped Actually" it is.'

Erica nods too. 'That's a great title.'

I roll my eyes again. 'Yes, I know it is. I hate myself.'

And with that, I close Erica's door again, leaving her to return to her laptop, this time with a broad smile on her face.

I amble over to my desk and plonk myself down.

That blank page stares back at me, just daring me to bloody well get on with it.

Suddenly, I am overcome by the same sense of vertigo I had standing at the top of the multi-storey car park. I'm contemplating the idea of jumping again, but this time there's no Wimsy around to stop me.

I write the title at the top of the page, right in the centre:

Dumped Actually

By Ollie Sweet

I feel a cold sensation settle into my stomach as I stare at these five words. The first of what could be many. The first of what *will* be many. Time to jump.

***

I told Erica that it would take me a long time to write 'Dumped Actually'. I figured it would be hard for me to do it, given how raw my emotions are.

However, by six o'clock that evening, I have already written three thousand words, and am still thundering onwards to a word count that will easily represent my longest ever feature for Actual Life.

I start quite slowly, talking about my life up to this point, by way of some background information, before leaping into the meat of the article.

I talk a little about how I grew up with parents who love each other without condition, and have the perfect long-term relationship. I mention how this gave me a very positive impression of what romance is like, even at a very early age.

Of course, their kindness towards one another extended to me as well, and I had what you would describe as an idyllic upbringing – surrounded by, and included in, all the love I could possibly wish for. Most of my childhood memories consist of me running around the incredibly beautiful sun-dappled garden they created together – laughing and giggling as I jumped over the geraniums, with them watching me from the patio with indulgent smiles on their faces.

Yes. It is enough to make you sick just thinking about it, isn't it?

When you have parents who are as emotionally available as mine were, it tends to rub off on you. I've never had trouble expressing or understanding my feelings, thanks to them.

I was pretty much a hopeless romantic myself by the time I reached adulthood. While a lot of my mates were off watching action and horror movies, I preferred to sit down in front of something by Richard Curtis.

I kept quiet about my love of romantic movies, as you would expect. The epic *taking of the piss* by all of my male friends would have been long, sustained and probably quite unpleasant.

In fact, the first time I ever really expressed my love for films like *Four Weddings* and *Love Actually* was when I wrote the speculative article that got me the job here at Actual Life. The fact it became a pretty popular read on the website meant that I wasn't the only bloke out there who didn't mind a bit of romance in his life.

Once I've provided the brief background about my upbringing, I start detailing my first break-up, and the words begin to spill out of me in a torrent. If you're going to clean out a wound, it's best to do it as quickly as possible.

Gretchen Palmer gets about seven hundred words dedicated to her. She was my first love, and my first heartbreak. We were together for six months when I was seventeen. Gretchen loved dancing. So *I* loved dancing too. Ballroom dancing, to be precise. If I didn't tell my mates about liking romantic comedies, I sure as hell didn't tell them about doing a bit of tango with my girlfriend in the church hall every Sunday afternoon. Can you imagine the response?

But Gretchen loved it, and I was more than happy to keep *her happy* by being her willing partner on the dance floor, whenever she wanted me to be.

I lost my virginity to Gretchen.

I then lost Gretchen to a twenty-one-year-old Asda assistant manager called Simon Pickings, who drove a restored 1978 Ford Cortina. I have never shopped in an Asda since.

Next came Yukio Sagawa. She was a student, studying cookery at my university, and I met her in the halls of residence. She spoke flawless English and dressed like a bohemian princess. My provincial little brain could barely cope. She opened my eyes to the world and showed me what was outside my comfort zone.

Yukio was an excellent cook, as you'd imagine. And she loved to cook and eat oriental food from every country in the Far East – with increasingly exotic ingredients as she got better at it.

Therefore, *I* also cooked and ate oriental food. Even though I don't like chilli. Or garlic. Or noodles. Or rice.

In fact, truth be told, I *hate* oriental food, but I wanted to keep Yukio happy, so I ended up eating a lot of stuff with a barely concealed grimace on my face. Do you know how hard it is to look happy about chomping down on a salty, wiggly octopus leg? Extremely hard, as it turns out. I must have got very good at it, though, because Yukio never seemed to notice that I'd go a slight shade of green every time she produced a new delicacy for me to try.

Watching me eat something that I'd probably be bringing back up again once she was out of the room always put a big, happy smile on her face, though, so the gastro-intestinal discomfort was worth it.

Yukio was unbearably exciting to be around . . . right up until the point where she wasn't around any more. At the end of our university courses, she announced that she was moving back to Tokyo. I, of course, offered to go with her. I would have gone anywhere with her, to be honest. But she said she wanted to be alone again. To be able to explore her own identity – or some such other bullshit.

Yukio gets over fifteen hundred words in my rapidly expanding article.

Lisa DeVoe was a sweet, sensible girl, who seemed to adore me. We met online, after a period of singularity for me that had lasted two years.

Lisa was an archaeologist, and loved her some dinosaurs. So *I* loved me some dinosaurs as well. To this day I can tell you all about the flora and fauna of the Jurassic and Triassic periods with no hesitation whatsoever, thanks to Lisa DeVoe.

This was all a lot easier to get along with than the ballroom dancing or the awful food, as it mainly involved looking at books and drinking coffee. It did also occasionally mean that I had to stand in a wet ditch with a trowel in my hand, but that was a small price to pay to see the happy look on Lisa's face when I dug up a Roman coin.

It was never a whirlwind romance with Lisa, but over time I became very fond of her, and I thought she felt the same way about me.

Right up until she dumped me in the middle of sex.

Yep. That's right. One minute I'm pumping away happily, the next I'm looking down into the crying eyes of a woman who it turns out doesn't want to be with me any more.

Her reasons? She said she wasn't excited by our relationship – which is just the kind of thing you want to hear while you're still inside someone. My unexciting penis withdrew extremely quickly at that point and became even less excited as I sat there while she explained how she felt.

It just didn't 'feel right' to her any more, apparently.

In much the same way as that knocking noise from the rear axle doesn't feel right, so you take it into the garage for a once-over.

No garage for me, though. I was sent straight to the scrapyard.

Lisa gets six hundred words in 'Dumped Actually'.

Which brings us back to the most recent disaster, of course – that of Samantha Ealing.

As has been established, Samantha was 'the one'. Funny, intelligent, beautiful, witty. I couldn't have created a better girlfriend for myself if you'd given me a test tube and access to expensive DNA sampling equipment.

It was love at first sight with Samantha. I'd only gone into the garden centre to buy some lavender for my balcony, and I ended up falling in love. It was the bees, you see. I wanted the lavender because I'd read in an article on Actual Life by one of my fellow writers that the bee population of the UK was plummeting, and one of the ways to help them out was by planting lavender. Also, I knew it would please my parents if I took more of an interest in plants.

I bumped into Samantha on my search for the lavender, and she showed me where it was. By the time we'd finished our impromptu discussion about the plight of the country's bee population, I was totally smitten.

So much so that I asked for her phone number there and then. It was an act of such brazen confidence that it made me quite light-headed. I nearly threw up when she actually gave it to me.

It was like something out of . . . yes, you've guessed it, a Richard Curtis movie. With Samantha, I really felt like I was in the best romantic comedy I'd ever seen. I also felt like she was the girl I would *finally* have the perfect relationship with.

So began the happiest period in my life. I walked around on cloud nine the entire time we were together. We never argued. We always had a good time together. Her interests coincided with mine quite a lot, and we were very much on the same wavelength. Everything just clicked into place right from the get-go. It was perfect.

Until it wasn't.

I still have no idea why Samantha finished with me. I thought we were *forever*.

I write over three thousand words about Samantha, until I realise I've gone way overboard, and cut it back by five hundred words.

With all of my heartaches laid bare, I then move on to the second section of the article – about how the hell I'm supposed to get over this latest split.

So far, I've done what anybody does when they get dumped. I've cried, I've wailed, I've got drunk, I've fallen into a miserable pit of depression.

. . . exactly the same way I did after Gretchen, Yukio and Lisa gave me the old heave-ho.

But I can't go on like this. It's becoming too much for me to cope with. It's also unbearably *cliché* when you get right down to it. And I hate to be cliché. In my writing, as well as my life.

Erica's idea to make 'Dumped Actually' a more interactive experience, by asking the readers what tips they could give me on getting over my heartbreak, was inspired. People *love* to contribute. More than anything. Everyone has their own tale of relationship disaster, and I have no doubt that a lot of people will be keen to share them with me – along with how they managed to get over them.

Once I've got a few good ones in, I can publish them in a follow-up article, with my thoughts about how effective they might be. It'll write itself! I'm sure I'll get enough responses to maybe do two or three additional features, which will keep me going for a few weeks of material.

I have no idea if it'll help Actual Life grow its subscriber base, but I'm sure it'll please those who already visit the site.

It's gone 9 p.m. before I have finished the first draft of 'Dumped Actually'. I've never been this late at work. It's quite an eerie experience. The office is empty other than me. Even Erica went home over an hour ago, handing me the key to lock up. I barely said two words to her, that's how intent I was on focussing on the article. She didn't mind. In fact, I'm sure she was delighted to see me so committed to it.

I finish the final line of the now lengthy feature and lean back in my chair, expelling the air from my mouth in a long sigh. I feel emotionally drained. Which is a first for me when I'm writing. It's hard to get emotionally invested in the décor at the Hayes Retro Cinema experience, unless you have a particular thing for chandeliers and red velvet carpet.

I also have a pounding headache, so it's probably time to get up from this desk and head for home.

I email the draft over to Erica, hoping she'll get a chance to look over it tomorrow morning. I have no idea whether she'll think it's any good or not, but it's the best I can do. I've put all of my energy into this one, and I don't think I have any more to expend.

By the time I get home, I am absolutely exhausted, and fall into the first deep sleep I've managed since Horst and his companions oompahed me back into the lonely single life.

***

'Ollie! This is brilliant!' Erica says to me the next morning, clutching a printout of 'Dumped Actually' as she walks over to where I've just sat down in front of my computer.

'Is it?' I say, rubbing one eye.

I slept like the dead last night and am having trouble shaking it off.

'Absolutely!' she says, perching herself on the end of my desk. 'It's the best thing you've ever written. Genuinely heartfelt, raw . . . and *real.*'

'Oh, it's definitely real, alright,' I reply with a grimace. 'More's the pity.'

'I've already been through and done an edit. Can you get the polished version back to me today? I want to get this live by this evening!'

'Really?' It's normally a good week or more before Actual Life articles are ready to go. Erica must really think this one is a winner.

I think it's a pretty good feature myself, but I'm not sure it's quite the revelation my boss wants it to be.

'Er, yeah. I guess so.'

'Excellent!' She pats me excitedly on the shoulder a couple of times. 'Well done, Ollie. This is very good stuff. Could be just the kind of thing that'll bring in more subscribers.'

Oh God. Now I feel something I hate when I've written an article – *pressure.*

Erica is obviously pinning quite a lot of her hopes to stave off Benedict and his desire to liquidate the website on this thing, but I think she might be exaggerating its potential a wee bit. I'm sure an article about being dumped will be quite popular, but popular enough to increase our subscriber base again? I don't see that happening.

And when it doesn't, will Erica blame me? Will she think I didn't do enough of a good job with 'Dumped Actually'?

You see? *Pressure.*

I hate it, and I don't cope well with it.

As I begin to go through the feature to polish it up for publication, I am starting to deeply regret the whole thing.

I am a man already consumed by regret these days – I don't need any more heaped on my shoulders.

But I've made my own stupid bed now, haven't I?

'Dumped Actually' is now officially a *thing.*

And to be fair, it's a thing I'm quite proud of. It *is* a good story, after all.

But good enough to help turn the tide at Actual Life?

I don't think so.

For that to happen, it would have to be read and shared by *tens of thousands* of people. I'd have to get *hundreds* of responses.

I just don't see that happening.

Not at all.

No way.

Fat bloody chance . . .

INTERLUDE

From: Monica Blake (MonMon82@outlook.com)

Hi Ollie!

Just finished reading 'Dumped Actually' and had
to get in touch. Poor you! I feel so sorry for what
you've been through! Can't believe that Samantha
would do that to you. You seem like such a nice
guy ☺.

You said you wanted to hear from people who have
been dumped before, and I am one of them! My
husband, Steve, left me a year and half ago, just
after our baby boy, Alex, was born. He told me he
wanted out during a nappy change, while his face
was covered in a load of Alex's fresh diarrhoea. I
guess that was the final straw. The joys of fatherhood just weren't for him, it seemed. I thought I'd
married a man, but he turned out to be a scared
little boy. He rejected me and our baby. Can you
imagine how horrible that was?

It was the hardest thing I've ever been through, so I know exactly how you're feeling ☹.

What I did to get through the break-up was I went and got a full makeover! It sounds silly, but it really helped me get some of my self-esteem back, and feel better about myself again. Steve always used to put me down. Told me I was fat a lot, especially after Alex was born ☹. But I went out and re-did my whole look, and it made me feel ten times better!

I know you're a bloke, and it probably doesn't sound like a good idea to you, but you should give it a go! The guy I went to was fabulous. I can give you his details, if you like!

Best wishes, Ollie. I really hope that you feel better soon, whatever you decide to do about it!

Lots of Love,
Monica

***

From: Edward 'Wolf' Moresby (WolfCamp@sky.com)

Dear Mr Sweet,

I am writing to you after having completed your entertaining story on the Actual Life dot com website. I was prompted to read it by my sister, who enjoys those types of websites. She felt that I might have some salient advice for you, since I myself have known the pain of a lost relationship, and subsequently discovered an effective way of moving past it.

When my Heather felt that her marriage to me was no longer workable and left me to move to the south of France, I was understandably upset. For some time I did not know how to cope with her loss. I eventually turned to the solace of the Cairngorms in the Highlands of Scotland for some sort of release from the upset. I spent two weeks up there with Davis and Roundhouse – my two best friends from my rugby club, and it was quite wonderful. It's good for the soul to spend time with like-minded people, doing like-minded pursuits, in like-minded clothing. Spending time in the embrace of Mother Nature is also extremely good for the soul. It offers the chance for contemplation and reflection. It really took my mind off Heather, especially with the support of my friends.

When I returned, I felt more able to carry on without her, and have never looked back since. I highly suggest you attempt something similar for your recovery.

Do let me know if you decide to follow my advice, and how you get on.

Yours,
Wolf Moresby

***

From: Callie Donnelly (CallieDonnelly@yahoo.co.uk)

Ollie,

Am in a bit of a rush, so don't have much time to write this, but just wanted to email you to say that I loved reading 'Dumped Actually' this morning on my way into work on the train. Really hit home how bad break-ups can be.

My advice? I've always found that the best way of getting over somebody is to get under somebody else! Sounds crude, but it's absolutely true.

Don't just sit on a shelf and do nothing. Get back out there and find another woman as quick as you can. It's what I've always done, and it's always made me feel a lot better. Your self-esteem takes a big hit when somebody gets rid of you, and there's no better way of building it back up again than finding someone else to climb into bed with!

Best of luck with it. I'll keep reading your stuff, and I'll get my friends to subscribe as well. You're really good!

Callie xxx

CHAPTER FOUR

THE IMPOSSIBLE ART OF SAYING NO

A fully grown man is about to tear a strip of sticky waxed paper away from my arsehole, and I'm not sure how I feel about it.

Oh, no. Hang on. I know exactly how I feel about it: nauseous and terrified.

'Now, Oliver, this might hurt a bit!' Laughlin McPurty tells me cheerfully. 'You may feel a wee sting.'

'Eeeeuuurrrggggggghhhhh,' is about all I can manage in response.

Why?

Because I've already been through several 'treatments' that I'm pretty sure are banned by the Geneva Convention. My cognitive abilities have been severely impaired by all of them. I almost don't want this waxing to be over that quickly, as I'm fairly sure the next thing on Laughlin McPurty's list is waterboarding.

***

But let us return to last Tuesday, to discover why I find myself in the position of a man about to become far less hirsute.

It turns out I wasn't entirely correct about how much of a response I'd get to 'Dumped Actually'. I may have underestimated things *just a tad*.

It hasn't been read by tens of thousands of people – it's been read by *two hundred and fifty thousand*. And I haven't received hundreds of responses. I've received *thousands*.

Most have been just well-wishers. A few have been people taking the piss, because that's how the world works.

But I've also had dozens and dozens of emails from people keen to tell me about their stories of heartbreak, and how they managed to move on with their lives.

It's been quite incredible.

The last time I remember anything taking off online like this was that 'Dry Hard' thing last year. That went viral in a matter of days. I ended up interviewing the Temple family for Actual Life. They seemed nice, if a little bewildered by the whole experience.

It took a little longer for 'Dumped Actually' to gather any pace. For the first week or so, it was bumping along quite nicely, the way I thought it would. It certainly got a lot of clicks, but nothing that out of the ordinary for one of Actual Life's more popular stories.

But then, inexplicably, after about a fortnight, it started to gather steam.

There's some weird alchemy to the way social media and the internet work that I don't for the life of me understand. One minute something can be just another feature in a sea of billions, and the next it can blow up – for no discernible reason.

Erica thinks it's because what I've written is a fantastic piece of work, but I'm sure there's something weirder and less tangible going on that none of us truly understand. There are probably scientists somewhere, dedicated to trying to make head or tail of it. Possibly underground at Facebook, where a picture of Mark Zuckerberg hangs so they can all pray to it in the morning.

By the time another two weeks had gone by, 'Dumped Actually' had been read and shared more than any other feature in Actual Life's entire seven-year history.

I had to stop looking at the website's statistics, because it was starting to give me vertigo.

I also had to stop googling my name. It's fun to start with, don't get me wrong. The thrill of seeing lots and lots of hits appear is quite incredible. But after a while it starts to become ever so *embarrassing*.

I poured my heart out to the world in that story. I didn't think it would be read by quite so many people. If I had, I would have never got past the first paragraph.

I have become something of a minor, and no doubt temporary, celebrity in cyberspace – all because I can't hold down a bloody relationship.

Some people get to be famous online because they climb a mountain, or record a song about a kitten riding on a miniature golf cart. I get to be well known for being a complete and total loser.

Oh joy.

But, I have to confess, a part of me was very happy to see 'Dumped Actually' do so well. The part of me that has to worry about the rent and electricity bills, mostly. Also, I have some professional pride as a writer and journalist, so to see something take off in such a fashion was a great boost to my cratering sense of self-worth.

Towering embarrassment and abstract pride are a strange combination, I have to tell you. It's like being nervous and on edge, while at the same time feeling relaxed and easy-going.

I've been taking a lot of ibuprofen the last few days.

I had imagined that I would be doing a follow-up feature to 'Dumped Actually' about all the feedback I'd received. A nice easy piece, highlighting the best of the responses, and my feelings about them.

Erica had other ideas.

'You've got to try them!' she tells me, over another cup of bean-to-cup coffee.

'Excuse me?'

'You've got to do them, Ollie! The ideas they've suggested. That's the best way to keep the whole thing going.'

'But . . . But I was just going to do a follow-up article about them.'

Erica waves her hand dismissively. 'Boring! That won't hold people's attention for long, I can tell you that. But if you actually give their ideas a go . . . Now that could be something we could keep going for *months*!'

'Months?'

'Yeah! Months and months!'

'Oh God.'

'Oh, come on, it's not like it'll be a new thing for you. You always go and do research for your stories.'

'Yeah . . . but going to a bar to drink a mocktail is not like camping for a month in Scotland, or getting an unwanted – and probably permanent – makeover!'

Erica smiles broadly. 'It'll be fine, Ollie! Trust me!'

'But . . . I . . . But . . . I can't . . . I don't . . .'

Oh *bugger*.

Bugger, bugger, bugger, bugger, *bugger*.

***

I emailed Monica Blake and asked her for the contact details of the man she went to for her makeover. Unfortunately for me, his salon was only a forty-minute drive away.

I tried to make one final protest to Erica, but she was quite adamant that I should follow up 'Dumped Actually' with some personal experiences of my own – and she is my boss, so I drove the thirty-mile journey with a resigned and heavy heart.

I have never had a makeover. I have never wanted to have a makeover.

I consider myself to be a tidy bloke. I have a decent haircut. I mostly wear clothes that are in good condition. I have clean teeth and use an expensive deodorant. I have never once felt that my physical appearance has been of detriment to my mental health, so the idea that having a bit of manscaping done could help me get over being dumped by Samantha is ludicrous.

And yet, here I am. Stood outside The Scissor Misters with a doubtful look on my face.

When I walk into the salon, I am immediately greeted by a man in a kilt.

Now, the word 'kilt' may conjure up images of a big, burly Scotsman with tree-trunk legs and a beard you could lose a red squirrel in, but that is not the person who has bounded over to me as I close the door.

You wouldn't think bounding was all that advisable for a man wearing a kilt, but this guy takes it all wonderfully in his stride.

'Ach! You must be Oliver!' he cries with excitement, in a lyrical Scottish accent, as he reaches me.

This is Laughlin McPurty. He looks exactly the way he does on the salon's website.

I ask you, have you ever seen such a moustache in your life? Look how it curls at the ends. Look how well maintained that tiny hipster beard is. Look at how thin the wire rims on those achingly fashionable spectacles are. Laughlin McPurty is every inch the bang-on-trend style guru.

His sporran is probably full to bursting with quinoa and chia seeds.

And yes, sporrans are not usually bright yellow, and kilts are not generally aquamarine in hue, but Laughlin is clearly not a man afraid to break with convention.

'It's sooo good to meet you!' Laughlin exclaims, and throws his arms around me like we're long-lost brothers. 'I was so excited to get your email!' he tells me, finally breaking the embrace. 'I read your article. Thought it was *terrific*. So sorry to hear of what happened to you and your lady. More than happy to show you some of the fantastic treatments we have. I'm sure they'll make you feel much better about yersel' . . . you'll see.' Laughlin throws his hands up above his head like he's just scored the world's campest touchdown. 'All free as well! Being on Actual Life will be great advertising for us!' He takes me by one arm. 'So, c'mon, c'mon, let's get a nice cup of bergamot, orange and mint rooibos tea in your hand, and we'll talk about what we're going to do with you today.' Laughlin looks me up and down. 'It's clear you badly need my help,' he tells me in a sympathetic tone.

Eh? I thought I looked quite good today. The skinny jeans are freshly out of the wash, I'm wearing my least battered pair of Adidas, and the chequered shirt is from H&M's most expensive range. What's he on about?

Laughlin leads me over to a row of chairs at the back of the salon, past another row in front of some enormous mirrors and a range of fiendishly complicated-looking contraptions that look like they've come straight off the set of a science fiction movie.

'Now, sit yersel' down here, and I'll get one of the girls to prepare you some tea. My partner, Clyde, is away for the day, so he sends you his apologies. But there's more than enough of us here to make sure you get the best level of service. The place doesn't start to get busy until about lunchtime, so we'll have plenty of time for you.'

Laughlin looks up as a young woman emerges from a door to my right-hand side.

'Ah, Tina! Get Oliver here a bergamot and mint rooibos, would you?'

Tina nods, smiles at me and scuttles back through the door.

Laughlin then comes and sits beside me. 'Now. What would you like to start with today, Oliver?'

I open my mouth to say something but, before I can, Laughlin lets out a little high-pitched gasp and thrusts out a hand.

'No! Don't you say anything! I know just what we should do for you first.' He then grabs my right hand and holds it up to his face. He's quite strong for such a scrawny bugger. 'These nails need a good work-over, Oliver! A good work-over, indeed!' He then points at my feet. 'And I bet the ones down there are no better, are they?' Laughlin then bends and starts to yank at my trainer. 'Off! Off with it, Oliver! Let's have a wee look at how bad things really are!'

Before I know it, I am divested of both Adidas trainer and Primark sock. Laughlin lets out another gasp. This one in horror. 'Look! Look at those, young man!' he cries, pointing accusingly at my feet.

I look down and inspect my toenails. Okay, they're not what you'd call particularly neat. That's what happens when you only have a pair of scissors with which to cut them, but they're not dirty or a weird colour, or anything else that would cause Mr McPurty such obvious distress.

At this point Tina returns with whatever the hell Laughlin told her to put in my tea. Burger mat orange and mint robot boss tea doesn't sound all that appealing, if I'm being honest.

Luckily, Laughlin's priorities have changed from making me drink a weird herbal concoction to doing something about my apparently hideous foot talons.

'No! No!' he says to Tina, waving her away. 'No time for tea! Oliver needs these nails taken care of . . . stat!'

Laughlin yanks me to my feet and drags me over to a large black leather chair, with an odd-shaped footrest on a metal stand in front of it. 'Sit!' he commands.

The chair is extremely comfortable, and I'd like to take full benefit from this comfort, but right now I'm too concerned about what's about to happen to my feet to do so.

'Stacy! Imogen! Bring out my personal pedicure kit! The special one I keep in the back!' Laughlin roars, before sitting himself in a chair in front of me. 'Right foot up, Oliver!' he tells me, whacking the footrest.

I do as I'm told, and the instant my foot is on the rest, Laughlin is immediately bent over it, examining it so closely and with such intent that he kind of reminds me of Gollum with the One Ring.

He starts to tut under his breath and shake his head. 'Ach, no. This is dreadful,' he intones. 'Oh dear, oh dear, oh dear,' he continues, under his breath. 'Would you just look at the state of – oh God.'

From the same door that Tina emerged from with my tea come two other girls – Stacy and Imogen, I presume. They are both carrying a large silk roll between them. This looks frankly ridiculous. The thing is only about eight inches wide. They resemble two disciples carrying an important religious artefact over to the high priest.

Laughlin grabs the black silk roll from them and opens it out on the floor beside him.

My eyes widen as I look down at what can only be something recovered from Guantanamo Bay. There are implements in here that I don't want to guess the use of. I don't want to, but I'm still going to.

That thing there – the one with the scoop at one end – that must be for prising out eyeballs. The long thin one with the spike on the end is no doubt used to stick into soft places in the groin area. The less said about the thing that resembles a bird's claw the better. I hate to think about where you'd stick that, and what would happen if you started to spin it around.

Laughlin grabs another implement, this one quite small, and with a flat scoop on the end. It's certainly not the worst looking of the bunch, by any means. Maybe I'm going to get away without too much—

'Bloody hell! What are you doing?!' I screech as Laughlin gets to work on my big toe. This is the first thing I've actually managed to say in this entire visit so far. It's taken an assault upon my cuticles to give me the chance to get a word in edgeways.

There is scooping going on. There is scraping going on. There is – and I can barely bring myself to say this – *rootling* being done upon my person.

Rootling.

Is rootling even a word?

I don't know, but it's what Laughlin McPurty is doing to me, of that I have no doubt.

None of it is actually *painful*. Not yet, anyway. But it is massively disconcerting. I feel like a small-scale, but very determined, invasion of my privacy is being undertaken.

A man's foot is his own private kingdom, and he should not have to—

'Uuurgggh! What's that??!' I exclaim, looking down at whatever it is Laughlin has just worked out from under my nail. It's kind of brown and squidgy.

Nothing under one's nail should be brown and squidgy.

'That, my boy, is what happens when you don't treat your poor feet well!' Laughlin says, disposing of the offending article in a small bin parked by his side. He then goes back to his Gollum-like examination of the rest of my toes, peering at each one intently before carrying on with his rootling and scooping.

This goes on for another couple of minutes until he seems satisfied. Then Laughlin brings out a small electric drill and the world goes grey.

AAAAAWWWWWWVVVVVVVVVVVVV goes the drill.

'Haaarruuugghhhh!' goes Oliver Sweet.

I've never had a problem going to the dentist, but from this day forth the sound of a dental drill will make my toes curl in terror.

I can barely bring myself to look down at what Laughlin is doing. Through trembling fingers that cover my eyes, I can see him going to town on my big toenail. His tongue is stuck out to one side in concentration, and I haven't seen a Scotsman's brow this furrowed since we knocked them out of the World Cup.

AAAAAWWWWWVVVVVVVVVVVV.

'Ah yes, here we go,' Laughlin mutters under his breath to my toes. I've never had someone directly address a body part of mine without including me in the conversation before. It's a strange experience.

AAAAAWWWWWVVVVVVVVVVVV.

'Come on, you beauty.'

AAAAAWWWWWVVVVVVVVVVVV.

'Get that right there, ye little bugger.'

AAAAAWWWWWVVVVVVVVVVVV.

'You'll no be giving us trouble any more, ye wee pernickety.'

Laughlin McPurty has now dropped into some hardcore Scottish patois that I have no chance of ever understanding. I just want this misery to be over with as quickly as possible.

AAAAAWWWWWVVVVVVVVVVVV.

'Aye. That's how we do it, ya little beggarin' mincer.'

I have no idea what a *beggarin' mincer* is, but I certainly don't want it anywhere near my poor old toes.

AAAAAWWWWWVVVVVVVVVVVV.

'Right! That'll about do it, then!' Laughlin eventually proclaims, stopping the drill.

I look down to see that, rather incredibly, my toes are not five bloody stumps. Instead, what stares back up at me are the shiniest of shiny toenails, each one more pristine than the last.

'Wow,' I say quietly.

'Aye! That's the way!' Laughlin laughs, before picking the scoop back up again. 'Now . . . time for the left foot, Oliver!'

Oh God.

We're only halfway done.

I sink into the chair as Laughlin forcibly removes my other shoe and sock. If I can just imagine myself somewhere relaxing and comfortable, I might be able to get through the rest of this.

A nice desert island somewhere.

Yes.

That's it.

I can feel the warm tropical breeze on my face. I can smell the scent of jasmine on the air. I can feel the warmth of the sun on my body. I can hear the gentle lapping of the waves as they caress the beach. I can—

AAAAAWWWWWVVVVVVVVVV.

'Aaaargh!'

I'd like to say that the pedicure was the worst thing to happen to me that morning, but it wasn't. Not by a long shot.

When Laughlin was done with my feet, he moved on to my hands. My fingernails received the same rootling and buffing as my toes, only this time the whole thing happened a lot closer to my eyeballs, and was therefore ten times worse.

When that was done, I was forced to endure a haircut and shampoo.

And I mean the word 'endure'. No one has ever been forced to *endure* a haircut and shampoo before. You *sit through* them. You *put up with* them. You even sometimes *quite enjoy* them.

But when Laughlin McPurty wields a pair of hairdressing scissors, it's like watching Freddy Krueger having a seizure.

Quite how I'm not decapitated is beyond me.

Even the shampoo that Tina gives me afterwards is something that will haunt me in my dreams for decades to come. Tina is rather large of breast, you see. And she really *leans into* her work. I'm not averse to a pair of breasts in my face, but when they are that fulsome, and accompanied by having your head squeezed like an over-ripe melon, it becomes incredibly claustrophobic, incredibly quickly.

For a few moments, I feel like I'm in danger of my sanity being lost in the embrace of Tina's bosom – forever to wander detached and alone betwixt those wobbling mammaries.

Before that can happen, though, I am thrust under a hairdryer by Stacy, who is thankfully flat-chested. My head gets boiled in hot air for a minute, and then Imogen starts to pull me towards the door at the rear of the salon.

'Where are we going?' I squeak, still trying to shake off the boob-related claustrophobia.

'Private room, luv,' Imogen tells me. 'Laughlin wants to give you a nice waxin'.'

'Waxing? What do you mean, *waxing*??'

'Well, you're too hairy, ain't ya?'

'Am I?'

'Yeah, 'course you are.'

I guess I'll have to take her word for it. The last time I shaved was two days ago, and I have to admit it's been a while since I trimmed my pubes, but how would Laughlin know that?

Does he have some kind of sixth sense about someone's levels of hirsuteness underneath their clothes?

A *pube-dar*, so to speak?

Imogen leads me through the door and down a long, expertly decorated corridor, to another door that leads into a small room containing a massage table. The room is tastefully decorated in a Balinese style, with a fair bit of decorative bamboo and at least two small stone Buddhas.

A gentle piece of calming oriental music is piped into the room from regions unknown.

Laughlin is nowhere to be seen right now. I can't tell if this is a good thing or not.

'Get undressed, luv,' Imogen tells me. 'When you 'ave, just lie down on the table with the sheet over you. Laughlin will be here in a bit to take care of you.'

'Er . . . what exactly is he going to do?'

Imogen rolls her eyes. 'Give you a nice *waxin'*, silly.'

'But . . . But . . . should he be doing that?'

Imogen's brow furrows. 'What do you mean?'

'Well . . . waxing's a . . . a . . . a job for *a woman*, isn't it?'

Somewhere, far off, the Sexism Fairy has just thrown up in her mouth a bit. Or his mouth, even. I've never met the Sexism Fairy before, so I certainly wouldn't want to presume his or her sex. It may lead to the reinforcement of negative stereotypes.

Imogen gives me a dark look. 'Laughlin is the best waxer in the south of England,' she tells me in a sniffy voice.

'Really? How do you know? Is there a competition?'

She pushes me towards the massage table. 'Just get changed. I'll tell Laughlin you'll be ready in five minutes.'

But I don't want to be ready in five minutes!

I'm not sure I could be ready in five *hours*!

Before I get a chance to protest, Imogen has gone, leaving me alone with my abject fear, and the not-so-soothing sound of pan pipes.

I don't want to be waxed. I have *never* wanted to be waxed in my life. I am not a piece of paper in urgent need of waterproofing, nor am I the bonnet of a sports car.

I'm thinking all of this as I nervously get undressed, lie on the massage table and cover my modesty with the sheet Imogen pointed out.

As I lie there, trembling slightly, my misgivings about this whole thing really begin to skyrocket.

This is ridiculous. I need to get out of this and get back to the safety of the Actual Life offices pronto.

When Laughlin McPurty comes in, I need to tell him in no uncertain terms that I will *not* be continuing with these beauty treatments. I will do it as gently but as firmly as I am able, so as not to offend him. I will thank him for his time, and his efforts, and promise to provide a very positive write-up of my experience on Actual Life.

Yes. These are the things I shall say when Laughlin appears. Definitely.

The door to the room swings open and in walks Mr McPurty, with Tina in tow. He's carrying a large box of waxing strips, and she's holding an equally large tub of what I presume is the wax.

Right. This is it. Time to end this farce before something really painful is allowed to—

'Okay, Oliver! Let's get you nice and bald!'

'But—'

'We're going to start with your lower back, and work our way down from there!' Laughlin wiggles his eyebrows as he says this. 'Luckily for you, the hair only starts about where your ribcage finishes.'

'But I don't want—'

'Now, you just lie back and relax, Oliver. This isn't going to hurt a bit.'

'Isn't it?'

'No! The wax and the strips we use are specially formulated not to hurt as much when they are removed from the body.'

He lies! He lies with the forked tongue of the lowliest demon from the pit!

'Oh, okay.'

'Good stuff! Are you ready for this, Oliver?'

'Um. I suppose so.'

'Great! Pop your head in the wee hole there, and we'll get on with it, then.'

I rest my head into the massage table hole, cursing my inability to say no to anything.

It's not the first time this has happened, and it surely won't be the last. Why am I such a bloody *doormat*? Why can't I just say no, and have done with it??

Tina starts to liberally smear my lower back with the cold, sticky wax, while Laughlin opens the box of strips, which look like they're made of a very heavy-duty, thick paper.

He then starts to apply these across my back, once Tina has finished, muttering to himself again as he does so.

'Aye, this'll do the minute. Should have the wee hairies off in no time at all,' he says under his breath. 'Down she goes into the crevices and nadgies. No time lost there, no problem.'

What the hell is he on about?

'And that'll about do . . .' he continues. 'Here we go . . . In a wee jiffy . . . One, two, three . . . and . . . gissat!'

RRRRRRIIIIIIIIIIIIIIPPPPPPPPP

'Oww!' I exclaim . . . more in surprise than actual pain.

'You alright there, Oliver?' Laughlin asks, patting me on the shoulder.

'Er . . . yes? I guess so.'

'You see? Not all that painful, eh?'

'No. I suppose not.'

Okay, my back feels warm and a little stingy – but it's nowhere near as bad as I feared it was going to be.

'Great! We've got another two or three here, before we move down.'

The prospect of moving down still sounds a little ominous, but my overwhelming dread has lessened considerably. Maybe this won't be so bad, after all.

Laughlin continues to divest my lower back of its remaining hair, before pulling the sheet covering my lower half down, and exposing my pale little bottom for all the world to see.

'Well, then,' he says in a thoughtful voice. 'Yer no' too bad down here, Oliver. Just a couple of strips in the crack will do you.'

I'm hoping that 'in the crack' is some sort of Scottish slang for doing something quickly and painlessly . . . but it really isn't, is it?

My eyes go wide as I feel Tina slather me in more wax.

Only she's not *slathering*, is she?

Oh no.

She's *inserting*.

Not deep, you understand. I'm pretty sure my rectum doesn't require a waxing . . . but she's definitely getting on down in there between my botty cheeks, with no apparent concern for my welfare or her personal hygiene.

I'm not going to describe what it feels like to have wax in between the cheeks of your bottom. Suffice to say, it feels like I've had *an accident*.

Then Laughlin applies the paper strips and I brace myself for the inevitable.

'Now, Oliver, this might hurt a bit!' Laughlin McPurty tells me cheerfully. 'You may feel a wee sting.'

'Eeeeuuurrrgggggghhhhh,' is about all I can manage.

'It's in there and ready,' Laughlin mutters. 'Off we go to the races . . . ready for anythin' and up to the wee smidgies . . . in one! Two! THREE!'

RRRRRRIIIIIIIIIIIIIIPPPPPPPPP

Of course, before this I knew – intellectually speaking – that the skin around the bottom area is more sensitive than that on the lower back. It only makes anatomical sense. I have not been aware of that fact on a visceral, purely emotional level until now, though.

'OH JESUS!!' I scream, probably loud enough for the bugger to hear me, whatever cloud he happens to be perched on.

My arse is on fire. My bottom is ravaged. My rear end is destroyed. My backside is ruined.

'Steady on there, Oliver!' Laughlin says, patting me on the shoulder again. 'That's the left side done, now jus' to get that right side sorted and we'll move on to yer penis.'

What! What?! *Penis?!* What is this talk of *penis*?!

There must be no penis involved! There can be no penis!

The penis cannot be part of this horror! Never! Never the penis! Never the—

RRRRRRIIIIIIIIIIIIIIPPPPPPPPP

'AAARRGGGHH!'

The world has ended. The universe has collapsed. Star Wormwood blazes in the skies.

'Tis the end! The End of Days is here! Everything is dust! All is lost!

'You okay there, Oliver?'

All I can manage is a quiet burble. My bottom is gone. All that remains is a burning supernova.

'Ach. Nice to see you've relaxed into it.' Laughlin lifts up the sheet. 'Now, swivel yersel' around, and we'll get that manzilian on the go.'

I want to say no.

I need to say no.

Every fibre in my being *demands* that I say no.

I do not want this thing he refers to as a 'manzilian'. It does not sound good. Not one little bit. It sounds like something Godzilla fights at the end of the movie.

He probably wouldn't stand for this. Not Godzilla. He'd say no to being waxed – before disintegrating the entire city, probably.

I need to be more like Godzilla.

Yes.

That's the ticket.

. . . as it turns out, I can certainly *sound* like Godzilla.

When a scrawny Scottish beautician rips a strip of waxed paper away from my pubic area, anyway.

RRRRRRIIIIIIIIIIIIPPPPPPPPP

'Reeeeeeaaaaaaaarrrrrrrrrrccccccccchhhhhhhhhh!'

See? Godzilla.

Definitely Godzilla.

For a few moments, I lie there, as ruined as the Incan civilisation. As I do this, Laughlin and Tina tidy away the used strips of waxy paper into a rubbish bag. The amount of hair on all of them doesn't bear thinking about. I will think about them, though . . . long into the night.

'Alright, Oliver. You're lovely and smooth now, in all the right places. We'll let you relax in here for a few minutes on your own. And when you're done, pop your clothes back on and we'll see you outside.'

'Oh . . . okay,' I reply with a sigh. 'That's . . . fine.'

'Good! Glad you're feeling nice and chilled out.'

Chilled out? Good God, man! My entire nether regions are blazing with the heat of a thousand suns. How could I be *chilled out*??

Laughlin and Tina exit the room, leaving me alone with my thoughts, and the pan pipes.

The one thing I'm principally thinking about is how much of a masochist Monica Blake must be. She's the one who suggested I come here, in order to help me get over my break-up with Samantha. It's what she did, after all.

If having all of this done is what got her over her own heartbreak, then she must be clinically insane.

Mind you, I can't say I'm feeling all that heartbroken at the moment. It's a little hard to pay attention to what's going on with your heart, when your arsehole has a red-hot poker shoved into it.

I heave another sigh.

Why didn't I just say no?

Why didn't I just get off the massage table before any of this?

What's *wrong with me*?

Why do I have this complete inability to upset people? Even when it comes at my own painful expense?

And I don't just mean surrendering to Laughlin McPurty's ministrations.

I wouldn't be here if I hadn't capitulated to Erica. If I had just said no to her in a firm but fair fashion, I'm sure she would have backed down.

But I didn't, did I?

No. I just went along with it. Just like I went along with the waxing.

Which is now why I'll be spending this evening with my arse parked in a cold bath.

Did this have something to do with why Samantha finished with me?

Did she want a more manly man, who can thrust one manly hand out and say no to anything he doesn't fancy getting involved with?

Am I *weak*?

Is that it?

I rub my hand over my face.

Bloody hell.

This has *not* been a good use of my time.

And it has certainly not made me feel better about losing Samantha.

If anything, it's made me feel even worse.

But never mind . . . Now I have to gingerly get dressed again, without letting any material touch my bottom or genitals, for fear of re-awakening the supernova, which has gone off the boil a little in the few minutes I've been lying here.

I slip my clothes back on slowly, wincing a bit as I do so. When I am fully dressed and upright, I walk over to the door, trying as hard as I can not to let too much material slide over the skin in the areas that Laughlin McPurty has just ritually abused for his own amusement.

This rather makes me look like I'm trying to hold in the world's most explosive fart, but I don't really care, as appearing massively flatulent is infinitely preferable to feeling denim rub across my red-raw skin.

Outside, Tina is standing by with another bogmot orange and minty rubadub tea. Part of me wants to tip it over her to see how she likes the feel of burning skin.

I take the tea with a weak smile and have a sip as I sit down in one of the chairs along the back wall. The salon looks like it's beginning to fill up now. Both Imogen and Stacy are dealing with customers, and Tina goes to join them to help out. I shuffle a bit on my seat, feeling the burning intensify around my poor bottom again. I am internally praying that the treatments are over for the day.

My prayers are answered when Laughlin hurries over to me and plonks himself down by my side. 'Okay, Oliver, how are you doing? Well, I hope.'

'Oh yes, I'm absolutely fine, thank you.'

'Enjoy all of the treatments, did you?'

'Yes, I certainly did.'

'And you liked the tea?'

'Oh my, yes. It tastes lovely.'

'Do you think you'll be back?'

'Yes. I probably will.'

'That's great. Hopefully today's little taster of what we have on offer will make you feel a bit better about yourself. We're in the self-esteem business here.'

'Yes, yes. I feel better already.'

I mean, Jesus Christ. *What the hell is wrong with me?*

'That's so wonderful. It was fantastic to have you here, and to help you out.'

Oh, for the love of God, he's going in for a hug.

Laughlin wraps his arms around me and gives me a tight, tight squeeze. I'm forced to lean forward so he can accomplish this, which squishes my red-raw bottom and my red-raw pubic area uncomfortably against my jeans.

And here I am, in a tender embrace with the psychopath who's just done this to me.

With the embrace done, Laughlin stands up and leads me over to the main door. As we pass his staff, I give them all a smile and wave. Tina and Stacy smile back, but Imogen gives me a dark look. I'm not entirely sure what I've done to earn this, but I have to guess it's my inadvertent sexism from earlier.

I would try to apologise, but I just want to get out of this salon as quickly as possible. Beyond its doors lies the outside world, wherein I shall find a nice cool bath and a cup of proper tea, without a bingo bango orange or any mint roybongos in sight.

'I'll look forward to reading your article about us on Actual Life,' Laughlin tells me at the door, with a meaningful look in his eyes.

Sigh.

I know what he'll be expecting. A glowing write-up of his beauty treatments that will send the hordes to his front door. That's what everyone wants. Laughlin has the same expectant tone to his voice that every single person I've ever spoken to has, after I've sampled their wares for the website.

But it's not really my job to write them an advert. It's my job to give a truthful account of what I've experienced.

I fear Laughlin may be a little put out with me once he reads my next feature . . .

'I'll be sure to give you an accurate and honest write-up,' I reply to him, as I always do in these situations.

Laughlin doesn't quite know how to respond to that. They never do, really.

I thank him for his time before I leave, though. He probably isn't aware that what he thinks are beauty treatments are in fact crimes against humanity, but I'm not going to shatter that illusion for him at his doorway. Much safer to do it from the confines of my office in about two hours.

The walk back to my car is more ginger than Geri Halliwell.

The drive back to the office is more ginger than the entire Weasley family stapled to Prince Harry.

Sitting back at my desk is as ginger as Ed Sheeran pumped full of Tizer to the point of bursting.

When Erica comes over to see how it all went, I am fantasising about inserting an ice pole into myself.

No one should ever fantasise about the insertion of an ice pole. Unless they're married to Mr Freeze.

'How did it go, then?' Erica asks. 'The haircut looks good,' she says, with an amused look on her face.

I return this with one of plaintive misery. 'They waxed my bottom.'

'Did they?'

'Yes. And rootled in my fingernails.' I waggle one hand up under her face to show her the results.

'Very nice.'

My brow creases. 'What's a pernickety?'

Erica shakes her head. 'I have no idea.'

'No. Me neither.' My eyes narrow. 'And the wee smidgies. Any idea what they might be?'

She continues to shake her head. 'Nope. You've lost me.'

I nod slowly. 'Okay. Just thought I'd ask.'

Erica laughs and pats me on the hand. 'I'll leave you to start writing the feature, Ollie. I'm sure it'll be extremely good . . . even if you never find out what the wee smidgies are.'

I shudder.

I hope to never find out what the wee smidgies are, to be honest. If I do, I'm afraid my sanity may be lost in less than a pernickety.

Gratefully, as I start to get into writing about what's just happened to me, the burning and stinging start to fade away.

By the time I actually get to writing about the experience of having my undercarriage waxed, I am feeling comfortable enough again to move around in my seat normally.

It's only when I pop to the loo that I am reminded of the results of my waxing. I look like a plucked chicken down there. It's a good job I'm not going to be having sex any time soon. I rather resemble a twelve-year-old boy in the sausage department, right now. This is not a sexy look for anyone who wishes to remain on the right side of the law.

But, of course, thinking about sex automatically makes me think of Samantha.

I wonder what she would make of my freshly bald bits and pieces, as I walk to my desk, and this drops me back into my pit of depression almost instantly.

Suffice to say, the beauty treatment did not do for me what it did for Monica Blake.

Nor did it convince me that attempting the suggestions sent in from our readers is the right way to go about following up on 'Dumped Actually'.

After all . . . who the hell really wants to read about me getting a manzilian, anyway?

CHAPTER FIVE

EYES OF A DISAPPROVING DOE

EVERYBODY.

That's who.

Oh, my good grief.

This is *insane*.

My second 'Dumped Actually' feature was even more popular than the first.

In the two weeks since I published the damn thing, it's been viewed over four hundred thousand times.

Nearly half a million people have enjoyed rootling, the wee smidgies and my supernova butthole.

You know how I thought Laughlin McPurty might be a bit upset when he read my truthful account of my visit to his salon?

Not in the bloody *slightest*.

He *loved* the article.

'But I don't understand it!' I say to Erica as she reads Laughlin's excited email. 'I basically slagged his business off!'

Erica shakes her head. 'Not really, Ollie. The way the story reads, you make it sound like it's your fault you didn't have much of a good time.'

I blink a couple of times. 'Do I?'

'Yep. You come across as awkward and out of your depth. Any criticism you may have of Mr McPurty's treatment methods gets swallowed up in your own sense of inadequacy.'

'Oh. Okay . . . *good* . . . I guess?'

'Oh, damn right,' Erica replies, slamming the lid of her laptop closed. 'Great work again. If you carry on like this, we'll have to give you a raise!'

'Really?' I say hopefully.

She rolls her eyes. 'Don't be silly, Ollie. Benedict is still only one step away from getting us shit-canned, even with "Dumped Actually" doing so well.'

'Oh.'

'So . . . what are you going to try next, then?'

'I'm sorry?'

'Well, the trip to the salon went very well. We need to get you off on another little adventure – as suggested by one of our loyal readers.'

'Went *very well*?' I say in a stunned voice. 'I've been through two tubes of E45, and my arsehole has only just stopped itching.'

'Yes, Ollie. And over four hundred thousand people *loved it*. So, I say again . . . what's next? How about the camping one? That sounds like it might be lots of fun!'

'I . . . But . . . You . . . I can't . . . I . . .' I purse my lips together for a second. 'I'll go take a look at my emails,' I eventually say with resignation, and trudge out of Erica's office with my head down.

***

Look, I'm not going all the way up to the bloody Cairngorms.

It's miles away, and after what happened to me with Laughlin McPurty, I want to be nowhere near anything Scottish for quite some time.

The New Forest will just have to do the job.

And I'm not doing it for a month.

I can just about manage two nights in a tent, and that's only under extreme duress.

And then there's the problem of finding a couple of friends to go with me. As I said before, I've never been good at keeping my friendships with other men going when I'm with a woman. It's a character trait I'm not particularly proud of, but it's just something that tends to happen. Yes, I can still maintain casual friendships, but nothing deeper than that. When I'm putting so much of my energy into a romantic relationship, I can respond to the odd, impromptu invite along to the pub with a mate, but organising anything more than that tends to go by the wayside.

Which creates something of a problem if I'm going to take Wolf Moresby's advice.

I would ask my dad to come along, but he and Mum are off on another cruise at the moment. This leaves Wimsy as just about my only option.

My only option, that is, until he turns my invitation down flat.

'I don't do tenting,' he tells me over the phone. 'It's uncomfortable, cold and boring. And with my luck, I'll be living in a tent soon, anyway, so I'd rather avoid doing it by choice, thanks.'

And that's the end of that. I may have persuaded Wimsy to remain on this earth, but he's still not exactly what you'd call *in a good place* mentally.

So that leaves me on my own, unfortunately.

What a sorry state of affairs.

Still, maybe a little self-reflection on my own would be a good thing, to be honest. It might give me the chance to get a few things straight in my head. And if I get lonely, I can always talk to a passing badger.

Also, this little adventure should give me more than enough material for 'Dumped Actually' volume three, so I'm going to go through with it . . . even though I will be on my lonesome.

Hell, I pretty much feel on my own all the time at the moment, anyway, with Samantha not around. I might as well do it physically, as well as metaphorically.

I manage to convince a local camping supplies shop to let me borrow the equipment I need for free, promising I'll mention them in the story. Writing an increasingly popular article for a website should come with some perks, after all.

Then it's just the matter of driving down to the forest and finding somewhere appropriate to pitch my tent.

Trying to recreate Wolf Moresby's off-the-grid trip to the remote Cairngorms as much as possible, I elect to ignore all of the formal campsites dotted around, and take myself off somewhere nice, quiet and remote.

I get as far as about a quarter of a mile off the road, before deciding that remote is a relative term, and as long as I can't hear a motorway, then that should be fine. The woodland glade I stumble upon seems perfectly acceptable to me, as the ground is nice and level, and the grass is quite short. It's pretty much the ideal spot to make a pitch.

You're not going to read a hilarious account of one man's bungled attempts to put up a tent at this point. These modern tents are dead easy to erect (more's the pity for anyone looking for some comedy value here), and within half an hour I have a nice little campsite all set up and ready to go.

There's the tent, a fold-out chair, a portable heater and a small stove – all laid out in the small clearing I found in the middle of a group of ancient-looking conifers. I am ready to rock and roll.

And by rock and roll, I mean sit quietly and wait for the boredom to render me unconscious.

Camping – as Wimsy pointed out – is *boring*.

There's no Wi-Fi, for starters.

And crapping in a bush may sound like a way to be at one with nature, but give me porcelain and a double-flush any day of the week.

Besides, there's probably poison ivy out there somewhere, and my poor bottom has only just recovered from being red-raw and itchy. I don't need a repeat performance.

But I will put up with it for a couple of days, because there are probably worse ways to spend a weekend – given that the weather is quite nice, the forest is very pretty and I have about three or four books I've been wanting to read for weeks now.

I have entertainment, a nice peaceful environment and several cans of gin and tonic to get through. All should be well.

And indeed, the first evening goes fine. Okay, I burn the sausage casserole on the stove a little bit, and the first book I've brought with me – a right old potboiler of a thriller from a first-time author – ends up being crap, but other than that, it is an extremely relaxing way to spend your time.

I can almost see what Wolf Moresby was on about. Being here in nature is a very therapeutic way to spend your time. It is when it's summer and the weather is on your side, anyway. Sitting on a chair long into the evening with a small heater keeping you warm as you make your way through the latest Neil Gaiman is a very soothing experience.

I even feel quite comfortable as I turn in for the night. Instead of sleeping on the floor, I have a rather nifty inflatable mattress, which isn't far off the same comfort level as my bed at home. I drift off in no time, and actually get the best night's sleep I've had in weeks.

That's the first evening.

By the time the second rolls around, I'm so bored I can hear my neatly manicured toenails growing.

I haven't looked at Twitter or YouTube in twenty-four hours now. I've already finished the Neil Gaiman book, and the remaining two – another couple of potboilers by authors I don't know – don't seem appealing in the slightest.

You can only spend so long cooking on a small camping stove before it becomes tedious, and the complete lack of human interaction is really starting to get to me.

At six thirty that evening, I am slouched in my camping chair, staring at a squirrel who is mucking about in the tree opposite without an apparent care in the world.

It's not that I'm particularly enamoured with the squirrel's doings, it's just that there's quite literally nothing else to look at that is in any way interesting.

Enjoying your natural surroundings is good for a couple of hours, but there's only so much stimulation you can get from a bunch of conifers and a few sparrows before you start to yearn for a bit of Sky News.

The squirrel gives me a look that seems to suggest that I am an ungrateful bastard, before scrabbling his way up the tree and out of my sight.

Sigh.

What the hell do I do now?

Sigh.

Go for an evening walk? Nah. I might get lost.

Sigh.

Get an early night? Doubtful. I haven't gone to sleep at seven thirty since I was five.

Sigh.

Get the laptop out and do some writing? *Ugh.* I don't think so. Besides, the battery life is terrible on the damn thing these days. I'd probably get into a nice little flow, and the bloody thing would conk out.

Sigh.

. . .

. . . . . .

How about I send Samantha a text message to see how she's doing?

103

My heart rate immediately speeds up at the prospect of doing such a thing. My phone has no Wi-Fi signal, but I can still send a text . . . or even make a call, should I wish to.

To Samantha.

Just to see how she is, you understand.

Nothing more than that. Nothing at all.

Would she answer? That's the question.

I've hoped and longed for her to call *me* these past few weeks (as pretty much everyone does when they get dumped – we all just want them to *come back*, don't we?) but it hasn't happened, of course.

So, why would she answer a call from me, if she hasn't tried to get in touch herself?

And even if she did pick up her phone, what would that mean?

I sit up in the camping chair, with suddenly sweaty palms.

This is the first time I've contemplated doing something like this. After the horror of Thorn Manor, the idea of getting in contact with Samantha again has made me feel physically sick. The embarrassment, humiliation and downright unfairness of it all is just too overwhelming.

And yet, here I am, thinking about getting in touch with her again for the first time since the break-up.

Aaaargh!

I should never have come out here!

This crazy notion wouldn't have popped into my head if I had enough other stuff to distract me.

But here in the forest, all on my own, with nothing better to think about, my brain has decided to throw up this most horrendous of options, and now I'm sat here on tenterhooks, considering it . . .

I pick up my phone.

I put my phone down again.

I pick it up once more.

I throw it down on to the ground, like it's done something wrong.

I pick it back up and actually open the iMessage app. I'd deleted all of my previous messages to Samantha through teary eyes a couple of days after the break-up, but I still have her number saved. Couldn't go that far, you see.

I start to write a message. I just ask her how she is, what she's been up to and how she's feeling. I keep it light, breezy and in no way representative of my actual feelings.

My thumb hovers over the send button, and the entire universe holds its breath.

Then I remember the horrified expression on her face as she said no. And that long, drawn-out note on the trombone that signalled my descent into misery.

No!

No!

NO!

I literally throw the phone across the glade in which I'm sat, watching it plummet into a thicket of tall grass.

My heart continues to race for a few more minutes.

I was *this close.*

This. Bloody. Close.

This close to making what would have been a *huge* mistake. What Samantha did to me was absolutely *awful.* She's the last person I should speak to.

Gah.

Loving and hating someone at the same time can really take it out of you.

It's a good half an hour before I've calmed back down completely – after I've given myself a good talking to. It would have been nice to have a friend out here with me to do this, but sometimes I feel like my own subconscious is another person, anyway, and has no problem berating me for any stupid decisions I make . . . or nearly make, in this case.

With that taken care of, another full hour goes by before I inevitably become bored again.

I deliberately don't look over at where I'd thrown the phone. Not even once. That way definitely lies madness.

. . . more madness, I mean.

But what the hell do I do with myself instead?

If I just sit here any longer, the temptation to go pick that bloody phone up might come over me, and that must be avoided under all circumstances.

I *have* to think of something to occupy myself with.

. . .

. . . . . .

I could, you know, *have a wank*.

I contemplate this idea for a moment, as I stare back up at the trees – and resolutely not at that tall thicket of grass with the mobile phone in it.

I am alone, after all. There's nobody around to see me. And if I go into the tent, I will have privacy, anyway, even if somebody did blunder past.

And there's nothing else to do, is there? Nothing else to occupy my mind sufficiently to prevent disastrous text message sending.

Wolf Moresby went out into the wilds for some constructive self-reflection. I'm damn sure I'm not going to achieve anything like that, but a little self-*abuse* probably wouldn't go amiss in its place.

Sod it.

Why not?

With my mind made up, I surreptitiously get out of the chair and turn back to the tent. Quite why I'm being surreptitious is beyond me. There's no bugger about to see what I'm doing, with the possible exception of the squirrel – and I doubt he'd cast much judgement on me having a quick shufty. After all, he does spend a great deal of his time playing with his own nuts.

I climb back into the tent and lie down on the inflatable mattress, cramming the sleeping bag behind my head to prop myself up a bit.

Then I divest myself of my jeans and boxers, looking down upon my penis after I have done so.

Here we reach something of a problem . . .

Because my laptop battery is knackered, and because there's no Wi-Fi, I'm not going to be able to find any pornography to assist me. That leaves me with just my imagination.

Now, ordinarily, this would not be an issue. I am the type of person who has no trouble conjuring up convincing daydreams in my head (I'm a writer, after all), and could certainly create a nice scenario that would help me.

The problem I have is that whenever I think about sex these days, I invariably think about the sex I had with Samantha. She liked to wear black lingerie. I can still hear the whisper of it as she crossed her legs.

Now, Mr Penis has no trouble with these memories *whatsoever*. The rest of Ollie Sweet isn't quite so happy about them, though. The last thing I want to do is think about Samantha any more than I already have this evening. That phone isn't all that far away, after all . . .

But Mr Penis cares nothing for such things.

He is indifferent to my heartache and mental pain. All he knows is that if I think long and hard about the sexiest times I spent with Samantha, it's infinitely preferable to any pornography that I could watch. Personal experience trumps other people getting down to it every time. And Samantha and I did have some truly epic sex, whether she was in lingerie or not. I've never felt as sexually compatible with anyone before. Not even Yukio, whose seemingly encyclopaedic knowledge of carnal pursuits was never-ending – and quite exhausting.

It's a cliché, but being 100 per cent in love with someone does make the sex better. And if that person has a kinky side that is not averse to wearing sexy black lingerie a lot, then all the better.

Sigh.

With a picture of Samantha in her finest lingerie unwillingly fixed in my mind, I begin to massage some life into Mr Penis. This doesn't take long, and before a minute has elapsed, I am standing proud.

Then something occurs to me. Samantha always liked to make love with a musical accompaniment. Something sexy, with a steady rhythmic beat. If I'm going to imagine being with her again for this, I might as well go the whole hog and recreate the experience as much as I can.

Leaving Mr Penis to twitch to himself for a moment, I reach into my rucksack, and pull out my MP3 player and earphones. Popping them into my ears, I select some Massive Attack to listen to. The hard, pulsating rhythm of their music is always good to have on in the background while you're getting naughty – even if you have to ignore some of the lyrics. I stick on *Mezzanine*, as it's still their best album, and return my attention to the task at hand.

It's incredibly easy to picture having sex with Samantha. She is so burned into my subconscious that it's no trouble at all to whisk myself back a few months to when my life was a happy place to be.

I close my eyes to better block out the world around me, making the memories even more intense. I can almost smell Samantha's perfume, and feel the soft, supple sensation of her skin under my fingers.

I now have an erection that you could pound nails in with. This wank is not going to last long.

As I continue to relive memories of sexy times past, I begin to feel the unwanted emotions encroaching again. This is the price I knew I would pay for using my memories of Samantha to masturbate over. All the pain and sense of loss that I've been attempting to keep at bay comes flooding out as I fall deeper and deeper into my memories of her.

This is becoming torture.

I really should stop.

But I'm approaching the point of no return, and stopping would leave me frustrated – as well as heartbroken.

This does mean that I have to conclude this wank with tears streaming down my face, though.

I must look like a sorry, sorry sight. Quite pathetic, indeed. A grown man with his pants around his ankles, his hand gripping his penis, and a look of abject anguish on his face.

I'm eternally glad no one is around to see me. It would be incredibly embarrassing.

The music begins to reach a crescendo, as I begin to reach my own. I really want to get this over and done with now. The combination of mental pain and physical pleasure is becoming too much for me. I just need to finish up and get back to squirrel watching.

It gets closer . . .

And closer . . .

And closer . . .

As I get into the home straight, I gasp and open my eyes.

Staring down at me, with large, liquid eyes, is the most beautiful deer I have ever seen.

Its head is poking in through the tent door, which I had neglected to zip up before commencing my masturbatory trip down memory lane.

I instantly freeze in place, gazing up into those luminous liquid eyes – which have a slightly disapproving look about them.

I do not scream. I do not flail around. I am simply too shocked and appalled by this turn of events to do anything other than sit there rigid – in every sense of the word.

How long has the deer been there?

I simply do not know.

Has it just popped its head in right at this moment? Or has it been staring at me with those disapproving eyes the entire time I've been flogging my winky for all I'm worth?

It really is quite a stunning-looking creature, and in other circumstances – where I wasn't gripping my willy for dear life, while 'Teardrop' comes to a conclusion in both of my ears – I would reach forward and give the deer a friendly pat.

I'm sure the deer would very much enjoy a friendly pat. And possibly a tickle under the chin.

Not from a raging pervert with tears coursing down his face, though. There are very few creatures on this planet that would enjoy that. With the possible exception of some Tory MPs.

I really should put my penis away.

This should be the first item on the agenda, following this strange and unwelcome turn of events. But there's a part of my brain that is refusing to accept that any of this is actually happening, and will not relinquish its grip on what it perceives is the only real thing left in the universe. It's as if letting go of my pulsing, purple member will force it to confront the unlovely new reality it has found itself thrust into.

It's at this moment that the deer's tiny offspring pokes its head into my tent as well, to see what all the fuss is about.

This is a *spectacular* turn of events, of course.

Now I am basically having a wank in front of Bambi.

Well, Oliver. Perhaps at this stage it might be a good idea to put your bloody penis away.

I have to wholeheartedly concur with my inner monologue. Nothing would give me greater pleasure right now than to pop the old chap back into my boxer shorts.

If only my boxer shorts weren't currently around my ankles.

'Could you go away, please?' I ask the deer politely.

You might think that shouting and wildly gesticulating at them might be a better way to get them to remove their heads from my tent – and you'd probably be right. But they look like such gentle creatures. I don't want to scare them. Far better I speak to them like an old English butler, with one shaking hand covering my rapidly shrinking penis.

'Shoo!' I say lightly, flapping the non-penis-holding hand about ineffectually.

They do not shoo.

In fact, Bambi now starts to root around in my rucksack with his nose. There's a Belvita soft bake in there somewhere I was planning on having for breakfast. That's probably what the little guy is after. I'm sure the scent of a chocolate oat soft bake is like manna from heaven to a herbivore such as he.

'Please shoo,' I say again. 'Shoo, shoo, shoo.'

The doe looks at me quizzically. She probably can't decide if I'm asking her to go away, or fetch me the nearest available footwear.

Neither is allowed to happen, because at this point, dad turns up.

This was inevitable. You don't get a doe and a baby deer in your tent for long, without daddy deer turning up to see what's going on.

Dad's got a big pair of antlers parked on his noggin, though, so he can't actually get into the tent with me. He settles for peeking in over his offspring's rump, sniffing and rolling his eyes.

That sodding Belvita. I knew I should have just bought a bag of porridge.

Speaking of said delightful breakfast treat, Bambi has now pulled it out of the rucksack and is trying to chew his way through the foil wrapping.

This distracts his mother from her continued inspection of my person. She turns her head and sniffs at the Belvita, just as the youngster finally manages to get at the soft bake within the foil.

All three are now distracted by the oaty bar of chewy goodness, which is probably a good time for me to get the hell out of here. Maybe if I evacuate the tent, the family of Belvita fans will do so as well.

I slowly turn around and start to pull up the tent canvas behind me. The canvas is very tight and taut, but I manage to open enough of a gap to squeeze my head and shoulders through.

At no point during this do I think to pull up my boxer shorts or jeans.

Which is why, about three seconds later, as I'm half out of the tent, I feel the cold and slightly wet feel of a small deer's nose upon my bottom – in an area still mostly devoid of hair, thanks to Laughlin McPurty.

'*Maaggahaana!*' I exclaim as the nose probes areas that no nose should probe.

It would appear that I am able to speak an alien language when I have a baby deer's nose up my bottom, as well as when I'm on a rollercoaster.

Good to know.

To get away from this unexpected and unwelcome development, I start to yank myself forward at high speed across the grass, like a soldier under fire. All the time I'm doing this, I'm screaming – also much like a soldier under fire, probably. The slow-moving virtual paralysis that consumed me with the initial shock of finding deer in my tent has evaporated, to be replaced by an energetic desire to remove myself from their vicinity with as much haste as the human body allows.

I cover a good ten feet of dewy grass in about three nanoseconds. It would have been even faster if I wasn't still dragging my boxer shorts around my ankles.

I really do need to pull those up at some point, before I have to start asking some serious questions about myself.

I do that very thing, and grimace as I yank the soggy black material up over my privates. My jeans are long gone. I think I lost them during the tent escape.

In the rapidly dwindling evening light, I can see the deer family starting to remove themselves from the tent. Dad backs away first, then mum, and junior brings up the rear, his face covered in Belvita crumbs.

The little bastard. I was really looking forward to that.

It's at this point I realise that my woodland glade is actually *full* of deer. I can count a good dozen surrounding my campsite. It would seem that I inadvertently chose a favourite foraging ground of some of the New Forest's finest fallow deer to make my camp. No wonder the grass was so trimly chopped.

I watch as the family amble their way back over to the other members of the herd. The father deer snorts a few times. And then he does something that makes my blood run cold. *He looks right at me.*

As soon as he does this, all of the other deer also *look right at me.*

Fifteen sets of ruminant eyes staring at you through the gloom of twilight goes way beyond disconcerting. We're entering the territory of being properly alarmed, here. And maybe even a little terrified.

Slowly, the deer all start to move towards me. Bambi is at the front of the herd, still licking his chops.

'I don't have any more Belvitas,' I tell him. 'All the Belvitas are gone now.'

I'm still speaking in that soft and irritating English-butler voice – because God forbid I actually do something horrible like spook the bloody deer, eh?

'Please leave me alone,' I entreat, without having any effect whatsoever. 'I really don't have any more food on me.'

By way of demonstration, I pull the sides of my boxer shorts out a few inches, in the time-honoured gesture, to show that my pockets are empty. As my boxer shorts don't have any pockets, I just look like I'm putting on some kind of bizarre display for the deer, like one of those tropical birds with its wings splayed open. I might as well start dancing around in a circle and have done with it.

Bambi and pals are having none of it, though. They are unconvinced by my display. They clearly believe I am the holder of more delicious Belvitas and will not stop until they have shaken me down for every last one.

'No more Belvitas!' I say, trying to sound harsh. I even jab a finger at them to show just how authoritative I am. It's the gesture of someone fully in command of the situation. Surely they must realise now that I am being serious about my lack of soft bakes? My finger is as pointy as it can possibly be!

Nope. The big sods are still coming.

It's probably time to run for it.

Bloody Wolf Moresby . . .

If I get out of this, I'm sending him an empty Belvita packet through the post.

What transpires next is not a high-speed chase through the forest. Far from it.

In actual fact, I only get about ten yards, with my arms flapping about like windsocks in a hurricane, before I realise that the deer aren't following me.

I am oddly disappointed by this. If I'm going to run away from something in terror, I'd prefer it to make some kind of effort at pursuit, otherwise I just look silly.

I turn and stare back at the deer, who are already dispersing into the forest, having come to the conclusion that I'm not going to be supplying them with any more oaty breakfast snacks any time in the near future.

The last deer to take their leave of me is the doe who caught me masturbating. There's still that disapproving look in her eyes, but it's now mixed with what I'm sure is a degree of pity. At least that's what it looks like in the fading light, from ten yards away. She could just be keying up for a poo, for all I know.

Still, at least I wasn't actually attacked by any of the deer. Not that this was ever really likely. Deer are placid and happy creatures, by and large. Especially ones who are quite used to humans tramping over their foraging grounds. I was never in any real danger.

No. Fallow deer are quite harmless, unless you do something to annoy them.

Not like wasps.

Wasps will have a pop at you just for being alive.

Now, this might seem like an odd thing to say. Why on earth have I suddenly started talking about wasps? It's *deer* we've been dealing with, so why the mental leap from large, foraging mammals to small buzzing insects?

Because I'm stood right under a wasp's nest, that's why.

Not two feet above my head – clamped to the branch of an overhanging oak tree is a nest about a foot long and a foot across.

And wasps don't need any excuse to have a go at you. Not even when you flap your hands around your head like windsocks in a hurricane.

I feel the first sting on the back of my neck.

'Oww! Bloody hell!' I wail, one hand instantly going to the back of my head. I look up and see the nest, from which several pissed-off-looking wasps are erupting.

Not that there's any other way to describe a wasp as anything other than 'pissed-off-looking'. It's kind of their *raison d'être*.

'Oh . . . for the love of pernickety,' I say in a tiny voice, as the buzzing maniacs fly straight at my head.

The next twenty minutes of Oliver Sweet's life can be accurately chronicled just by relaying the sounds that accompany them. They are as follows:

Buzzing.

Two loud screams.

Bare feet running through a forest.

Three more screams.

More buzzing.

A zip being quickly pulled up.

Another scream.

The rustling of canvas.

The clanking of metal.

Lots of buzzing.

Yet another scream.

The unzipping of a large bag.

Scream.

More sounds of rustling canvas and clanking metal.

Buzzing.

Scream.

Heavy, fast footsteps.

A large bag being dragged across snapping twigs.

Buzzing.

A blood-curdling scream.

A car door slamming.

Another car door slamming.

A car door opening.

The sound of fast footsteps.

Buzzing.

The noise of a man rummaging around in a tall thicket of grass for a mobile phone.

Yet another scream.

Incredibly fast footsteps.

A car door opening and banging closed again.

A car engine revving loudly, before fading away.

The sound of buzzing growing distant.

The tweets of a single bird.

Silence for a moment.

The sound of a rough tongue licking a foil wrapper.

A small but satisfied mammalian grunt.

***

Of course, there's no way I'm writing any of this up for 'Dumped Actually'. What do you take me for? A bloody madman?

Can you actually imagine what the reaction would be to me telling people all about my experience of masturbating in front of a family of New Forest deer?

What on earth would people think of me?

What would Wolf Moresby think of me, specifically?

It was his suggestion to take myself off into nature to rediscover my happiness. If he were to know that I took his innocent suggestion, and twisted it into an event bordering on accidental bestiality, what would his reaction be?

And anyway, 'Dumped Actually' is supposed to be about my attempts to find things to help me get over the heartbreak of Samantha leaving me. People don't need to hear about how much I am failing to do this, by nearly sending her a bloody text message. It's not uplifting – or helpful in the slightest.

It just makes no sense whatsoever for me to go into the office on Monday morning, sit at my desk and write a feature for Actual Life about this weekend.

No.

I shall not write the truth about my camping experience. I will make something up that is a lot less embarrassing, and a lot more helpful to my reading audience.

There's no way I'm mentioning the text message, the deer or the Belvitas.

Okay, it probably won't be as interesting, funny or as exciting, but that's just the way it is.

I do not need to describe my excruciating thirty-six hours in the New Forest just to get a bigger readership.

I mean, what kind of person would do that? What kind of person would want hundreds of thousands of people to know he sat in front of the eyes of a disapproving doe, grimly clutching his penis for dear life?

It would have to be the kind of person who has a near-pathological need for attention and affection.

Someone who has weighed up the embarrassment that it would cause him against the thrill of being popular with an audience, and come out in favour of the latter.

What kind of deep-seated need for approval and recognition would this person be cursed with?

They'd have to have severe emotional problems, wouldn't they?

CHAPTER SIX

VANITY, THY NAME IS WOMAN (WITH APOLOGIES TO SHAKESPEARE)

The Deer Porker.

That's what someone on Twitter called me.

Somebody else called me Captain CampyWank.

A third christened me The Belvita Bandit.

I also got a tweet from the British Deer Society. They weren't happy with me, let me tell you. Not because I pointed my gentleman's sausage at a family of their beloved creatures, but because I allowed Bambi to eat human food. They told me at length how foods such as soft oat bakes can be very bad for the deer's digestion.

I felt awful.

For the rest of the day, I went around with a mental image of Bambi yakking up all over his mother.

So, not only do I get to feel the hot, pulsing embarrassment I have brought down on my own head, I also get to feel the shame of hurting an innocent creature.

I truly am blessed in life.

Needless to say, the third edition of 'Dumped Actually' went down a storm again. Partly due to my masturbatory shenanigans, but also due to the way I described nearly sending Samantha that bloody text message, and how I thought about her during my ill-fated five-knuckle shuffle.

I was deeply shocked to find out that I am not the only person who has tried to have a fiddle with themselves after being made single again, only to find themselves crying like a baby.

I was equally as shocked to realise that so many people wanted to share this kind of intimate information with me.

It's like 'Dumped Actually' has uncorked a vast mental dam in the subscribers to Actual Life. The outpouring of heartbreak from across the country has fair taken my breath away.

And all because of *me*. All because I wrote a silly article.

What a *wonderful* feeling.

I am basking in the glow of all the attention. I just wish it hadn't come with being called The Deer Porker.

Erica is obviously delighted with all of this. I've hit upon a rich seam of zeitgeist here, and she's cartwheeling down the hallways because of it.

Actual Life's engagement figures are way up, the new subscriber count is the highest it's been in three years, and we're even starting to get calls from advertisers again.

Benedict Montifore scowled at me like I was the Antichrist yesterday when he came into the office to talk to Erica. He still wants to shut us down – for reasons I can't quite fathom at the moment – and I've now become the number one reason that's not happened yet, largely because ForeTech's board of directors are a lot happier with Actual Life's financial returns these days. You'd think Montifore's desire to get rid of us would have softened somewhat because of all of this – but no. He still wants shot of us all, the bastard.

This means I am a marked man.

Never mind, though . . . People in the office are starting to treat me like a *hero*.

As far as they're concerned, my silly little feature is keeping the wolves from the door, and that makes me Captain Popularity around here. This is infinitely preferable to Captain CampyWank.

It's all incredibly strange, incredibly embarrassing and incredibly marvellous.

So . . . why am I sitting here chewing on a fingernail, with a cold, hard ball of frozen steel in my gut?

Because of Callie Donnelly, that's why.

I've read through her email to me about a hundred times, and each time I do, an internal war takes place in my mind.

On the one hand, the prospect of actively trying to find another woman makes my toes curl with horror . . . but on the other, it would make an excellent fourth feature for 'Dumped Actually'.

After all, who hasn't tried to find a new love, as a replacement for the old?

We've all done it. All attempted to fill that void with a fresh face.

I remember when Yukio flew back to Japan, I went online and joined a dating website called A New Love.

I went on precisely one date.

It was with Charlotte.

Charlotte enjoyed knives.

I didn't know how much Charlotte enjoyed knives until she pulled one out of her jacket about an hour into the date.

I can still see its gleaming tip in my nightmares to this day.

Up to that point, Charlotte seemed like a normal girl, even if she did wear quite heavy and dark eyeliner.

I sat there for a further twenty minutes while Charlotte expounded at length on how she forged the knife herself from some melted-down spoons and a leaf spring from a 1987 Vauxhall truck.

Then I faked a bowel obstruction and ran away.

Given this, you'll understand my reticence to go out and find myself somebody new.

One part of me wants nothing to do with the dating scene again.

. . . and I'm not even the type of person who *has* rebound romances. I tend to be 100 per cent committed to the damn thing, or not at all. Could I even cope with meeting another woman so soon after Samantha, and maybe going through all of it again? I don't think so.

But the other part of me – the part that enjoys being called Captain Popularity and having lots of new readers – thinks it's a *great* idea. It's the same part of me that was insane enough to write all about my run-in with Bambi. The side of me that wants to keep the ball rolling, to keep the readers happy, to *please them* above all other things . . .

If I chew this fingernail any more, I'm going to need a plaster.

I need advice about this.

If I'm going to attempt such a thing, I need someone to help guide me through it. Somebody I trust.

Erica is alone in her office. I think I'd better go have a chat with her.

'Knock, knock,' I say, opening her door.

She looks up at me and smiles. As well she might. I am the golden boy around here at the moment, after all.

'If you've come looking for a Belvita, I'm fresh out,' she says, grinning like a loon.

I roll my eyes. 'Very funny.'

Erica holds up a hand. 'Hang on, I have something cued up for just such an occasion as this . . .'

She taps a few keys on her laptop and looks up at me again, an expectant expression writ large across her face.

From the laptop speakers comes a song from *The Sound of Music*.

You know which one it is already, don't you?

Yep. Julie Andrews singing her little heart out about does and deers.

I pinch the bridge of my nose and stand there with my head down as my boss sings along with Julie about rays of golden sun, and appropriate pronouns with which to describe oneself.

'Okay, okay,' I say, finally walking into the office, wincing.

Erica whacks another key, and Julie Andrews ceases her musical litany. 'Sorry, couldn't resist. I've been waiting for you to come in here for two days now.'

I slump in the chair opposite her desk, as I have done a thousand times in the past. 'I suppose I shouldn't be too mad. I have rather brought all this upon myself.'

Erica nods. 'Well, yes. But I'm eternally grateful you have.'

'You might be, but Mr Montifore clearly isn't.'

Erica's smile vanishes. 'Don't worry about him, Ollie. He's *my* problem. You just keep doing what you're doing.'

I give her a thumbs-up. 'Will do.' I sit up in the chair. 'That's actually why I've come in here. To ask you something.'

'Go on,' Erica responds, looking curious.

'It's like this. I've had an email from a woman called Callie Donnelly . . .'

'I saw it. She's the one who suggested you get back out on the dating scene again.'

'That's right. I've been sat at my desk in two minds about the whole thing, because on the one hand I know it's a great idea for another article, but on the other hand I have no desire to try to date anyone new right now. That's when I thought of you.'

Erica blinks a couple of times. 'You thought of *me*?'

'Yeah. Of course. You're the perfect person to ask.'

Erica's jaw drops open. 'Ollie . . . are you asking me out on a date?'

It's my turn for some jaw droppage. 'What?'

'You don't want to date anyone new, so you thought of me?'

'What? No! That's not what I meant!'

Oh God. How exquisitely *awful*.

'It isn't?' Erica has got over the shock very quickly, it seems, and is now looking highly amused.

'No! I just meant that I should talk to you about it all, and get your advice!'

'Oh . . . okay.' Erica's eyes twinkle as she says this. This is a cruel, cruel woman. To revel in my discomfort like this.

At that moment, my stupid treacherous brain throws up a suggestion.

Why not ask her out, Ollie? She's an incredible woman. You know her well. And you've always had a great relationship with her at work, so . . .

'Why? Would you . . . Would you go out on a date with me?' I ask hesitantly.

Erica's eyes go wide, before she starts to shake her head slowly. 'No, Ollie. I won't. And I don't think that's really what you'd want, anyway, is it?'

I also start to shake my head. 'No. Probably not.'

Stupid brain. Making stupid suggestions. Why weren't you so proactive when the deer was staring at our bloody erection?

Don't blame me, pal. You should have fed me more Omega 3.

I have to rescue this excruciating situation before it gets any worse.

'I just . . . I just wanted to ask if you think it's a good idea to go ahead with it, and if you do, what advice you could give me about meeting someone!' The words fall out of my mouth in a torrent.

Erica leans her chin on her hand and regards me with the look of someone who owns an adorable puppy that has just done a shit on the carpet. 'That sounds a bit more sensible,' she says, and ponders my request for a moment. 'You know what, Ollie? I *do* think you and I should go out together.'

'What?' For some reason my heart rate has sped up.

'Not on a date, of course. But if you're going to meet a new woman, it might be a good idea for you to have some help. I've known you long enough to know that without it you'll go out searching for new love . . . and come home with a new injury.'

I'd like to protest, but she's 100 per cent correct.

'What are you suggesting?' I ask.

'There's a place I know that might do the trick. It's quite upmarket. Lots of eligible singles for you to meet. It could be perfect.' Erica smiles. 'It's certainly somewhere I've enjoyed frequenting on occasion.'

There's a whole side of Erica Hilton I know nothing about. I feel more than a little nervous about finding out about it.

'Okay. I guess that sounds . . . *good*.'

Erica laughs. 'Oh, don't look so worried, Ollie. We'll just go along, have a couple of drinks and see if we can catch you someone nice. If not, you can just do a brief write-up on the bar itself and call it a day.'

'Yeah. Yeah, that sounds fine. Absolutely fine.'

Erica's words calm me down a bit, but the prospect of even talking to a strange woman in a setting like the one she's just described fills me with trepidation.

At least I won't be going along alone. There's something ever so comforting about Erica's levels of self-confidence. With her along for the ride, I should be able to get through the evening without too many disasters befalling me.

***

It takes three attempts for me to settle on an outfit to wear.

I start off with a blue polo neck, black jeans and my least scuffed pair of Adidas. I send a picture of myself in this get-up to Erica, who almost instantly sends back a message saying, 'NO, Ollie. Try again!'

My second attempt is, if anything, even worse. I pull out a pair of beige chinos that I haven't worn in ten years, a purple shirt – because at one point it must have been fashionable, I guess – and a pair of black work boots.

Erica's response to this ensemble is, 'You look like you're either searching for psychological help, or your next victim. Try again, Ollie. Put on something smart that you feel really uncomfortable in!'

Which sounds like strange advice to me.

However, I understand the genius of it, when I yank out the Moss Bros coal-grey suit I wore once to a wedding with Samantha and put the damn thing on. It's awful. I feel deeply uncomfortable in it. Especially when I pair it with the slim-fit white shirt that Samantha made me buy to go along with it. And then there are the shiny black shoes, with the tops that cut into my ankles. I hate them so very, very much.

When I send a picture of me dressed in all this awfulness to Erica, I almost immediately get a response saying, 'Great! That's perfect! See you outside the bar in an hour!'

Why do I put myself through these things?

Because you know you might get a good story out of it.

I can't really argue with that logic.

The taxi ride across town to the club is conducted with much chewing of fingernails. It's probably a good job we arrive outside the place in less than half an hour, otherwise I'd be trying to chat somebody up with bloody stumps.

The club is called Manucode.

This sounds more like an order given to an IT worker by a caveman than the name for a nightclub, but what the hell do I know?

The club's exterior looks exquisitely expensive. Which is to say, it's minimalist in the extreme. This is not a nightclub that feels the need to advertise itself to all and sundry.

Its long, tinted-glass frontage is lit with cool blue spotlights, and I can just about see inside, to where the moody blue lighting appears to be continued around the whole club. It's hard to make out much through the glass, other than the fact the place looks quite full.

It's a wonder I've never heard of Manucode before – but then I remember who I am, and it makes perfect sense that I've never heard of it before.

There's a simple but elegant sign above the double doors set at the right-hand side of the glass exterior, bearing the club's name in that same cool blue. Standing in front is a bouncer in an equally elegant black suit. He has a pleasant, welcoming expression on his face, which is unusual for a bouncer, and is therefore quite worrying.

I bid the bouncer a good evening.

'And to you, sir,' he replies with a smile. Somebody working on a door who is this polite is probably incredibly dangerous.

I offer him a shaky smile in return and look out into the road to see another cab pulling up.

From it emerges Erica Hilton, and my heart sinks.

There's no way I'm going to even get the chance to talk to another woman this evening, not with Erica looking like that. They won't be able to stand the comparison.

Erica is wearing a dark-green evening dress that clings to places I didn't know she had. I've only ever seen my boss in an efficient and straight-cut business pantsuit before. This dress tells me where all her curves are, and it's making my knees tremble.

The redness of her hair is particularly deep this evening, and she's worked it into a long elegant wave that must have taken hours to get right.

She walks up to me with the kind of grace usually reserved for endangered species on the savannah.

'Evening, Ollie.'

'What are you doing?' I respond, forgetting my manners.

She looks taken aback. 'What do you mean?'

I hold out my hands. 'Well . . . look at you!'

Her eyes narrow. 'What do you *mean*?' she repeats, her tone sharpened to a point.

I let out a gasp of exasperation. 'How am I supposed to meet another woman with you looking that incredible? They'll avoid coming anywhere near you!'

Erica smiles and pats my cheek. 'Oh, Ollie. I think it'll be absolutely fine.' She turns to the bouncer. 'Good evening, Carlo. How are you?'

'I'm well, thank you, Ms Hilton,' Carlo replies, opening the door as he does so. Beyond is Manucode's main bar and dance floor, full of people who look like they most definitely belong in a swanky gaff like this.

'I am not nearly cool enough to go in there,' I say in almost a whisper.

Erica rolls her eyes and snakes one arm into mine. 'Don't worry, Ollie. I'll be by your side, for as long as I need to be.'

'That's what I'm worried about. Next to you, I look like a bin bag full of cold sick.'

Without saying anything else, Erica shakes her head, and then drags me through the door.

The floor of Manucode is all polished grey concrete flecked with gold. The walls are a crisp white colour, with the occasional expensive painting hung on them. The long bar that sticks out into the centre of the expansive room is replete with every single alcoholic beverage under the sun, and is lit with that same cool blue that dominates the entire club.

The most dominant feature of the place is a waterfall that runs across the whole back wall, down a vast sheet of glass and into a long canal at the bottom that's full of what look like gemstones. Their water bill must be bloody astronomic.

The comfy-looking black chairs that sit around the shiny chrome tables have that simple sophistication about them that you just know would cost you an arm, a leg and most of your children's future.

There's a low stage in the far right-hand corner of the club, where a four-piece band is filling the air with a sweet-sounding Latin number. No cheesy DJ for Manucode tonight, it appears. Live music is the sophisticated order of the day for this place.

The whole club screams wealth and stylishness.

I scream doubt and reluctance right back at it.

And it's full of exclusive-looking people, drinking exclusive-looking drinks, with exclusive-looking expressions on their faces. I bet when they need to relieve themselves of those exclusive-looking drinks they'll go into exclusive-looking toilets and have an exclusive wee.

The only thing exclusive I've ever been near is a VAT bill.

'Let's go sit up at the bar,' Erica suggests, before gently leading me over to it.

'This is horrible,' I tell her in a low voice.

'Why?'

'People might think we're . . . you know . . . together.'

Her eyebrows shoot up. 'And you think that's *horrible*?'

'For *you*, yes.'

Erica doesn't even dignify that with a response. Instead she turns to the barman, who has miraculously appeared in front of us. 'Hello, Hector. A bourbon sour for me, and for my friend here . . .' Erica looks at me expectantly.

'A pint of Carling?' I venture.

Hector looks like I've just wiped a bogey down his nose.

'Get him a Peroni, Hector,' Erica interjects. I look at her for a moment before nodding at Hector, who squints at me, before going off to get our drinks.

'Now, Ollie,' Erica says, laying a hand on my shoulder. 'Just relax, and stop worrying too much. You don't look out of place at all. Have a few drinks, chill out and we'll see what happens.'

I nod my head again, uncertainly. Erica must be mad if she thinks I don't look out of place in this club, but then if these people do think

I'm her date tonight, then maybe I won't look *all* that bad. Anyone with a woman like her on their arm can't be a complete loser, can they?

As the evening starts to tick by, however, I come to realise that nobody thinks I am Erica's date. Erica's *pet* maybe, but definitely not her date.

She appears to be extremely well known by the club's clientele. Not a minute seems to go by without somebody new and exclusive coming up to talk to her. Erica doesn't need to move from our spot once to get into a conversation with somebody. They all just come to her.

I am roundly ignored as much as possible, except when she drags me into the conversation.

You know when you're chatting to someone quite happily, and then they bring up how well their dog is doing after the rubber band was surgically removed from its bowels?

Yeah. That.

By the time an hour and a half has gone by, I'm frankly amazed I haven't been given a pat on the head and a dog biscuit.

Erica keeps buying me Peroni beers, though, so I can't complain too much, even though this is more or less akin to having my water bowl refilled every once in a while.

The chances of me meeting a woman with which to test Callie Donnelly's thesis on getting over heartbreak are becoming less and less likely. Nobody wants to kiss the pet dog, do they?

Colour me totally surprised, then, when I'm suddenly confronted by Vanity.

Vanity is the name of a person dressed in a very tight black cocktail dress, rather than a general description of the crowd of people here gathered, I hasten to add. Though, come to think about it . . .

Vanity is tall, willowy, raven-haired and ever so exclusive. She's also way, waaaaaaaaaay out of my league. The odds of me pulling her are about as high as the bar stool I'm sat on becoming self-aware and running for prime minister.

That isn't stopping my boss having a good go, though. 'Ollie, I'd like you to meet Vanity O'Hare,' she says. 'Vanity is a good friend from my yoga class.'

I nod dumbly.

'This is Oliver Sweet, Vanity,' Erica tells her. 'He writes for me.'

Vanity looks suitably unimpressed by this.

'He's probably my most talented member of staff. Has a real way with words.'

It's clear that Vanity thinks having a way with words is about as important to her continued happiness as the economic outlook for the nation of Azerbaijan.

'He's the one who's behind "Dumped Actually",' Erica tells her in a confident tone.

At this, Vanity's interest immediately perks up.

Aha. Erica may have found an inroad here . . . whether I like it or not.

Suddenly, Vanity's attention is squarely fixed on me.

'*You* wrote "Dumped Actually"?' she asks me, in an excited tone.

'Er . . . yes. That's me.'

Her eyes light up. 'Oh God, I love it! You're so funny!' Vanity's exquisitely manicured hand touches me lightly on the chest.

What?? What?? What's happening here??

Go back to sleep, Mr Penis.

What?? No! Something has just happened!

No, it hasn't.

Oh yes, it bloody has! She just touched you! The dark-haired beauty with the million-dollar figure just touched you!

It doesn't mean anything.

Bollocks it doesn't! Don't screw this up! I've never been anywhere near someone like this before.

She's not going to be interested in having sex with us, you cretin. If she's read 'Dumped Actually', she'll know about you being hard around a baby deer.

131

Shit. I hadn't thought of that.

No, I didn't think you had. Now go back to sleep.

'Ollie's work is keeping Actual Life afloat, Vanity. I really couldn't do without him,' Erica says in a gushing manner, before she squeezes my arm gently.

What's going on here with all this female touching?

I'm starting to feel like an avocado being inspected before purchase.

'Oh. I'm so glad you have someone like this working with you, Erica,' Vanity replies. 'You know how we all *adore* you and your website. It's great to see it doing well again.'

'Thank you, Vanity!' Erica says, continuing to gush. Erica Hilton gushing is a slightly strange thing to behold. It's like I'm with a totally different person to the one I'm used to.

'Your break-up sounds like it was a really hard thing to deal with,' Vanity tells me, eyes full of sympathy.

'Yes. Yes, it was,' I reply, starting to feel uncomfortable.

. . . sorry, *more* uncomfortable.

I may be okay with writing about my disastrous love life, but talking about it with someone I've only just met is another thing entirely.

'I know how you feel,' Vanity says. 'I've been through much the same thing myself.'

'Oh. I'm sorry to hear that,' I tell her, a bit perplexed. Who the hell would dump this woman?

Vanity moves a little closer to me and touches me on the chest again in a playful manner. 'Thanks, Ollie. It's lovely to meet someone who knows what it's like. You've really made me feel better about everything.'

'Oh. Okay. Pleased to hear it.'

She cocks her head slightly to one side. 'Is anyone helping you feel better?'

'Chas! Chas Molineux!' Erica suddenly exclaims, pointing a finger towards one swarthy-looking individual across the bar. 'You owe me a cocktail, you naughty boy!' Erica turns back to Vanity and me. 'Excuse me, you two. I have a free drink awaiting me over there.' She gives me a meaningful look. 'Enjoy yourselves.'

Oh good lord.

Oi! Oi! What was that??

It was nothing, Mr Penis!

Yes, it was, you lying git! Erica leered. *She bloody well leered at us!!*

So?

What do you mean, so?? She thinks we're in here!!

Don't be ridiculous. This type of thing doesn't happen to *us*. One-night stands with beautiful women *don't happen to us*. It's just not the way we're built.

It might not be the way you're built, but it's what I was put on this earth to do, you ignoramus!

'Shall we go and sit at a quiet table in the corner?' Vanity suggests as she watches Erica walk over to the bearer of her free cocktail. 'We can talk more easily there.'

See?? See?? We're totally in, here!!

I have a suspicion that my penis may actually be right on this occasion. Unbelievable as it may seem, Vanity is giving me extremely strong signals. Ones that even I am able to understand.

An instant feeling of deep regret and shame pulses through me. For some reason, I inexplicably feel that if I go off with this incredible-looking woman, I will somehow be betraying Samantha.

It's an incredibly silly thing to think. It makes no rational sense whatsoever. But it's still right there at the centre of my mind, unwilling to go away.

No!! No, you don't!! You're not going to ruin this for me!! I need this after what happened with Bambi, you bastard!! Smile at her, agree and let's get this show on the road!!

For a moment I am frozen in place, not knowing what to do. Then I remember that I have a story to concoct about this evening . . . so I had better at least make an attempt to do something worthy of the write-up.

This gets me going.

'Okay, that sounds like a great idea,' I tell Vanity, in a slightly shaky voice.

She takes my hand. 'Great. I'm sure we'll have a *lot* to talk about,' she says, voice now huskier than Lapland.

As she leads me into a dark corner of Manucode, which is relatively empty compared to the rest of the bar, I spot Erica looking at me with a self-satisfied expression on her face. I return it with one that is partly grateful and partly scared to death.

I don't see much more of Erica that evening. Vanity holds my complete attention for a good hour over in the corner. The conversation ranges around a variety of subjects, but I would have a hard time relaying any of them to you now, because Vanity is quite a mesmerising person to be with. Her voice is melodic, her smile is captivating and she smells like thirteen kinds of wonderful. You try remembering what you're talking about when your opposite number in a conversation is like that.

I think I just about manage to hold up my end of the chat (whatever the hell we talked about), but it's touch and go, to be honest. Mostly, I just try to avoid gazing at her cleavage too much. This is slightly more difficult than inventing a perpetual motion machine out of three bottle caps and a Smarties tube.

By the time she asks me if I'd like to come back to her place for a nightcap, I am in such a state of utter bewilderment that it takes me a moment to get my mouth to work. This simply doesn't happen to people like me. Incredibly beautiful, exclusive women do not invite us back for a nightcap. We get to see them once every so often going past at speed in a Ferrari. If we're very lucky, we might get splashed by their puddle water.

'Er . . . yeah. That'd be cool,' I say, draining the last of my Peroni with a slightly trembling hand. I'm still not sure I'm ready for this kind of thing, but I'm pot committed now, so had better get my arse in gear.

Vanity then leads me out of Manucode, past Carlo, who just about manages to conceal his amazement that someone like Vanity is leaving with someone like me.

We then walk down the road about two hundred yards.

'Are we going to call a cab?' I ask her.

She smiles and delves into her cleavage, pulling out a single silver door key. 'No need. We're already here.'

Well, of course Vanity would live close to the exclusive club, in an extraordinarily expensive Georgian townhouse . . . What was I thinking?

Okay, maybe it's only the ground floor flat of the Georgian town-house, but if it costs less than a million quid, I'd be flabbergasted.

Vanity enjoys the minimalist look.

Once we're past the ornate frontage of her flat, we enter a world of clean lines and simple colours.

There's a lot of black in here, along with an equal amount of light grey, some flashy red, and a bit of white. Everything is colour-coordinated to within an inch of its life. The black couch looks like it was made just to sit on top of that red rug – which, come to think about it, it probably was. Vanity seems the type to enjoy bespoke.

The rest of the flat is similarly decked out. Vanity obviously appreciates the same kind of artwork as Manucode, as there are some very similar paintings on her light-grey walls.

The kitchen is all gleaming steal and marble counter tops.

The whole place is a good 483 per cent cooler than I could ever be.

The only thing coordinated in my flat is the coffee stain on the carpet that matches my dusty, second-hand Ikea TV stand.

'Would you like a gin and tonic?' Vanity asks me as she pads lightly over to one of her gleaming kitchen cupboards.

Nick Spalding

'Yeah. That'd be good,' I tell her, still looking around the kitchen with wide eyes.

'Okay. Go make yourself comfortable and I'll be right in.'

I do as I'm told, and go back into the lounge, where I sit on the black couch and try my hardest not to touch anything. I especially avoid going anywhere near what looks like a brand-new ultra-thin TV that's hung on the wall in front of me. It looks like it cost a year's wages, and I don't think Vanity would be very happy if I—

OH MY GOOD GOD IN HEAVEN.

Vanity has come into the lounge with two tall glasses of gin and tonic. She has also lost her dress somewhere, the poor girl – hence my blasphemous exclamation.

All Vanity is wearing now is a pair of black hold-up stockings, a black G-string, a plain black bra and a smile that says she's getting precisely the reaction she wanted.

She sashays over to me with a wicked smile on her face and hands me my drink. 'You don't mind me looking like this, do you?' she asks.

This is rather like my bank manager asking me if I mind him putting an extra one hundred thousand pounds in my bank account.

I shake my head very slowly. I'm slightly worried if I do it any quicker, my tongue will fall out.

Vanity sits down and looks at me with smoky eyes as she takes a sip of her gin. 'I hope I haven't shocked you,' she says, knowing full well that she has, 'but I'm not the type of girl who likes to beat around the bush.'

'No. That's fine!' I reply. 'I'm not, either.' I blink. 'Not that I'm a girl. But what I mean is that I don't like to beat around it, either. The bush, that is. No beating it for me. Absolutely not.'

I drain half of the gin in one gulp.

Vanity smiles and takes the glass out of my hand. She places it alongside hers on the black coffee table next to the couch, and straddles me in one smooth movement.

136

'Why don't you carry me to the bedroom, Ollie? We've talked a lot this evening, and now I want to do something else with you.'

'Okay,' I reply in a feeble voice.

This is *insane*. Completely and utterly insane. I'm in the house of an absolutely gorgeous woman, and I'm now 100 per cent sure she wants to have sex with me.

With *me*.

This is the type of thing you'd expect to find happening in one of those romantic movies I spent my youth watching, not here in the real world. You know, one of the ones where the boy from the wrong side of town gets to fall in love with the girl from the right side. Billy Joel's 'Uptown Girl' would most definitely be on the soundtrack album.

And yet . . . here we are. This is actually *happening*. This is a thing that is happening to Oliver Sweet *in real life*. No Billy Joel necessary.

And maybe if something as unbelievable as this can occur, then something *equally* unbelievable could come from it. Maybe being with Vanity *could* help me get over Samantha. Maybe being with her *could* make things so much better for me. Maybe Vanity could be 'the one' – instead of Samantha. That sounds like a good story, doesn't it? A story that hopefully starts with some lovely sex.

This really is all too much for me.

So is trying to stand up with Vanity clutching at me like a spider monkey on a fig tree. I have a go at it, but when it becomes quite clear that I can barely lift my bottom off the couch, Vanity climbs off me and instead pulls me to my feet. So much for showing her what a big, strong alpha male I am.

Oh, who am I kidding? She's read a story about me getting my arsehole waxed. I'm sure she's under no illusions.

Vanity then leads me into her bedroom, where a red bed, light-grey walls and a black carpet await. She sits herself on the bed, yanks me towards her and starts to unbuckle my belt.

It suddenly hits me that I'm about to have sex with someone for the first time since Samantha. It's a surreal and bizarre thought. I'm also struck by that irrational sense of betrayal again – but I manage to push it aside, as Vanity has just reached into my boxer shorts.

Right, now you shut up and go sit in the corner while I get my mojo on.

Okay, Mr Penis.

Good boy.

I gratefully let him take over. It's so much easier when you just think with your penis. This is why men tend to do it ninety per cent of the time.

Vanity stops rummaging, and instead decides to peel me like an orange. Before I know it, I am completely naked. I haven't been undressed this fast since I wandered into the kitchen at the age of six covered in dog shit from the Alsatian next door.

Vanity appraises my naked form and, by golly, this girl should be an actress. The way she gazes at my body with hungry lust is quite incredible. I am not an unhealthy person physically – but neither am I what anyone would consider 'buff'. A slight paunch and a distinct lack of pectoral muscles are not things that people usually gaze at with hungry lust. Mild interest, possibly. But never hungry lust.

Still, that's what Vanity is doing . . . and now she's grabbing hold of my penis, so I am rendered instantly unable to think straight – and will be completely incapable of relaying my thoughts for the next few minutes.

Please enjoy whatever light music you may have to hand while this goes on.

. . .

. . .

. . . . . .

. . . .

'Uuuuuuhhhh,' I moan in ecstasy as Vanity comes up for air. This evening really has taken a most unexpectedly pleasant turn. I will have to send Callie Donnelly some flowers.

Vanity looks up at me, still with that hungry expression in her eyes. 'Will you do something for me, Ollie?' she asks.

This is the perfect time to ask a man to do anything – up to and including handing over both kidneys.

'Yeah, yeah,' I reply, nodding vigorously.

Vanity smiles and leans back over the bed to her white bedside cabinet, from which she pulls a pair of silky red-and-black boxer shorts. She holds them out to me. 'Put these on for me?'

Okay. This is a bit strange, but the girl can apparently breathe through her ears, so I'm not going to argue.

I slip the underwear on, and it's immediately apparent they are meant for a man who has no issues with his body image. They are so tight and clingy that you'd have to be very confident in the size of your junk to get away with them. You'd also need a fine set of abdominals parked above them to pull them off properly. I have neither, so slightly resemble an overstuffed sausage.

'Oh God,' Vanity says breathily, caressing the pants and my penis through them. 'Lie down on the bed for me,' she orders.

'Okay.'

I do so, somewhat awkwardly, as the tight silky boxer shorts don't allow for much freedom of movement.

Vanity then climbs on top of me and starts to grind like she's making a loaf of bread from scratch.

If she goes at it much harder, the static electricity between her G-string and these boxers is likely to give us both third-degree burns.

My penis, so happy a few moments ago, is starting to get a little concerned about both the build-up of friction and how much he's being squashed.

Vanity is having a whale of a time, though, so I grit my teeth and try to enjoy myself.

She continues to slide up and down for a while longer, before gasping and looking at me with the kind of raw, animalistic sexual aggression that I have only ever seen before in my dreams.

I wish she'd get back to stroking, actually. All this grinding is starting to give me chafed thighs.

'Would you wear something else for me, Ollie?' she asks, one hand snaking into areas that are guaranteed to get her a positive answer.

I nod dumbly, and watch as she leans over me towards the bedside cabinet again and pulls out a cardboard mask.

Right. This is starting to get downright peculiar.

The mask is one of those photographic jobs you can order online, of either celebrities or of people you know – if you have a photo of them good enough to use, that is.

The carefully cut-out face on the mask Vanity wants me to don is of an extremely attractive man, with very dark hair and the kind of designer stubble that must take ages to get just right. He's a beautiful chap, of that there is no doubt. Kind of a Latin-looking Ryan Reynolds – if such a thing were possible. Deadpoolio.

'Who is that?' I ask Vanity, but she does not answer, and is already yanking the mask over my head.

I look out through tiny pinprick eyeholes as the tight elastic band constricts my ears and rubs against my hair. What on earth is going on here?

Never mind. Vanity is busying herself with my downstairs area again, so we'll just go with it. If me wearing a cardboard mask of Ryan Reynolds's European cousin is what floats her boat, then so be it.

Vanity pulls out little Oliver and starts to coax him back into full preparedness again. This works a treat, and in no time at all he's accomplishing one of the very important tasks he was put on this earth to do – after the application of a condom, of course.

I'd like to see what Vanity is doing on top of me, but all I get are fleeting glances of various parts of her jiggling anatomy through the entirely inadequate eyeholes.

'Would you do something else for me, Ollie?' she asks in the middle of this.

Oh good grief. What else does she want me to wear? You're supposed to get undressed for sex, not the other way around.

'What do you want me to do?' I respond in a muffled voice, hoping it doesn't involve a hat, boots or a thick winter jacket.

'Do you know any Italian?'

'Italian?'

'Yes! Do you know any Italian words or phrases?'

'No, sorry.'

She looks vaguely disappointed at this news. 'Can you speak in an Italian accent?'

'An Italian accent?'

'Yeah! Just start talking in an Italian accent for me.' As she says this, Vanity squeezes her thighs, sending pulses of pleasure through my entire body.

'O-kay. I guess I can do that.'

'Great. That's great, Ollie,' Vanity says, increasing her pace on top of me a bit.

'Er . . .'

Jesus. How do you speak in an Italian accent? I don't know any Italians. My only regular interaction with anyone who could remotely be considered Italian is Super Mario – and he's a horrific stereotype, created by Japanese people.

But he is my only real frame of reference, and Vanity wants me to speak like an Italian, so . . .

'Hello! It's a-me, Mario!' I exclaim, in the single worst Italian accent ever attempted, from beneath the confines of the cardboard mask.

'Oh yeah!' Vanity moans.

Bizarrely, this appears to be working.

'Er . . . how are-a you-a today-a?' I venture.

'Oh God, I'm sooooo good,' Vanity tells me, closing her eyes tightly.

'Um . . . would-a you like-a da pasta salad-a?' I ask . . . for some bloody reason.

'Mmmmmm,' Vanity groans as she starts to increase her pace even more.

'Ah . . . I must-a collect-a da golden coins-a, and-a save-a the Princess Peach-a.'

'Uuuhhhhh.'

I'm not sure Vanity is really listening to me now, which is probably just as well. There's nothing less sexy than a fat plumber with a thick moustache and a thing for jumping on tortoises.

'Eh . . . I getta da Bowser, and I-a unlock-a da secret level-a with the warp-a whistle.'

'Aaahhhh.'

'Um . . . You like-a da hat I'm a wearing-a?'

'Uuuhhhh.'

I figure I'd better try saying something a bit sexier at this point.

'Ooh yes-a. That-a feels-a so good-a. Ride-a me hard-a. You have-a da lovely pussy-a.'

Oh, for God's sake. That's just *creepy*.

I can't think of much else to say, now I've discovered how much Super Mario sounds like a sexual predator when you try to speak dirty as him, so in mild panic, I just start to do the *Super Mario* theme.

'*Da da da, da da da da, da da da da da da da, da da daaaa*,' I sort of sing, possibly completely out of tune. Fearing this may not be exciting enough for Vanity, I also throw in a loud and happy 'Woo hoo!', much like Mario does when he collects a particularly large stack of gold coins.

'Oh God,' Vanity continues to moan. 'Oh God, you're so good, Alessandro! You're so good!'

Wait, what?

'Fuck me, Alessandro!' Vanity cries, eyes still tightly screwed shut. 'I've missed you so much! I love you, Alessandro!'

Hang on a bloody minute . . .

'Oh God, Alessandro . . . you're so good to me! Keep going, Alessandro!'

Who is this Alessandro person??

It doesn't matter!!! Just let her call you it, you idiot!!!

It *does* matter, Mr Penis!

No, it doesn't!!!

Yes, it bloody well DOES!

I rip off the mask, snapping the elastic band as I do. At the same time, I start to scrabble out from under Vanity, withdrawing myself quite painfully in the process. She tumbles off to one side with a squawk.

'What are you doing?' she wails in frustration. 'We were so close!'

'Who the hell is Alessandro??' I wail back, looking at the face of the cardboard mask again. 'Is this him?'

Vanity grabs the broken mask out of my hand. 'Yes! Yes! This is Alessandro!' She beats a fist on the bed. 'Why couldn't you have just carried on for a few more moments??'

I go wide-eyed with horror. 'Because you kept calling me by another bloody name! Who the hell is Alessandro?' I repeat, climbing off the bed.

Vanity stares at me for a second, before bursting into tears.

'He . . . He's my boyfriend!' she wails between great wracking sobs. 'He left me a month ago!'

Oh hell.

'And he's Italian, is he?' I say, putting two and two together.

'Yes! From Naples.' She wipes her nose with one long, slender forearm. This is the first completely unsexy thing she's done all evening. 'He drives a Maserati!' This revelation sends Vanity off into another flood of tears, as I fully come to understand why I was invited back to her flat this evening.

Vanity is not interested in *me* in the slightest. This was never going to be the beginning of a whirlwind romance that would get me over the disaster of the last one. This was all about Vanity clinging on to the vestiges of her own lost love. I was merely the nearest and easiest surrogate. This evening was not about new romance. It was all about the old.

I was a fool to think anything different.

I whip off Alessandro's silky boxer shorts and start to put my own clothes back on. It's time to get out of here. I may not have a huge amount of pride, but even I can't accept being used as a substitute penis for another man.

I can.

Shut up, you stupid bloody cock!

'Where . . . Where are you going?' Vanity asks, her tears reducing somewhat to sniffles now.

I give her an indignant look as I pull my shirt back on. 'Home!' I tell her.

'Why?'

'Why?! Because the only reason you brought me here was to pretend I was your ex-boyfriend!'

'He's not my ex! He'll come back to me!'

I roll my eyes. This all sounds *extremely* familiar.

'Well . . . I don't know what to tell you, but using me like that is just . . . It's just not bloody on!'

I march out of the bedroom, fully intent on getting out of here as quickly as possible. Hopefully I can flag down a taxi, otherwise I'll have a very long walk home.

Vanity follows me out, pulling on a light-grey dressing gown as she does so. 'I'm sorry! I'm really sorry!' she cries as I approach the front door. 'I just miss him so much! And I thought . . . I thought you'd understand!'

'Why?!'

'Because of "Dumped Actually"! You know . . . You know how much pain I'm in!'

Vanity slumps on to the couch, all the strength gone from her legs.

I've got one hand on the front door handle as I look back at her sitting dejected on the couch. I should just leave. I should get out of here and try to forget about this bizarre experience.

But then, Vanity is right, isn't she?

I *do* know how much pain she's in.

It's a pain I still feel every day myself.

The pain of loss. The pain of rejection. The pain of emptiness.

I sigh heavily and hang my head for a moment, making a decision I don't know if I'm going to instantly regret.

Then I walk back over to where Vanity is slumped on the couch and sit down next to her, putting one arm around her shoulders, as they heave with the crying fit she clearly needs to get out of her system.

When that passes, I make us both a coffee in the exquisitely expensive kitchen.

'Thank you,' Vanity says in a quiet voice when I hand her a cup. 'I'm so sorry I did this to you. I'm not . . . not normally that manipulative.'

'We all do things we regret when we've been dumped,' I reassure her.

'Do we?'

I laugh once. 'You've been reading my stories, haven't you?'

Vanity nods. 'Oh yeah. The thing with the deer . . .'

'Yeah. The thing with the deer.'

I sip my coffee and internally cringe for about the millionth time this month.

Vanity sniffs. 'How do we move on, Ollie?' She sounds so lost and lonely that any remaining resentment I may have had for her falls to pieces in an instant.

'I don't know,' I tell her. 'I'm trying my hardest to find out, but so far I just don't know.'

Now *I* feel like crying.

Again.

Vanity shakes her head. 'Everything I do, everything I see. It just reminds me of him.'

'Yeah, I know that feeling.'

She looks up at me through tear-soaked eyes and gives me a small, vulnerable smile. 'Thank you for not leaving. It's nice to have somebody I can talk to about this . . . finally.'

And that says a lot, doesn't it? That this beautiful, rich and apparently self-confident woman can feel so messed up by heartbreak that she can't bear to speak about it with the people she knows.

Losing the people we love breaks all of us, no matter who we are. That's the thing about proper love. It's a great leveller.

This feels like an appropriate moment for a nice hand hold.

Yes. That feels very nice indeed.

Vanity squeezes my hand and drinks more of her coffee as we sit in silence for a moment.

'Will you . . . Will you write about this?' she eventually asks me.

'Um . . . probably. But I won't if you don't want me to.'

She nods. 'No. No, you should. I think that . . . I think that it would be a good story for you.' She smiles. 'And I probably deserve it, after what I've done.'

Bless her. She's obviously trying to make it up to me, by giving me permission to make a fool out of her on the internet.

'I'll change your name, Vanity,' I tell her. 'No one needs to know it was you.'

She nods. 'Okay.' Her hand squeezes mine again. 'Would you like to talk about her? Samantha, I mean?'

I puff out my cheeks. 'Would you really want to hear about her?'

'Yes. And maybe I can tell you about Alessandro. It might . . . It might help us both?'

'To talk about it all, you mean?'

'Yes. Maybe . . .'

What a strange and incredible night this has been. I start out as somebody's pet, in a club I have no business being in, I meet the most beautiful woman in the world, who I have some extremely awkward sex with, and now I'm actually considering an impromptu therapy session about heartbreak with that same woman.

Incredible.

And so, for the next *four hours*, Vanity and I talk. And talk. And talk.

It's like we're both opening our wounds as much as we can, so we can clean them out, and get some fresh blood in there.

It's painful. It's cathartic. It's draining. It's quite wonderful.

I end up putting Vanity to bed with a kiss on the cheek at 4 a.m., and get a few hours' sleep on her exceptionally comfortable black couch.

I then leave at ten o'clock the next morning . . . feeling ever so slightly renewed.

Callie Donnelly advised me to go out and try to find a new romance, so I would feel better about myself. I didn't think it would work at all . . . but I've been proved wrong – even if it's not for the reasons Miss Donnelly thought.

For the first time I feel like there might be a life for me beyond Samantha. I think Vanity feels the same way about Alessandro.

I still hold the pain close to my chest, but maybe something has shifted in me, after the night I've just had.

Call it a slight change in perspective, if you will.

I am not alone in this.

That's what I've learned.

Even the best and boldest of us can be brought low by our heartache. That is something that I find strangely comforting.

We're all prey to the vagaries of our quest to find the right person to love. Every single one of us. But sometimes I think we all need reminding of that – instead of believing that we're the only ones in the deep, dark hole.

Vanity proved that isn't the case for me, and I am eternally grateful for that. That's the main thing I will take away from the last twenty-four hours of my life.

That, and the fact I will never be able to play *Super Mario* again without getting an erection.

INTERLUDE

From: Ahmed Rahami (Rahami82@hotmail.co.uk)

To Mr Sweet at Actual Life,

'Dumped Actually' is a fantastic read, Mr Sweet. It's a lot of fun reading it. It also reminds me of a very bad time in my life. But now things are better and I can look back on it without feeling the hurt! My marriage ended in very bad circumstances. My first wife, Rafia, had an affair with my cousin, Syed, when I was out of the country, visiting the rest of my family. Syed had always wanted Rafia, but I never thought she would leave me for him, as I am taller, more handsome and have better prospects. But then Syed was once in an episode of *Casualty*, so maybe she was blinded by fame.

It felt like I would never get over it. The thing that worked for me, though, was throwing myself into my work as much as possible. I hadn't made much effort with my job as an IT consultant before my marriage failed. It was just a way to make money. But after I was single again, I made a lot more of it. This led to a promotion and the praise of my boss. All of this made me feel much better about myself. I was strong enough to go on with my life. I now have a new wife, and a three-year-old son. I met my wife at work! So my suggestion to you is to work hard and make the people you work for proud of you. This will make you feel proud too! Impress them as much as you can. Make yourself valuable to them and your work. Nothing is better at making you feel better.

Best of wishes,
Ahmed Rahami

***

From: Dominic Carter (CartmanRules@virgin.com)

How do, mate,

You lucky bastard. I read about what happened with you and that posh Charity girl. She sounds amazing. Any chance you could get in with her long term? I think she sounds much hotter and better than that Samantha. I tried the same thing when Lisa left me. I ended up shagging my sister's best friend against a wheelie bin in Rochester. Neither of them have spoken to me since, so that went really well.

Getting over Lisa was really hard, anyway. She was my one and only, you know? I thought we'd be together forever. Especially because of our little boy, Jack. But then she left me. At half-time during the England-Portugal match at the World Cup. Talk about bad timing.

I didn't know why she left for ages. She wouldn't talk about it. Just upped and left with my baby boy. I started drinking when it happened. More than ever before. Got into a few fights because of it, that were all my fault. I was in a really bad place. And I don't just mean up against that wheelie bin.

The worst thing was not knowing why. Not knowing why she'd done it. It was tearing me apart because I didn't know what I'd done to make her leave. I always thought I was a good husband and a good father. Why would she leave me the way she did?

So I went to her work to have it out with her. At first she didn't want to talk to me at all, but I made her talk to me, because I had to know. She's a lovely lass, as well. She could see how bad I was. I think she felt a bit guilty about not talking to me more.

And you know what she tells me? She tells me about all the things I was doing that ruined our marriage. It wasn't one big thing. It was just loads and loads of little things. The nights out with the boys. The drinking. I never did anything romantic with her. We never went out together. I forgot her birthday a couple of times. I didn't show her enough attention.

You know. All that usual woman stuff. At first, I thought she was bloody mad and bang out of order. But after a while I started to realise that she probably had a point. And I thought that if I changed, I might be able to get her back.

So I did everything I could to be better. And it worked, after a while. I stopped the drinking. Stopped the big nights out. All of that. Felt a lot better about myself.

Me and Lisa still aren't back together, but we get on well now. See each other quite a lot, mostly with Jack. It's nice. I don't know if she'll ever take me back, but I know that if I hadn't talked to her about her reasons, I would never have changed.

So that's what you should do if you really want that Samantha back. Go and speak to her. Find out why she got rid.

I'd go off with that Charity, myself, but we're all different.

Anyway, cheers, mate. I'm off to KFC with Jack for a bargain bucket.

Dom

***

From: Elizabeth Moore (Lizzy_Moore@gmail.com)

To Ollie,

I can't tell you how much I've laughed reading your article on the website, Ollie! I'm sorry you've had to go through so much, but if it helps to know that you've really put a smile on my face, then maybe that's not so bad!

I think it's so cool that you've asked to hear from other people about how they got over their break-ups. Even cooler that you're actually trying the things they suggest. Although, I guess you probably wish you'd never gone camping, eh? ☺

I just had to get in touch, because I think I have the answer to your problems. When my relationship of seven years with my boyfriend, Alfie, fell apart, I thought the world had ended. Couldn't even get off the couch.

But then my doctor suggested I try some mindfulness exercises to see if that could help. I was really sceptical, but had a go at it anyway, as what did I have to lose? At first it didn't do much, but as the weeks went by I really started to change. Things began to feel a lot better. Not just about Alfie, but my life in general.

Mindfulness teaches you to communicate better with yourself, and live more in the moment. Through it I discovered that I suffered quite badly with anxiety, which the mindfulness really helped with. I basically got my life back because of it.

I also got a new job, because I now teach mindfulness classes, as well as classes in meditation techniques, cognitive behavioural therapy and other methods of relaxation and self-improvement.

You would be more than welcome to come along to try some of them out, if you like!

Anyway, hope you are well, and are not doing too badly. Best wishes and lots of love,

Lizzy Moore

CHAPTER SEVEN

THE TRAUMA OF THE TINY WHITE BALLS

I'm not a great believer in serendipity these days.

It sounds like the kind of thing that only happens in badly written novels. Life may be full of coincidences, but they rarely result in a happy ending, in my experience.

I'm not saying they all happen with disastrous results either, though.

They just tend to *happen*. That's the thing about coincidence. Nine times out of ten it will be completely inconsequential to your life.

You'll try to get into a Volkswagen Polo in the car park that's exactly the same as yours, with nearly the same number plate, parked a few bays away from where your actual car is.

Or you'll bump into that same couple from Lancashire on holiday in Greece that you met last year on holiday in Tenerife.

Strange and head-scratching coincidences that might seem important at the time, but in actual fact have no impact on your life whatsoever.

But then there's the one-in-ten case that actually *does* have a massive effect on your life; and for me – at least in recent times – that's only resulted in bad news all round. Without what I thought was 'serendipity', I wouldn't have been stuck at a theme park with a bogey wiped down my nose.

Given all of this, I tend to ignore coincidence as much as I possibly can, especially the sort that looks like serendipity. Nothing good can come from it. I've learned that lesson.

Finding appropriate feedback from my audience is not as easy as I'd like it to be. I get hundreds of responses from the continuing run of 'Dumped Actually' stories I'm writing, but there's actually not a lot of them I can turn into the *next* story.

I get a lot of emails and social media messages that are either congratulating me on the feature, or taking the piss out of me for all of my mishaps. I still get an unhealthy amount of pornographic pictures of Bambi in my inbox every week. I don't know what's more disturbing, the fact that I keep getting sent them, or that there are people out there making so many of them in the first place.

I've also started getting an awful lot of men contacting me, asking me to pass on their phone numbers or social media profiles to Vanity. I ignore all of these, of course. They think she's just an object of sexual desire, but I know she's actually a real, living, breathing human being, who still needs time to heal.

Of course, I am also continuing to get a lot of people contacting me with their suggestions on how to get over Samantha. Most of them run along similar themes: Get drunk. Go on holiday. Shag somebody else. Move away. Etc., etc. All of these are fine – and I've even tried a couple of them already – but my journalist's nose does not twitch when I read any of them.

It's come to the point where writing a good story for 'Dumped Actually' is as important to me as getting over Samantha. I don't know when this happened, but it's definitely the case now. My desire to distract myself from heartbreak has been joined by my desire to fill out three to five thousand words with some quality storytelling. Of course, this is a distraction from the heartbreak in and of itself.

Or at least it would be, if I could actually pin down some suggestions from the punters out there that I could go and experience for another write-up.

I've bounced a few of them off Wimsy, to see what he thinks of them. I'm finding that underneath all that misery and self-pity, my new friend has an extremely sharp mind. This is proving very useful, as it's always nice to have someone to chat to about these things.

He agreed with me that nearly all of them weren't worth exploring, though, more's the pity.

So, at the moment I only have three ideas that seem like they could turn into something I can use for more material. Sadly, one of them is right out, as it involves confronting Samantha about the reasons why she dumped me. This is not happening. Never in a million years. I will masturbate in front of an entire herd of fallow deer before I do that.

Then we have Lizzy Moore's idea of doing a bit of mindfulness. This sounds like so much new-age blather to me, so that one gets shoved to the bottom of the pile as well . . . for the moment.

This leaves Ahmed's proposal that I bury myself in my work and win the approval of my peers and seniors.

Sadly, I feel like I'm already doing this.

'Dumped Actually' continues to be a massive success. Actual Life's subscriber numbers are still climbing – even though they've levelled out a bit, as all things do after the initial rush.

I am still popular with my peers around the office, although I'm starting to detect a little jealousy emanating from some of them – particularly Helen, who writes lifestyle features like mine, and is probably cursing the fact that she has a happy marriage with a wonderful man called Mark.

Erica is also very pleased with what I'm doing. She was absolutely *delighted* with the story about Vanity – not just because she found the whole *Super Mario* thing hilarious, but because she was impressed with the way I portrayed Vanity (or Charity, for the purposes of the story).

'That girl has a lot going on, underneath all that make-up and breast augmentation,' Erica told me. 'Sometimes I think people like her just get lost in the pressures of that social scene. I only think she turns up to yoga because it fits the lifestyle she thinks she needs to have. Everyone has to be gorgeous and perfect all of the time. It doesn't leave much room for being a flawed, interesting human being. It was a pleasure to see that side of her, and lovely that you were so nice to her.'

Vanity adored the article as well. She called me the day it came out and told me that she loved me for it. Which was very nice.

So, the *last* thing I wrote for 'Dumped Actually' has been a success all round. Which now makes it even harder to top it with the next feature – hence my stress and anxiety over picking a subject worthy of the follow-up.

I'm sat chewing on a knuckle at my desk, trying my hardest to think of a way I can take Ahmed's suggestion on board (and failing completely) when my office phone rings, and that awful serendipity thing I was talking about comes a-calling.

'Hello?'

'Ah . . . is this Oliver Sweet?' The voice on the other end of the phone is deep, baritone and speaks of supreme self-confidence, self-belief and possibly self-love.

'Yes,' I reply, hesitantly.

'Good. I wasn't sure if my secretary had your number right, and I didn't want to have to go through Erica.'

'Okay.'

I don't yet know who this person is, but I have a feeling that my testicles do, as they are starting to crawl up into my belly.

'How are you, Oliver?'

'I'm well, thank you. Um . . . who may I ask is calling?'

There's silence on the other end for a moment. It's probably of the offended kind.

'I'm Benedict Montifore, Oliver. I own y—' He stops himself. 'I own Actual Life.'

Yep. My testicles were right on the money.

'Oh, hello, Mr Montifore. It's nice to hear from you.'

What would be nice is if I could throw the phone down and dunk the whole thing in holy water, but I'd better be on my best behaviour with this man, as his capriciousness is well known, as is his desire to throw me and my fellow Actual Lifers out on to the street.

'I'm sure. I hope I haven't interrupted you from writing another *wonderful* feature, Oliver.'

'No, no. I certainly wouldn't say that . . . sir.' 'Sir' is always good to use in these kinds of circumstances, isn't it?

'Good. Good. That "Love Actually" feature of yours is doing *so well*. I wouldn't want to be the cause of any hold-ups.'

'It's "Dumped Actually", actually.'

'Excuse me?'

'The feature, Mr Montifore. It's called "Dumped Actually". It's a clever riff on the movie title.'

'Is it?'

'Yes.'

'Very well.'

'Okay.'

I'm not entirely sure Montifore thinks it's all that clever, given the tone of his voice.

'Do you golf?'

'I'm sorry?'

'*Golf*, Oliver. Do you play?'

'Ah . . . not really, sir. I once came fourth in a pitch-and-putt contest on holiday in Plymouth. Does that count?'

'No. It does not.'

'Okay.'

'But you can hold a club, yes? Hit a ball?'

'I suppose so. After a fashion.'

The fashion being one from twenty years ago, when my favourite T-shirt was Mighty Morphin Power Rangers, and the golf club I was carrying was largely made of plastic.

'I wanted to invite you out for a round. It's the way I like to get to know my employees.' There's a meaningful pause. 'The ones I admire, anyway.'

Oh dear. This can't be good.

'Oh. Okay.' I have little else to say on the matter right now, as I'm still trying to process several things.

First, that Montifore would deign to reach down from his highest of high perches to call me on the telephone. Second, that he is trying his very best to come across as pleasant to someone he must actually hate deep down inside. Third, that he wants me to come and play golf with him. And fourth, that he says he *admires me*.

Me.

Oliver Sweet.

The person who is probably preventing him from convincing his entire board of directors to close Actual Life down tomorrow and sell off the assets.

What strange and curious machinations are these?

'So, would you like to come?' Benedict repeats in a tone on the verge of becoming impatient. 'I part-own a course not too far away. It's called Sheldon Brook. Have you heard of it?'

I have, indeed. It's the kind of place people from Manucode probably wish they could get into. The women, anyway. Sheldon Brook is exclusively for men. And by men, I mean fat, old rich, white men, who voted for Brexit, think abortion is wrong for anyone but them, and don't understand why people can't just know their place like they used to.

I'd rather use one of my crawling testicles as a golf ball than visit such a place.

My mind instantly starts to conjure excuses not to go.

. . . I have severe hay fever that means I can't be in the countryside for more than ten minutes every six months.

. . . I'm scared of large concentrations of sand.

. . . I'm in the middle of transitioning into a woman, so I doubt the members of Sheldon Brook would want me anywhere near the place. It'd only confuse and worry them.

. . . I have a deadline for my next feature that I just can't miss.

The last excuse would be the most sensible – and the only even remotely believable one – if I actually had a feature to write.

Which is when it hits me. The pure, unlovely, unwanted serendipity of it all.

It's bloody *perfect*, isn't it?

For so many reasons.

Not only would I get to have the chance to win the approval and respect of my boss – like Ahmed Rahami suggested – but I might also be able to convince Montifore that keeping Actual Life going is the best thing for him to do. Just think how much people around here would love me then!

Also, I'd have an extremely good basis for a further 'Dumped Actually' story, wouldn't I?

Those are three large, fat, squawking birds that I can confidently hit with one expertly aimed stone – if I'm about myself enough.

And yet – in much the same way that I never wanted to go out on the pull, as Callie Donnelly told me I should – I do not want to spend one second in Benedict Montifore's company, and I do not want to visit a place like Sheldon Brook. There is no conceivable way in which any of that could make me feel better about my break-up with Samantha.

. . . but if I hadn't gone out on the pull, then I would never have met Vanity, and had the most cathartic and rewarding experience of this entire process so far.

Sometimes, I have learned, you just have to risk going outside your comfort zone for something good to happen.

I have tried to firmly remain in my comfort zone my whole life for one reason or another, so this can safely be considered quite a large shift in my outlook on the world.

Bearing all this in mind, my hand tightens on the phone as I respond to Benedict's offer.

'Yes, Mr Montifore. I would like to come. It would be nice to see your golf course.'

'Excellent, Oliver. I'm very pleased. It will give us a chance to discuss how you're feeling about the future of Actual Life, and your place in my company. I'll have my secretary call you later today to arrange a time and sort out all the details.'

'Okay, Mr Montifore.'

'I look forward to meeting you.'

'As do I, sir.'

Try telling my balls that. They've now climbed back up into the cavity from which they dropped three decades ago and are attempting to burrow in even further.

The other end of the line goes dead, indicating that Montifore is done with me . . . for now.

I sit back in my chair and purse my lips together.

Whether this is a good idea or not, I have no clue, but at least I now have a sense of focus and purpose again. I'm not worried about what I'm going to write about next any more. I *am* comprehensively worried about spending a significant amount of time in Benedict Montifore's company – but that is infinitely preferable to having nothing to tell stories about. I've got to keep my audience happy, whatever it takes.

I want to keep Erica happy as well, so I'd better tell her all about this latest development. I'm sure she'll be delighted I have a new angle for 'Dumped Actually'!

'You're doing fucking *what*?!' Erica exclaims when I pop in to tell her about my date with Montifore.

'You don't think it's a good idea, then?'

'A good idea? A good idea?!' she snaps, and jumps to her feet. 'No, Ollie. I do *not* think it's a good idea!'

My face flames red with shame. The last thing I want to do is upset Erica, and it looks like I've managed to do that in spades.

'Why not?'

'Because . . . Because . . . Aaaargh!' She throws her hands into the air. 'Because he's a *bastard*, Ollie! A morally bankrupt, self-centred, money-grubbing bastard!'

The venom in Erica's voice could kill a herd of elephants.

'I know! But Ahmed thinks I should get to know him better!'

Her face drops in confusion. 'What?'

I go on to explain the contents of Ahmed Rahami's email, and why this is the reason I've reluctantly agreed to spend the day golfing with Montifore at his resort of eighteen holes and gross misogyny.

Erica starts to pace up and down in front of me when I'm done. 'It doesn't matter. You shouldn't do this, Ollie. Pick a different email.'

'I don't have another good email,' I reply – which is a lie, of course. I have the ones about the mindfulness and confronting Samantha, but Erica does not need to know about either of them. This golf date with Montifore *feels* like the right thing to do. I just have to convince her of that. 'Look, I don't like the idea of spending time with him any more than you do, but think of the story I can write about it. And maybe, just maybe, I could talk him round into keeping us. And if I could do that, we'd all end up winning.'

Erica looks at me darkly. 'He won't change his mind, Ollie. Trust me on that.'

'Why, though?' I ask in confusion. 'If we're making him money, and the site is popular, why would he want to get shot of us?'

Erica leans on her desk. 'There's more going on with him than you know about. But it's stuff you don't *need* to know about. It's just between him, me . . . and the rest of the board of directors.'

I throw my hands up. 'Well, if you won't tell me, then what am I supposed to do?'

'Pick another story.'

My shoulders slump. This really isn't fair. I know there's good material in this. Erica is shooting me down for reasons she won't go into and it's very, very frustrating.

Ah well. I guess I'll just have to think of something else to write about.

. . . you could tell her you're going to do it.

I couldn't do that.

Why not? Let's face it, you're her best asset right now. She needs *you.*

Yeah, but she's the boss.

So is Montifore – and he makes a good subject for a story, doesn't he?

I can't do it.

Yes, you can.

No, I can't.

YES, YOU CAN.

'Ollie? Are you alright?' Erica asks, sounding puzzled. 'You're twitching a bit and staring off into space.'

I look at her. 'I want to do this story, Erica. It's right. It's good. It'll go down well with the audience.'

Erica goes to open her mouth to argue, and sees the resolute look on my face. This is no doubt quite shocking to her. My face doesn't do resolute. It's happier with things like apologetic and capitulatory. I probably look like I'm having a seizure.

My boss taps the bottom of her chin thoughtfully for a moment, regarding me closely. 'Alright, then, Ollie. Go spend the day with Benedict. I don't think it's a good idea . . . for many reasons, but you seem quite determined.'

I thrust out my chin. 'I am.'

She rolls her eyes. 'Well, all I'd ask is that you keep your guard up, and remember what kind of man you're dealing with.'

'I will.'

A strange sense of satisfaction washes over me. I've just had a disagreement with Erica Hilton . . . and have come out on top. This never happens. Not the coming out on top bit – I mean *having a disagreement*. With anyone. *Ever.*

'Can you play golf?' Erica asks, very doubtfully.

'I came fourth in a pitch and putt once,' I tell her confidently.

Her eyes narrow and she reaches into a desk drawer. She pulls out a small box of pills and throws it at me. I catch it and look at its contents. '*CalmFast*,' I read, '*for when you need a relief from highly stressful situations.*'

I give Erica a flat look.

I think she's going a bit overboard here. It's only a round of golf with the man. I'm not scaling the north face of the Eiger, or engaging in a wrestling match with him. I know he's a bad person, but I'm pretty sure I can handle a few hours in his company. Hell . . . maybe I can get to the bottom of why he hates Actual Life so much, while I'm at it. That'd be a scoop, wouldn't it?

No. This is going to go fine, I'm sure. And even if it doesn't, it'll make a good story whatever happens, and that's the main thing!

I intend to approach this whole thing with a new-found sense of confidence and purpose. I figure it makes a nice change from nervous and flailing.

***

Sheldon Brook is every bit as awful as you've imagined from my previous descriptions. The clubhouse looks like Wayne Manor, without the benefit of an incumbent superhero to give it a valid reason to exist.

The second I pull up in the taxi laid on by Benedict's secretary, I am regarded with suspicion and dislike by all of the fat, rich, white men. I am far too young and poorly dressed to be here. These men probably think Adidas is a place in Africa.

Having announced my presence to the bored-looking male receptionist in the club's foyer, I am then forced to stand around like a spare you-know-what at a wedding for ten minutes, while Benedict wraps up some kind of impromptu business meeting in a room somewhere in Sheldon Brook's recesses.

This gives the old men a really good chance to examine me for my many imperfections as they come and go between golf course and clubhouse. I now know what it's like to be an animal at the zoo. One of the crap ones. Maybe a pig of some description. Probably from Africa.

Whatever sense of self-confidence I may have temporarily experienced in the office with Erica has evaporated under their judgemental glare. Maybe this was a bad idea. Maybe I should have just gone and done some meditation.

No, Oliver! This is what you were expecting! Now just gird whatever loins you may have hidden about your person and get through this!

'Ah! There you are, Oliver!' Benedict Montifore says in that rich, expensive baritone as he emerges into the foyer from a dimly lit bar area, where many of his fellow Sheldon Brookers are enjoying some lunchtime brandy and casual racism.

He's wearing golf clothes, and therefore looks like a plonker. It's impossible for anyone to look like anything other than a plonker in golf clothes. Feel free to line up Chris Hemsworth, Bradley Cooper, Idris Elba and Ryan Gosling, and put them all in golf clothes. They will all look like plonkers of the highest order.

I have a great deal of love and respect for my dad, but the one he time he tried to play golf he had to dress appropriately for it, and he looked like a plonker as well.

'Hello, Mr Montifore,' I reply as my boss-plonker approaches me – a man I have absolutely zero respect for.

'Please. Call me Benedict!'

Do I have to?

'Okay, Benedict. Feel free to call me Ollie, if you like.'

'Thank you, Oliver. I may do at some point.'

. . . if I've been a very good boy, no doubt. What is it with these exclusive rich people and their desire to treat everyone else like a pet dog? If this goes on for much longer, I might as well change my name to Ollie the Collie.

'Ready for some fun on the links?' Benedict asks.

'Yes!' I reply, trying to fake some enthusiasm. What are the links? Or does he mean lynx? Are we going to ride a feral cat at some point?

Benedict slaps me on the back. 'Excellent. Let's get you some clubs, and we'll be on our way.'

Benedict leads me back out of the enormous clubhouse, and around to an equally prestigious building to the side of it. This one looks brand new and modern, in stark contrast to the clubhouse. A long and low structure made out of black aluminium and glass, it appears to house the golfing equipment of all the men sat a few feet away, drinking Hennessey cognac and complaining about how many brown people there are at their private hospital nowadays.

'You can use one of my sets of Callaways, I think,' Benedict informs me, before barking orders at a young Asian man in a white uniform, who runs off to get our equipment for the day.

A few minutes later he returns with two sets of golf clubs, both of which look more expensive than my last three cars combined.

'So, let's go grab ourselves a cart and get out there,' Benedict tells me, striding off. This leaves me and the young Asian man standing with the golf clubs, staring dumbly at each other for a moment, before he picks up Benedict's set and scuttles off after him. I have to carry mine, of course. I don't get my own Asian slave. This is something I feel profoundly grateful for.

I'm going to need several baths when I get back from this place to wipe the stench of privilege and bigotry off myself, before it stinks up my flat.

I follow Benedict and his caddy over to a long row of gleaming white golf carts, plop my Callaways in the rack on the back and sit myself in the passenger seat.

'Off we go!' Benedict roars, and puts his foot down, transporting us quickly across a carefully tended grass expanse to the first hole of eighteen.

'I'll tee off,' he tells me, climbing out of the cart. The young Asian man – whose name I really must learn soon – brings out a large driving club, a small black tee and a shiny white golf ball. He hurries over to the patch of ground next to a sign with a giant number one on it and busies himself placing the ball on the tee. All the time he does this, Benedict is staring down the course with a meaningful look on his face. The caddy then hands Benedict the club and steps back.

'A good three hundred and twenty yards this one,' he tells me. 'It's a fine way to start a round.'

He then spends a good forty or fifty hours repeatedly making practice swings next to the teed-up ball. At least that's what it feels like. If England players took this long to take a penalty, they might win a few more of the shoot-outs, because the opposition would have died of boredom.

Eventually, Benedict whacks the little white ball with his big black stick and receives a hearty clap from the caddy. I join in, because it seems like the appropriate thing to do.

'Straight down the middle, sir,' the caddy says. 'Well done.'

'Thank you, Hung,' Benedict replies, not actually looking at him for one second. Poor Hung might as well be invisible. Which, in a very real and deliberate sense – for the people who belong to this golf club – he absolutely is.

My turn.

Oh, fabulous.

I tentatively rummage around in the front pocket of my golf bag, retrieving a tee and a ball in much the same way as Hung did.

I then copy his movements over by the big number one sign, and stick my tee in the ground, with the ball lightly placed on top.

Then I go back and select a club from the bag.

I choose one of the big bulbous ones, feeling that a big bulbous one is the right one to pick for the first whack of the little white ball. The skinny metal ones are for later, and the short flat one is for the green. I know this, for I have seen it done thusly on Sky Sports.

'Going with the big dog, eh?' Benedict nods approvingly as I walk over to the tee. 'Brave man!'

I look more closely at the club I have chosen, and it is enormous, of that there is no doubt. It's like somebody has stuck a pole into a big black whoopee cushion. On it are written the words 'Big Bertha'.

I fear I may have bitten off more than I can chew here. I'm sure Bertha would agree.

Just because I saw Benedict doing it, I take a few experimental swings of the club, trying my hardest to remember what I did all those years ago at the pitch and putt when I swung the tiny plastic club, on my way to that victorious fourth place.

Something about squaring your shoulders, rounding your hips, thrusting your bottom out and bending your knees, I believe it was.

Or maybe that was how you're supposed to prevent haemorrhoids. I can't quite remember.

After three rather half-hearted attempts at swinging the Big Bertha, I figure I'd better get on with it, and step up to the tee.

Right, then.

Bottom out.

Shoulders square.

Knees bent.

Hips round.

Was I supposed to do something with my elbows? I'm sure I was.

Are they supposed to be in or out? If it's out, I'll look like a chicken, but if it's in, I'll look like somebody in dire need of a toilet. We'll go with out, I think. Golf people don't seem too concerned with looking like plonkers, given the way they dress – I'm sure they have no qualms with resembling barnyard fowl, as long as it gives them a good drive off the tee.

And here we go, then . . .

One. Two. Three.

WOOSH.

I miss the ball completely – which is exactly what we were expecting to happen. Let's make no bones about it.

Such is the weight of the Big Bertha, I am facing in completely the opposite direction to the ball by the time I manage to get my body to stop moving. Inertia is a bitch, in such circumstances.

Benedict Montifore looks quite smug. That's got to be some kind of measure of a man, hasn't it? That he'd take actual pleasure in the mistakes of someone he knows has no experience of playing golf. I am zero competition to him, and yet he's completely unable to show anything but smugness about my lack of ability.

Hung is pursing his lips together and trying not to laugh. We'll let him off, though, as he has it bad enough already. I'm only being forced to spend a few hours with Benedict. This poor bugger probably has to see him on a weekly basis.

Giving them both an awkward smile, I square up to the tee again, and take a deep breath. If I can just hit the damn ball, that'd be enough. Even if it only goes ten feet, at least that's something.

This time I swing the ridiculous club a bit slower and with more control – and what would you know, I actually *hit* the golf ball!

Okay, it doesn't fly anywhere near as far as Benedict's did, but neither does it just dribble off into one of the nearby bushes. The shot is relatively straight, relatively high and relatively hard. Einstein would be proud of me.

I watch as the ball hits the fairway about two hundred yards away, and comes to a stop in the middle of the lush, green grass.

When I look back at Benedict, I am pleased to see he looks like he's chewing on a wasp. Hung is wide-eyed with amazement. As well he might be.

I bend over and pick up my tee. 'Shall we?' I say to them both, walking back to sit in the golf cart.

The confidence I had back in Erica's office swells in my chest again. This might not be so bad, after all. I'm not going to beat Benedict, but at least I'm not going to make a complete fool out of myself, with any luck!

I tell you what, though, I'm doing more than not making a fool of myself. Nine holes in, and I'm actually starting to get good at this silly game. That pitch-and-putt fourth place is starting to make a whole lot more sense now.

I've only bogeyed four holes, hit par on a further four and have just sunk my putt on the second par 3 of the course to get a birdie!

I'm only two shots behind Benedict!

And can you hear him grumble? Oh my, yes. Yes, you can.

Look how his brow furrows. Take joy in the tense set of his shoulders. Rejoice in the near constant look of combined frustration and befuddlement on his face. I'm sure he brought me out here to lord it over me all afternoon, but no lording has been done. There's been less lording done here than at an atheist's convention.

He's on the back foot. He's shaken and stirred. He's out of sorts.
Wonderful.

'Nicely done,' he tells me as we walk back to the golf cart. He's trudging. I have a spring in my step.

'Thanks, Benedict. That putt from eight feet was quite good, wasn't it?'

'Yes,' he replies, begrudgingly, ramming his putter back in the bag. He then pulls out a packet of cigars. 'Time for a break, I think.'

I smile inwardly. He wants to mess up my rhythm. It's an obvious tactic.

Benedict pulls out a cigar, and then offers the packet to me. I shake my head, but thank him for the offer. He shrugs his shoulders and snaps his fingers. Hung moves to his side with a lighter. I cringe and feel a bit nauseous.

'So, let's talk Actual Life,' Benedict says, blowing out a wreath of smoke. 'You've done very well, Oliver . . . *Ollie.* The website owes all of its recent success to you. Well done.'

'Er . . . thank you, sir.' I don't know what to do with these compliments from this man. It's rather like being confronted by an enormous and dangerous grizzly bear, who pats you on the head and offers you some chocolate.

'No doubt about it, you're a man on the rise.'

'Am I?'

'Yes, indeed. I've been keeping my eye on you.'

This announcement makes my skin crawl, and my sense of self-worth sky-rocket. It's a weird combination.

'That's why I asked you to come out here today,' Benedict continues. 'To discuss your future with ForeTech.'

'My future?'

'Indeed! And what a future it could be, Ollie! I have many projects on the go, and many fingers in many pies.' He smiles at me . . . shark-like. Or should that be spider-like, given how many fingers he appears to have. 'I've just put a rather sizeable investment into Condé Nast, actually. You know who they are, don't you?'

Of course I do. No self-respecting journalist doesn't. That company owns a vast array of some of the world's most successful magazines – a lot of which I'd kill to work for.

'Yes, Benedict, I know who they are,' I say, a bit dumbly. My brain is trying to leap forward a few seconds in this conversation, scarcely able to believe where it might be going.

'Excellent. Well . . . that gives me a lot of sway with them, as you might imagine. So much so that I'm sure I could put in a good word for somebody like you. Maybe at *Wired* magazine . . . or *GQ*?'

He leaves this hanging in the air, as heavy as his cigar smoke.

Bloody hell. Writing for something like *GQ* would be a *dream*. It's why I got into this business in the first place.

'Um. Wow. I don't know what to say.'

'Oh, don't worry. I'm just spitballing here,' Benedict replies, voice dripping honey, 'but I'm sure you'd slot in quite well somewhere like that . . . a man with your talents.'

'Thank you.' I couldn't be more buttered up right now if I crashed into a truck of Kerrygold.

'And for me to have a word in the ear of the right person, Ollie, all I'd need from you in return is a small favour.'

Ah.

'A small favour?'

'Yes.'

'What kind of small favour?'

Benedict takes another drag on the cigar, inspecting me. 'I won't beat around the bush, Ollie. I want Actual Life gone from my portfolio of companies. It was a mistake to buy it in the first place, and I want nothing more to do with it. Sadly, the way ForeTech is set up, I need the approval of a majority of our board of directors to liquidate it, and I can't get that at the moment – all thanks to your . . . *considerable efforts*.'

He's trying very hard not to be angry. I'm not sure he's doing all that well. There's a venom in his voice that makes me squirm.

'Then why not just sell it, then?' I ask, which seems like the obvious question.

He shakes his head slowly. 'No, Ollie. No selling. Not this one. I want it *gone*. I want it *dead*. And you can help me do that. Would you like to know how?'

I can't answer. The rage coming off this man in waves is quite terrifying.

'I'll tell you how, Ollie,' he continues without waiting for me. 'All you need to do is march into that bitch Erica's office and hand in your resignation. No more "Dumped Actually", no more Actual *bloody* Life. You can take your little feature and go write it over at *GQ*.' He grabs me by the shoulder. The stench of cigar makes me heave. 'Wouldn't that be wonderful, Ollie? Your story, your article, your *baby* . . . at one of the country's most popular magazines? I can make it happen, Ollie. I can make it happen . . . if you *help me*. Help me end that stupid website, and crush that fucking bitch.'

So.

There we have it.

The reason for this little outing across the rolling English countryside. Benedict wanted to get me somewhere alone, and on his turf, so he could bribe me with the best job in the world – as long as I betray my boss (and more importantly, my friend) of the last six years.

My hand starts to tremble. Anger and loathing course through my veins. As does a mounting sense of shame.

Erica was absolutely right.

I should never have come out here.

I should have *listened to her*.

In my overwhelming desire to be proved right about a stupid story, I have placed myself in a truly awful position.

I'm out here, in the middle of nowhere, alone with the biggest bastard on the planet and his manservant, Hung, both of whom are looking at me expectantly. Hung contrives to also look a bit sick himself, though. This probably isn't the first time he's had to witness Benedict Montifore conducting his loathsome business practices on the ninth hole, and I doubt it will be the last.

For some reason I am instantly transported back to the courtyard outside The Blitzer at Thorn Manor. The same feelings of shame, stupidity, embarrassment and disbelief wash over me. The situation is entirely different, but the emotions are exactly the same. So are the overriding thoughts that crash through my brain like wrecking balls:

What the hell is wrong with me? Why did I do this to myself?

And what the bloody hell do I DO NOW??

'So, what do you think, Ollie?' Benedict asks, blowing yet another cloud of cigar smoke into the calm air.

I want to punch him. I want to kick him. I want to swear, scream and rage at him.

But that's just not Oliver Sweet, is it?

He's not a man who does well with confrontation. He's not a man who knows how to vent his emotions. He's not a man who knows how to stand up and be strong.

He *is* a man who will allow someone to rip the hair off his arsehole, though. He's also a man who will squeeze his erect penis in front of a baby deer. He's a man who will agree to wear a face mask during sex.

And above all, he's a man who will let the woman of his dreams slip through his bloody fingers.

'Can I think about it?' I say in a trembling voice.

Benedict's eyes narrow and his lips turn themselves into a cold white line. 'Very well,' he eventually says, with mild disgust. 'Though . . . you shouldn't think about it for too long, *Oliver*. I don't make these offers very often, and when I do, I'm very careful about them. I can help the people who help me, Oliver.' He leans a little closer. 'And destroy those who don't.'

Wow. He really is a gold-plated monster, isn't he? I wonder if he's friends with Donald Trump?

'Okay. I won't,' I reply, hating myself with every fibre of my being.

Why don't I just stand up to him? Why don't I just tell him where to go?

Because he'll make your life hell. Because he'll take 'Dumped Actually' away from you.

Oh God.

He could do that.

I'm not sure he could actually straight out fire me here and now on this golf course – he'd have to go through Erica, and she'd never agree – but he could ruin everything anyway, though, I'm sure he could. He has the power to do that, without a doubt. Any man who owns a big enough stake in Condé Nast to hold sway with them would probably be able to destroy me if he wanted to, wouldn't he? Benedict hasn't actually said that I'd never work in this town again if I don't do what he says, but he wasn't far off it.

'Let's carry on with the game,' he suggests, climbing back into the golf cart. 'Perhaps while we're on the back nine, you could think about my offer a little more, and give me an answer by the time we hit the eighteenth.'

I nod slowly, not trusting myself to speak.

As Benedict ferries us towards the next hole, I sit beside him, seething in a cauldron of mixed, negative emotions. I am colossally angry. At Benedict and, inexplicably, at *Samantha*. It's a double-header of repressed rage that threatens to burst a blood vessel in my head.

I also feel stupid. *Incredibly* stupid. Stupid for coming here today, stupid for not listening to Erica and stupid for asking Samantha to marry me.

It's quite shocking just how much bottled-up emotion I still have about the break-up. I thought I was moving on a bit. I thought my recent experiences, and the success of 'Dumped Actually', were helping me to get past Samantha – and yet here I am, reliving all of it like it was yesterday. All because I've just been asked to betray all of my principals and morals by a shark dressed in golfing clothes.

'You're up first on this hole, Oliver,' Benedict tells me as we come to a halt.

I don't answer him. I can't trust myself to say anything right now.

I don't want to play this stupid game any more, either. I hate golf. I thought I liked it when I came fourth in the pitch and putt, but now I am entirely sure that I will never step foot on to a golf course again after today, for as long as I live.

I snatch the driver out of my golf bag. I yank a tee and a ball from the front pocket. I see Hung looking at me from his perch on the back of the cart and I glower at him. This is completely unfair of me. None of this is his doing. But I glower at him all the same.

Walking over to the tenth hole, my grip is so tight on the club that my hands have gone white. I can feel my jaw clenching hard as I look down the narrow gap through the trees to the fairway beyond. I'll have to hit this ball as straight as possible to avoid the thick row of pine trees that runs along either side of the teeing ground. But what's even more important is that I'll have to hit the ball as *hard* as possible.

Extremely hard.

That little pimpled bastard is about to experience all of the rage I cannot direct at Benedict – and certainly cannot direct at Samantha.

With hands still shaking with fury, I stab the tee into the ground and put the ball on to it. Benedict and Hung stand behind me, watching.

Yeah . . . you just watch. You just watch me hit this little white bastard five hundred yards.

As I swing the driver back, I actually emit a grunt of frustration, and as I propel it towards the ball with all of my strength, I let out a full-blown cry of rage that makes the birds rise from the surrounding trees.

The club hits the ball with almost Herculean might. It flies off the tee at supersonic speed.

Because I have sacrificed all technique for unrestrained anger, the swing I delivered was completely cack-handed and therefore the golf ball does not fly straight and true off the tee. Not even close.

Instead, it fires off to the right, straight at one of the thick pine trees that surround us.

It hits this at a vast rate of knots with a loud crack . . . *and comes straight back at us.*

Hung screams. I shriek. Benedict says nothing.

It's a little hard to immediately express yourself when a golf ball has just hit you in the testicles at three hundred miles an hour.

He does let out a cry of pain as his hands go towards the most vulnerable part of his body. Then his legs sag, all the strength gone out of them.

Such is the shock and trauma of it all, Benedict loses complete control of his body, causing him to face-plant into the grass beneath his limp feet. This leaves him with his bottom pointing upwards, proud to the sky.

He then emits a high-pitched whine of agony and starts to twitch spasmodically.

I look at Hung. Hung looks at me. We both look down at Benedict.

'Mr Montifore, are you alright, sir?' Hung says.

He gets no reply.

'Benedict? Can you hear us?' I venture, getting much the same response.

Hung moves closer, and gently pokes Benedict on the rump. You'd think that this would get a reaction, but nope . . . absolutely nothing. Even the painful whine has ceased.

'I think . . . I think he might be *unconscious*,' I say in disbelief. It shouldn't be possible to fall unconscious with your arse hanging in the air, but Benedict has somehow accomplished it.

'He's unconscious?' Hung says, poking him again.

'I'd say so.'

'So, he doesn't know what's going on?'

'No. I would say that he doesn't.'

Hung gives me a look of such ferocity, I have to take a step back. If I have been holding on to a ball of repressed anger, then this man has apparently been holding on to an entire planet of it.

Hung also takes a step back, sets himself . . . and then kicks Benedict Montifore so hard up the arse that I'm amazed his foot doesn't appear from between the man's perfectly white teeth.

'Fuck you, you piece of shit!' Hung screams.

For a second I don't know what to do with myself. I've just witnessed an assault on an unconscious man. I really should be reporting it to someone.

Instead I roar with approval and throw up a high-five, which Hung slaps with aplomb, grace and the triumph of a man who's just got his own back for the first time in many, many years.

Benedict makes a burbling noise, and does very little else.

'I suppose we'd better call the doctors,' Hung says regretfully, and goes over to the golf cart. There he pulls out a small corded telephone from somewhere under the dashboard.

I hold out a hand. 'Maybe . . . Maybe just give it a few minutes,' I suggest. 'I don't think he's actually in any real danger. Look . . . he's twitching a bit. I'm sure he's fine.' I look up into the crisp blue sky overhead. 'Let's just enjoy a few minutes' peace.'

Hung smiles at me and deposits the phone back into its recess. I go over to where he's now sat in the driver's seat and plop myself down next to him.

'We're probably both going to get in trouble for this, you know,' Hung tells me.

'Most assuredly, I'd say.'

'Totally worth it, though.'

'Absolutely.'

'I bloody hate golf.'

'So do I.'

'I think I might get a job in a bookshop. They seem nice and quiet.'

'Yes. And there's absolutely no chance of someone like him coming into it.'

Hung smiles beatifically. 'Very true.'

We both lapse into silence and listen to the birds for a few moments. If we both smoked cigars, no doubt we would have raided Benedict's supply by now.

After another minute or so, Benedict Montifore farts, and slowly topples over to one side. He hits the dirt, and this seems to bring him out of unconsciousness. '*Wstfgl?*' he says, spitting out a clump of grass as he does so.

I look at Hung. Hung looks at me.

We both do the exact same resigned sigh . . . and spring into action.

'Oh my God!' I cry, faking concern for all I'm worth. 'Benedict! Benedict! Are you alright?'

'I'm calling the clubhouse, Mr Montifore!' Hung cries in equally faked urgency.

'What happened?' Benedict says, spitting out more grass. 'One minute I'm watching you, the next . . .'

Oh my. This is *wonderful*.

But what tissue of lies can I weave that will point the blame away from Hung and me before Benedict's head clears?

What might have happened here in this forested area of the golf course that could have given rise to his current malaise?

Then it comes to me.

'Ah . . . you were attacked by a deer!' I exclaim, helping him to his feet. 'It rammed you. From behind.'

Benedict winces and clutches his balls.

'And in front,' I add. 'It really was a very *angry* deer. Big antlers. Funny black colour. Probably foreign.' I figure I might as well appeal to Benedict's baser instincts at this point – it can only help.

Hung runs over and helps me pull Benedict to his feet. Angry, truthful Hung is long gone now. The act of the servile caddy is back in force. 'Please go slowly, Mr Montifore! You must not hurt yourself more! Doctor is on the way!'

Hung winks at me over Benedict's slumped back as we take him over to the cart's passenger seat and gingerly place him in it.

As Benedict looks down, with hands still clasped over his genitals, Hung lifts his hand above the man's head, and we share a surreptitious high five, before I climb into the driver's seat and take us back to the clubhouse.

I whistle a bit as I do this.

My anger – so sharp and hot a mere few minutes ago – is more or less gone, for now, anyway. The fact I've managed to injure this arsehole and apparently get away with it makes me *very* happy.

Yes, it's hugely passive-aggressive, but I think we've handily established that I don't do *aggressive*-aggressive, under any circumstances.

By the time we do arrive back at the clubhouse ten minutes later, though, and Benedict is carried away gratefully by an awaiting on-site doctor, my happy mood has rather coloured again.

The anger is back, but now it's being overridden by a more familiar emotion – worry.

Not about Benedict's memory returning. If that happens, it happens, and it was an accident, after all. I'm pretty sure Erica would stop him making my life too much of a misery . . . I hope.

What I'm worried about is how the break-up with Samantha still has the power to leap into the forefront of my mind when I am under emotional strain. I'm obviously not getting over it anywhere near as fast as I'd hoped.

And I'm obviously very angry with her, for doing what she did to me. Far angrier than I thought I was, if I'm being honest. The confrontation I've just had with Benedict about Actual Life has made me realise this.

It's also made me realise that maybe 'Dumped Actually' is not quite the helpful therapy session I thought it was. My pain, shame, anger and sense of defeat are still right there – just waiting to jump out of the closet whenever I get a bit het up.

Speaking of 'Dumped Actually', my other worry is that there is no way I can write up this silly jaunt to Sheldon Brook into a story. If I do, I'll have to lie pretty much about the whole thing, and even then I might run the risk of jogging Benedict's memory, which is something I can ill afford to do.

I have wasted my time entirely today.

How monumentally *frustrating*!

All this round of golf has done is make me upset, angry and tormented by my own demons.

. . . just like every other round of golf anyone's ever played in the whole of human history.

CHAPTER EIGHT

It's Not You – It's Most Definitely Me

I can't move.

I can't breathe.

I can't see.

I can't speak.

I can't hear.

I can't feel.

Why?

Because I am *stood outside a garden centre.*

Oh, the horror.

Now, there might be many men in the world who find themselves rendered unable to function when presented with the idea of having to walk around a garden centre. They will be married men, and it will be the first warm Sunday afternoon in spring. The fear will stem from the fact that they are about to spend three hours walking around the most boring shop on earth with their wives, while she spends all the money they have on plants and interesting decorative features for the patio.

There will be a football match on that the man will be missing. His team will be three-nil up by the time they reach the petunias. If there is a hell for middle-aged, married men, this is it.

But none of that is the reason *I* am feeling such fear, as I stand in front of Griston's Garden Centre on this particular warm Sunday afternoon. I cannot move, simply because I know that the assistant manager of the garden centre is a woman called Samantha Ealing, who I last saw running away from me in tears at a theme park.

I did not want to do this. I can't believe I *am* doing this.

Of all the reader suggestions I have received for 'Dumped Actually', Dominic Carter's was the one I was absolutely going to ignore with extreme prejudice, and never, *ever* even consider doing. Nothing good can come from confronting Samantha about our break-up, I thought. Nothing whatsoever. Who wants to live through that kind of trauma? Only a fool, that's who.

But then came a conversation with my depressive new best friend Wimsy, and my perspective has been irrevocably shifted.

This conversation came about in the pub (as they often do when it comes to Wimsy and myself) a couple of days after my ill-fated trip around the golf course with Benedict Montifore.

Benedict's memory didn't come back, by the way. That's one bullet dodged, at least.

The smile on Erica's face came back though, when I told her all about it. I had to get her a small cup of water when her hysterics turned into a choking fit.

After that, I received very many *I told you so*'s from her, which was more than fair enough.

I was also ordered, in no uncertain terms, to go back to my desk and pick a different subscriber's email to work with – just like Erica had told me to do in the first place.

I tried to do this. I really did. But it's very hard to make sound judgements when you're so bloody angry.

And trust me folks, I was *extremely* angry.

Angry at myself, angry at Benedict Montifore – but mostly angry at Samantha Ealing.

My boss's boss managed to unlock a vast seam of rage in me that I have barely any control over.

Anger is better than self-pity – as I'm sure you'd agree. And I have spent the past few weeks and months in an almost constant state of self-pity about Samantha. Being angry at her makes a welcome change.

Or at least it did for a few hours.

But replacing one negative emotion with another is not helpful in the slightest, and within the space of twenty-four hours my newly unearthed rage at my ex-girlfriend had created a knot in my stomach that all the milk of magnesia in the world wouldn't cure.

I figured a stress-relieving trip to the pub with Wimsy might calm me down a little.

It didn't.

It just riled me up even more.

All thanks to Wimsy – and his annoying ability to talk perfect sense.

'Why don't you just go and have it out with her, then?' he asks me as he sips on his second pint of Carling – which I paid for, needless to say. Wimsy is still bordering on the destitute.

'Don't be ridiculous,' I reply, rolling my eyes.

'Why is it bloody ridiculous? She's obviously still under your skin in a big way. Maybe the only way you get past her is to go thrash it out with her – like that bloke said you should in his email. What was his name again? Dave something?'

I have made the extremely silly mistake of speaking to Wimsy about my job at length, during these trips to the Old Queen's Head. A mistake that is coming back to haunt me right at this moment.

'Dominic Carter . . . and like I told you before, there's no way I'm doing that. No way in hell.'

I take an enormous swig of my own pint of Carling and regard Wimsy through an expertly furrowed brow.

'Why not?'

'You know why not.'

'Do I?'

'Yes!'

Wimsy sits back and folds his thin arms over the old Fat Face jumper I gave him last week. 'Oh yeah. That's right. You're a chicken.'

'I am not a chicken!'

Wimsy nods. 'Yeah, you are.' He points a finger at me. 'Mr Chicken, that's you. Oliver Chicken. You live at No. 1 Chicken Street, in Chicken Town, Chickensville.'

'Stop saying chicken.'

Wimsy just stares at me for a moment with a grin on his face, before raising both elbows to his side. '*Bwak buck buck buck*,' he intones as he waves his elbows up and down slowly.

I grit my teeth for a moment. 'Why do I bother hanging out with you, again?' I ask him as I grip my pint glass.

'You enjoy my refreshing honesty and candour,' he replies, still continuing to slowly wag his elbows up and down.

'Stop doing that.'

'Alright, but my point bleedin' stands. You should go grow a pair and go see your bloody Samantha. You might get some answers – and it might stop you being such a grumpy bastard.'

'*I'm* a grumpy bastard?' I say to him in disbelief.

'Yes. You are. *I* am thoroughly and comprehensively depressed. This is a very different thing. *You* are just a grumpy bastard. And you need to talk to Samantha!'

'I can't! It's just too damn hard!'

Wimsy waves a dismissive bony hand. 'Oh, for fuck's sake. It won't be that bad.'

'Yes, it will!'

Wimsy leans forward. 'You don't know that, you hairy brass pillock!' He points a rigid finger at me. 'That's your whole problem, Ollie. You build things up in your head way too much.'

'No, I don't!'

'Yes, you do! Just go and see her! It might make you feel better!'

'No, it won't!'

'Won't it?' He shrugs. 'I don't know . . . maybe it won't. But tell me this' – Wimsy leans forward even more, so much so that his head now hovers over my pint – 'would it make you feel any *worse?*'

Which is an extremely good point.

I rub my hands across my face. 'I just don't think I've got it in me to confront her like that, Wims.'

He sits back in his chair and folds his arms again. 'Then I don't reckon you'll ever move on, chief.'

Oh Christ.

He's probably right.

This is why I hang out with Wimsy. Having his life comprehensively ruined has given him a blunt attitude towards the entire universe that I find very refreshing – even if his advice does make me nauseous.

The idea of confronting Samantha makes me want to vomit up my kidneys, but it might be something I have to do, so I *can* move on with my life.

I'm angry at her – and what's more, I'm *confused.*

Confused as to why she ended our relationship – and why she chose to do it in such a humiliating way.

The frustration and agony of not knowing why Samantha dumped me has eaten away at my very soul. I've tried to ignore it, I've tried to suppress it – but it's clear I can't do that any more. If I am ever to move past this, I need to know why it happened.

Which brings us bang up to date, with me stood outside a garden centre, my anus quivering like a scolded dog.

I look back over my shoulder at my car. Wimsy is sat in the passenger seat giving me a huge thumbs-up. I offer him a watery smile and stare back towards the garden centre entrance.

With a final, long drawn-out breath, I gird what loins I do possess, and start walking towards Griston's Garden Centre, with a look of bleak determination on my face.

This look drops off like the pound did after Brexit as soon as I'm actually in the garden centre, though. As I move from the large undercover shopping area, and out into the broad expansive courtyard, where they keep all the actual plants, I am swamped by happy memories of strolling through this very same set of doors, on the way to surprise my lovely girlfriend at lunchtime.

The intoxicating smell of plants assails my nostrils, sparking off flashbacks to far happier times. Over there, by the hanging plants, is where I gave her a box of her favourite Monty Bojangles chocolates. Way over at the back there, by the ponds, is where I stole a secret kiss when nobody else was looking. That big trestle table covered in lavender? That's where I told Samantha I had tickets to the opening of Thorn Manor.

All of this batters me in the face in a split second, and all of the determination and strength I had outside dribbles out of my body, and down the nearest drain.

I have to leave. I have to get out of here. I have to *save myself!*

I turn on my heel, fully intent on getting out of Dodge as fast as my legs will carry me, when I see her.

Samantha is walking through the big undercover shop, just past one of the enormous standees selling Resolva weedkiller. This is somehow quite apt, as I am a weed, and if she sees me, I will be instantly killed.

I actually let out an audible gasp of terror.

Samantha is deep in conversation with one of the other staff members – an older lady who I recall as being a Jan. Or a Jane. Or something else beginning with J. It was definitely a J – without a doubt.

Who cares what her bloody name is! We have to get out of here!

But now Samantha and JanJane are walking directly along the aisle that leads through the shop, to the exit. If I go that way, I will definitely be seen.

Hide!

Hide, you fool!

Letting out another gasp of horror, I scuttle sideways like a crab, in search of a large rock I can crawl under. Griston's isn't known for its rock selling, though – unless you count the decorative pebbles – so I have to find something else to shield myself behind, before my ex-girlfriend sees me, and the world ends.

I could duck under that trestle table full of lavender, which I mentioned earlier. But this would leave me far too exposed, so I immediately rule it out.

There's some definite merit to secreting myself behind the box hedges. They should certainly be large enough to conceal me – but then they are in a high-traffic area of the garden centre, and I might be spotted by someone else, who might then inform a staff member that there's a man secreted about the box hedges. I will instantly be dubbed a pervert and arrested.

The only other area I can reach before Samantha and JanJane see me is the one that contains the garden sheds. This is, of course, the perfect place to go, and I really should have put it at the top of the list. What can I say? I'm not functioning with high mental efficiency right now.

The sideways scuttle brings me to a selection of three sheds large enough for me to hide myself in. I then go through a hasty game of Goldilocks and the Three Bears in my head.

The one on the left is too small to get into. It's more one of those storage bin things you throw the shears and gardening gloves into after you've had a hack at the buddleia. The second is a Wendy house, and is therefore not appropriate in the slightest. If hiding behind a box hedge might make me look like a pervert, what would hiding in a *Wendy house* do for my reputation?

Don't answer that.

The third shed is perfect, though. It's a bog-standard job, complete with shingle roof and solid-looking pine walls. It should do the trick, no problem. I can pop myself in there and wait it out.

Or at least, I could, if the bloody thing wasn't locked with a padlock!

Who padlocks a sodding shed in a sodding garden centre?! What possible purpose could it serve? Are they perhaps afraid that someone may try to steal something from the probably empty shed? A cubic metre of pine-smelling air, for instance? Or have they had a lot of desperate men trying to hide from their ex-girlfriends over the course of the last few months, and have decided that enough is enough?

Regardless, that option is not open to me, so off I go into the bloody Wendy house, and the risk of a possible future reputation as a bit of a Rolf Harris.

And it's just in the nick of time too. If I had dawdled a second longer, I would have been seen by Samantha and JanJane, of that there is no doubt. It's a miracle I manage to get away with it at all.

I crouch down, hastily squeeze myself through the small front door of the Wendy house, and immediately spin around to look out of one of the tiny windows. I stare up and out of it as the person I thought I was going to spend the rest of my life with – and JanJane – go walking past, talking about the shipment of garden gnomes they are expecting in an hour.

My heart pines openly as I look at her in the flesh for the first time in way too long.

Samantha, that is, not JanJane.

I'm sure JanJane is a very nice person, but if I can't actually remember her name, I'm not really going to be that in awe of her, am I?

Samantha looks beautiful, of course. This was as inevitable as death, taxes and the lies of politicians.

She's wearing her dark-green Griston's Garden Centre polo shirt like it's something from a catwalk, and the way her hair is tied back in a rushed ponytail is a study in effortless style.

This is what my eyes see, anyway. For anyone else on planet earth, she probably looks like an attractive blonde girl in a dowdy work shirt, who would rather be talking about anything other than garden gnomes with her assistant JanJane.

But to me – as I gaze up at her from my crouched hiding place – she looks like a million dollars.

Oh bloody hell, I think I'm about to start crying in a Wendy house. This must be some kind of new personal low for me. It even tops grasping my erect penis in front of a baby deer. If not by much.

As my emotions roil and bubble away inside my chest, I watch Samantha and JanJane come to a halt right in front of my Wendy house, as they are joined by another person – a tall young man wearing a pair of green combat trousers, big black work boots and a Griston's polo shirt, much like Samantha and JanJane's.

'Hi guys!' he says as he joins them. 'Sam? Can I speak to you about that problem we were having with the main fish tank? If we don't get the filtration sorted out soon, we're going to lose some of the tetras.'

'Yes, of course, Riley,' she replies.

'I'll go see if I can find out when the delivery's coming, Samantha,' JanJane says. 'See you later.'

'Thanks,' Samantha replies, and watches JanJane disappear back where she came from, before turning her attention back to Riley the fish tank man.

'Is there anything wrong with the fish tank?' she asks him in an amused voice.

Riley grins and shakes his head. 'Nah. Course not. I just wanted to get you alone, so I could do this.'

All the universes collapse in on themselves as Riley leans forward and kisses Samantha square on the lips.

'No,' I say to myself, in the smallest voice imaginable. It's probably the same way a tiny shrew would say 'no' in the confines of its mammalian brain, as it sees the hawk descending from above.

'No, no, no,' I repeat, tears sprouting from my eyes. 'No, no, no, no, no, no,' I continue to babble as I watch my beloved swap spit with another man.

Samantha giggles and puts one arm around Riley's waist. 'You'll get us both into trouble, you know,' she tells him.

Riley looks around. 'Who with? The place is almost empty! And Jeff is off today, so there's nobody stopping me.'

Riley kisses Samantha again, this time passionately – and probably with tongues.

No! No! I kiss her with tongues, you bastard! It's my tongue that should be in her mouth!

'It should be . . . *my* tongue. It should be my tongue. *It should be my tongue*,' I moan as quietly as I can – obviously now in the midst of a huge emotional breakdown. 'It should be my tongue. It should be my tongue. It should be *my bloody to—*'

'I'm sorry I wiped bogies on you, mister.'

'*Mb.*'

Now, then.

If somewhere in this broad and exciting universe of ours (the bits that didn't collapse when Riley kissed Samantha) there is some race of aliens, far away in the vastness of existence, who have taken it upon themselves to catalogue every single word ever uttered by any sentient creature across the cosmos, then surely they would have catalogued the word '*mb*' by now.

Quite why they would be constructing such a gigantic tome of knowledge is beyond me. Perhaps in their huge, alien intellect, they have become bored with the trivialities of Euclidean geometry, and the search for a unifying theory for the atomic and subatomic worlds, and have instead turned their attention to writing a really, really bloody good dictionary. The kind that contains every single word ever uttered, including the one I've just said – which is '*mb*'.

Now, you can't just have a list of words in a dictionary. You also require a description of their meaning. And our alien friends – being the creatures of vast and unknowable intellect that they surely are – would no doubt have made sure that they had an appropriate description for what the word '*mb*' means.

I therefore have no doubt that the entry into the *Dictionary Galactica* would read something like this:

> *Mb (pronounced* mb*) – the sound a human male makes when he hears a small child's voice right behind him, while trapped in a Wendy house watching his ex-girlfriend play tonsil hockey with a new man.*

A strained noise escapes my vocal cords. I have to slap a hand over my mouth to prevent the scream that's rising up from the recesses of my soul erupting into the world, and giving away my hiding position.

Slowly – ever so slowly – I turn my head to see a small girl, parked in the gloomy corner of the Wendy house, staring at me with wide, innocent eyes.

She has obviously recognised me, but it takes me a few moments to register who she is.

'*Lauren?*' I venture.

'Yeah?' Lauren replies, one finger starting to probe the inner workings of her left nostril.

'You're here,' I say in disbelief. Lauren does not reply. 'You're here . . . *now.*'

Lauren continues to stay quiet and rummage around inside her olfactory cavity.

'How?' I mutter – not to Lauren this time, but to whatever deity or supernatural monster is out there. The one who has contrived to place me in the middle of the single most awful and unlikely coincidence in the history of mankind.

I am trapped in a Wendy house, with my ex-girlfriend right outside kissing her new boyfriend. In the self-same Wendy house is the tiny girl who wiped bogies down my face, just after that ex-girlfriend had broken up with me, in front of a Bavarian oompah band.

Can I go insane now? Is that okay with everyone?

'What are you doing?' Lauren asks me, squeezing into the corner a bit more. 'Why are you in here?'

'Er . . .' Oh my God, what exactly am I meant to say to her?

I'm in here, Lauren, because I don't have the guts to confront my ex-girlfriend, due to a crippling lack of self-esteem?

Will Lauren understand that? Or would I have to try to explain to a six-year-old what self-esteem means? That could take some time, as she's lucky not to be old enough to need self-esteem yet, and will therefore have no idea what I'm on about.

I instead elect to lie, because lying to small children is always the best approach.

'I'm playing a special game of hide-and-seek with my friends,' I tell her.

'Are they your friends outside?' Lauren asks, pointing at Samantha and Riley. I can't bear to look, just in case they're still going at it hammer and tongs.

I swallow a large ball of bile. 'Yes. Those are . . . *my friends.*'

'You must not be very good at hide-and-seek, then.'

'Why's that?'

Lauren points again. 'They've found you.'

I spin around to see the worst possible thing imaginable. Samantha and Riley are both bending down outside the Wendy house and are looking at me through the tiny windows.

'*Prb,*' I say.

Prb (pronounced prb) – *the sound a human male makes when he's been discovered hiding in a Wendy house with a small girl he isn't related to, by his ex-girlfriend and her hunky new lover.*

'Ollie?!' Samantha exclaims in horror.

Ohgodohgodohgodohgodohgodohgodohgodohgodohgodohgodohgod ohgodohgod.

'Hi Samantha!' I say in a voice full of manic cheeriness. 'Fancy seeing you here!'

Then another voice pipes up. 'Sam? Have you seen Lauren anywhere? I can't find her. Is she in there again? She is, isn't she! Lauren Grosvenor, you come out of that Wendy house right— *Oh Jesus Christ, she's in there with a pervert!!*'

I shake my head vociferously and start to gesticulate wildly. 'No! No! I'm not a pervert! I'm not a bloody pervert!'

Riley's face falls in horror. 'Aren't you that bloke who wanks off in front of baby deer?'

'What? No! That was just . . . That was just . . . Oh bloody hell!'

I have to get out of this Wendy house before I'm arrested for accidental Rolf Harrising.

Samantha, Riley and the angry-looking mother of Lauren the bogey monster all step back, allowing me to squeeze myself out of my impromptu hiding place. Lauren follows me out, and immediately runs into the arms of her mother.

I stand straight and hold out both hands. 'Look, there's been a massive misunderstanding here.' I am no longer terrified of confronting Samantha. That has been comprehensively eclipsed by the terror of being arrested for Rolf Harrising.

'What are you *doing here*, Ollie?' Samantha asks. 'Why were you hiding in there?'

'Because . . . Because . . .' It's probably time I just told the truth. It may be embarrassing, but at least it'll stop them calling the police. 'Because I came here to talk to you, and then I bottled it, so I hid in there, hoping you'd go by without seeing me, so I could get out of here.'

'You wanted to hide in a Wendy house with a little girl so you didn't have to talk to Sam?' Riley says, bristling.

'No! No! That's not what I meant! I didn't know she was in there!' I look at Samantha with utter disbelief. 'How is she here? *Why* is she here?'

Samantha grits her teeth and glares at me before answering. 'Lindsay was kind enough to drive me home after you . . . you . . .' She can't bring herself to finish that sentence. 'We struck up a friendship in the car on the way back.'

'Oh.'

Well, at least I haven't got to worry that there's a mischievous and hateful deity above my head causing all of these godawful coincidences.

'Hang on,' Lindsay – mother of Lauren the bogey monster – says, looking at me properly for the first time. 'Isn't this Oliver? The bloke who asked you to marry him?'

'Yes,' Samantha says, shifting uncomfortably. This reminds me of why I am here today. I am extremely glad to see her shift around like that. She's obviously still totally ashamed of what she did to me!

Lindsay regards me with a mixture of revulsion and pity. It's quite something to behold, especially coming from someone who has a child who likes to wipe their nose product down people's faces. 'I'm going to take Lauren over to the café,' she says, starting to back away.

'Okay,' Samantha says, smiling down at Lauren as she does.

The three of us watch the girl and her mother withdraw, and then regard one another again. This is starting to feel like something of a stand-off – and it's very definitely two against one.

Samantha sighs. 'You look . . . well?' she hazards, trying to keep things polite.

I give her a flat stare. 'Do I?'

She looks deeply uncertain.

It's funny, but now I'm actually talking to her, I don't feel anywhere near as scared. Anticipation is always worse than reality – Wimsy was 100 per cent right.

. . . though, I suggest you don't apply that logic to sticking your hand in a gas fire any time soon.

'Why have you come here, Ollie?' she asks me, getting to the root of the matter.

'I . . . I wanted to come here to ask *you* why, actually, Samantha.'

Her eyes narrow. 'Could you please call me Sam, Ollie? Everyone else on the planet seems to have no problem with it. I'm not sure why you do.'

'I thought you liked Samantha.'

'Not really, no. It sounds so bloody formal.'

Well, that's a shock. I genuinely thought she loved it.

Something deep within me shifts. I always believed I knew Samantha as well as anyone could know another person. In all the time we were together, I thought I'd come to know her completely.

Apparently not, though.

'Okay . . . *Sam.*' It sounds so alien in my mouth. 'I came to ask you why.'

'Why what?'

'Why you did it to me, *Sam.*' Oh dear. Starting to feel that anger now. And I don't have a golf ball I can fire at Samantha, so I might as well just tell her how I'm really feeling, and get it over with. 'Why you dumped me in front of all those people! Why you ended a beautiful relationship! Why you broke my heart, *Samantha!*' I look at her incredulously. 'Why did you break my *heart*?!'

Yes!

Look how taken aback she is! Look how guilty she is!

No!

Look how angry Riley is! Look how much taller and broader he is than me!

'You'd better get out of here, mate, before I knock your fucking block off,' Riley says, stepping forward.

I sneer at him. 'You sure you want to go out with her, buddy? She'll only end up dumping you too!'

'You *bastard!*' Samantha cries.

I'm amazed. 'Me?? I'm the bastard?? I *loved you*, Samantha! I did everything for you! And you just led me down the garden path, didn't you? I thought we were going to be together forever! You made me think you felt the same way!! You LIED TO ME!'

'I didn't bloody lie to you!'

'Yes, you did!' All the anger and frustration of the past few months is boiling over now. 'You fucking dumped me! When I asked you to *marry me!* Who does something like that, Samantha? Who?'

Tears are starting to well up in her eyes now. *Good.*

'I had to end things with you, Ollie!' she wails. 'It was all too much! YOU were too much! It was all going way too fast for me!'

'Too fast?! Too bloody fast?!' I scream. 'We were in love! We were meant to be! We were together for all of that time!'

And now it's Samantha's turn to look at me with utter disbelief. 'What do you mean *all of that time*?'

'Oh God!' I exclaim, exasperation filling every pore of my being. 'All the time we were together!'

'Ollie . . . we only went out with one another for *THREE MONTHS*!'

She screams the last two words so loud, they echo around the garden centre walls, and cause a couple of startled pigeons to take flight.

For a moment there is nothing but silence. And then I speak again.

'SO?' I scream back at her. 'So bloody what? That was *long enough*, Samantha! That was more than long enough for me to know it was right! That it was perfect!'

'Oh my God!' she wails, head going into her hands.

'Are you fucking *mental*?' Riley interjects.

'What?' I spit at him.

'Are . . . you . . . mental?' he repeats slowly, so I can understand.

'No! I . . . am . . . not,' I reply, parroting him.

'Really? So, you thought that it was fine to ask a woman to marry you when you'd only been seeing her for three months?'

'Yes!'

'*Three* months.'

'Yes! What part of that don't you understand?!'

He blinks a couple of times. 'Jesus Christ. I've had things in the fridge for longer than that, and I didn't ask them to marry me.'

'But . . . I . . . ah . . . wh?' I stammer, unable to get any words out.

Samantha looks up at me again, distraught. 'Don't you *see*, Ollie? Don't you see how it was all too fast for me?'

'Gh . . . mh . . . I . . . eh . . .'

'It was all too much! I liked you . . . Maybe I was even starting to love you, but you came on too strong. Too fast. I felt . . . *trapped*. I felt rushed. I just couldn't do it any more.'

'But . . . But I loved you. You were *the one*.'

'I know, Ollie.' There's sympathy in her voice now. I hate her and love her for it in equal measure. 'And I'm sorry. I really am. But it was too much. *You* were too much. You were just so . . . so . . . *needy*.'

I stare at her, bottom lip trembling. 'I am not *needy*!'

And then it all flashes in front of my eyes . . .

My relationship with Samantha. The one I had with Yukio. And Gretchen. And Lisa.

'Dumped Actually'. Erica. Vanity.

All of it.

'Oh fuck me,' I say in a rush of breath. 'I *am* bloody needy!'

Well, *of course* I am.

I'm pathologically needy.

I'm a people pleaser. A man constantly in need of affection and attention.

All the things I've done in the past few weeks to open my eyes to the kind of person I am have crystallised in this one moment of absolute clarity about my break-up with Samantha.

I look at her anguished face. 'Oh bloody hell, Sam. I'm really, really sorry.'

A weight I didn't know was there is instantly lifted from my shoulders. The truth of it. The clear, honest, horrible truth of it, is there for me to witness for the first time.

And bizarrely, the understanding feels *wonderful*. Wonderful to have an answer at last. Wonderful to know why it all went wrong. And most of all, wonderful to realise that the woman I'd fallen in love was absolutely worth it . . . even if I wasn't.

It's not you, Samantha. It is most definitely *me*.

I look at Riley and point to Samantha. 'Give her a hug, mate.'

He stares at me for a second, before nodding, and wrapping his arms around her.

There's still pain in my heart as I watch him do this. But it's muted now. It's *less*.

I feel like I'm closing the door on something in my mind and in my heart, and the relief is quite palpable.

Mixed in with this sense of relief is a heap load of gut-wrenching *guilt*, though. Guilt that I put poor old Samantha through all of this.

I then let out a gasp as I realise something for the first time.

'Dumped Actually'.

I've been writing about Samantha in 'Dumped Actually' all of this time, and I've made her out to be the bad guy. I've written about her like she was the one to blame for all of my heartache.

And she's probably read it.

'Oh my God,' I exclaim to the heavens as Riley continues to hug his girlfriend. 'Samantha – I'm so, so sorry for all the things I've written about you!' I blurt. 'I wasn't . . . I wasn't thinking straight. I haven't been for a very long time.' The deserved shame in my voice makes me want to vomit. I am an awful human being.

Riley gives me the dirtiest look imaginable. 'Yeah, well. This isn't the first time I've had to hug her like this because of you. She's been *humiliated*, thanks to your bloody stories.'

'I didn't mean to do that!' I wail, almost feeling like I could burst out crying.

I think I'm fully realising how impactful 'Dumped Actually' has been. All this time I've been concerned about how it affects just *my* life . . . and I've completed ignored how it could negatively affect the lives of the people I've been talking about. I don't ever remember mentioning Samantha's surname in the articles I've written, but anyone who knows that she dated me would know it was her in an instant.

Oh *God*.

'Sam . . . I'm so sorry,' I repeat. I could say sorry a thousand times and it probably wouldn't be enough. 'I was hurt . . . and in pain . . . and I haven't been thinking straight.' Now I'm the one putting his head in his hands. 'I haven't actually been thinking straight for a very long time . . .'

Sam regards me at first without much compassion, but as she watches me trembling on the verge of tears again, I can see her face softening somewhat.

Sam looks at her boyfriend. 'Riley? Can you . . . Can you go and let Paula know I need a few minutes off? She can handle the store for a bit.' She then looks at me. 'I think I need to sort something out with Ollie . . . once and for all.'

Riley nods, gives me a look of a million daggers and makes his way off to inform Paula (or JanJane, as I inexplicably dubbed her) that their boss will be a little preoccupied in the immediate future, talking to the man who has trashed her character online.

Once Riley is gone, Sam turns back to me and folds her arms for a second. 'What the hell to do with you, Oliver Sweet,' she says, shaking her head. Then she reaches out a hand and points at the Wendy house. 'In there, you.'

'Pardon?'

'Back in there. I want to do this in private.'

My face flushes. What does she want to do in private?

I don't answer her, but crouch back down and crawl into the Wendy house again as I've been ordered to do, swiftly followed by Sam, who does it with a lot more grace than me.

I sit cross-legged on one side, while she does the same on the other. We can both sit up like this fine. It's quite the expansive Wendy house. No wonder Lauren likes being in here.

Sam looks at me silently for a few moments, no doubt thinking of the best way to start this awkward, but necessary, conversation.

'You don't need to apologise, Ollie,' she eventually says. 'And that's because I don't have to apologise to *you*, either. I know what I did at Thorn Manor was a shitty thing, but I was trapped and confused, and didn't handle it well.'

I hold out a hand. 'Please. You were absolutely right to do what you did. I was clearly coming on way too strong. I should never have put you in that position. Not that fast, anyway. I should have . . . I should have . . .'

I don't know what I should have.

The absolute worst thing about all of this is that if I wasn't such a needy little sod, then maybe my relationship with Sam would have flourished properly, over the right amount of time, and maybe my marriage proposal would have had a far more positive answer.

That way I wouldn't be sat cross-legged in a Wendy house across from a beautiful, intelligent and good woman – who I lost because of my stupidity.

'Stop it,' she says.

'Huh?'

'Stop it, Ollie. Stop beating yourself up.'

'What else am I supposed to do?'

'*Forgive.* Forgive us *both*. I have. It's not your fault that you were the way you were with me, and it's not *my* fault I had to end it with you. I don't want to spend a moment more resenting you, and I don't want you to resent me, either.'

I nod slowly. 'Look, I am so sorry for the way I've written about you.'

Sam shakes her head. 'Don't worry about it. You were never *that* awful, Ollie. I don't think you could be, even if you tried. It's one of the reasons I was attracted to you in the first place. I was just upset that I was being made out as the villain of the piece.'

'I'll make it up to you!' I blurt. 'I'll do a write-up about what happened here today, and I'll make sure everybody knows what the truth is! If . . . If you want me to, that is.'

Sam's eyes narrow as she thinks about this. 'That'd be nice, yes. Thank you. Though maybe don't say anything about hiding in here with Lauren. People might get the wrong idea.'

I shake my head. 'People have had the wrong idea about me for months now, don't worry about it. Thankfully they just all think I'm a fumbling idiot, rather than a pervert. I can't leave Lauren out, anyway. She's kind of the star of the piece.'

Sam actually laughs at this. Her face lights up, and my heart starts to break all over again.

I look at Sam and heave a deep sigh. 'I was never good enough for you,' I tell her.

Sam shuffles forward and does something that takes me completely by surprise. She wraps her arms around me.

'Yes, you were,' she says into my ear. 'You were – and are – a lovely man in so many ways, Ollie. I knew that then, and I know it even more now from what I've read about you.' She then moves her head slightly away from me, so her face is right in front of mine. 'You just need to . . . I don't know . . . find your *centre*. Do you know what I mean?'

'I think so.'

'You tried to make *me* your centre.' She shakes her head. 'But it'll never be right, Ollie. It'll never be right until it . . . until it comes from *inside you*. You know what I mean?'

I can't believe I lost this girl. I can't believe it at all.

'Yeah, I know what you mean. But . . . But I don't know how, Sam. I don't know where to find it.'

'You will.'

'Will I?'

'Yes. You just need to get to the bottom of why you feel the way you do. Why you . . . push things too hard. That's all.'

That's all, she says. Like it's the easiest thing in the world.

'Okay, Sam. I'll try.'

'Good.' She smiles and looks around for a second. 'Now. If you wouldn't mind, I want to give you one last kiss.'

'What?'

'You heard me. I love Riley to pieces, but I did love you as well, Ollie. Even if it was only for a very brief moment in my life. I want the last memory I have of you to be a good one. Do you want that too?'

No, Sam. I want the last memory I have of you to be when I die an old and happy man.

'Yeah,' I tell her. 'That'd be nice.'

Sam leans forward and plants her lips on mine.

It is the best and worst kiss I will ever receive in my life.

The ghost of it will stay with me for the rest of my days.

I will go many places and do many things in the time I have left to me – and I will do them all with this moment carried in my heart throughout. It will sustain me in times of pain. It will make me smile in times of peace. It will be a moment I will never forget.

One of many moments, caught between a void.

Sam leans back again, smiles, but then looks startled as she thinks of something. 'Please don't put that in "Dumped Actually".'

I smile. 'Don't worry, I won't. I think that moment stays between you and me – and nobody else.'

'Good,' she replies, grinning.

And then we're hugging again.

This hug *will* go into the next chapter of 'Dumped Actually'. In fact, it will be the way I'll end it, I think.

Because what better way can there be for Samantha to depart this story than with the warm embrace of friendship and forgiveness?

And make no mistake, she does depart this story now – *forever.*

Because the story is not about her. As much as I would have loved it to have been. As much as I *needed it to be* – it's not. Nor is it about Yukio, or Gretchen, or Lisa. Or anybody else.

This story is about *me*.

It's about bloody time I accepted that.

I'm going to try my hardest to stop being so needy. I'm going to try my hardest to put myself first for a change. I'm going to try my hardest to please myself, for once.

I'm going to try my hardest to do all of these things – but I am scared out of my mind that I'm going to fail, unless I get to the bottom of what makes me tick. Unless I get a better understanding of why I've acted the way I have – not just with Samantha, but with all of the women I've been with – I'm never going to have a successful relationship. That much is clear to me now. What is making me so desperate to please? I have to find out. I just *have to*.

That all starts with climbing out of this Wendy house, saying a last farewell to Sam and leaving this bloody garden centre.

I might buy a pot plant for my parents on the way out, though. They like those.

CHAPTER NINE

A One-Way Trip into a Weird Little Mind

'That geranium you bought us last week is flourishing by the pond, Oliver. A really lovely addition to the garden. It's very bushy!'

You see?

They did like it.

'That's great, Mum,' I reply down the phone as I wander back to my desk with a fresh cup of tea in my hand.

These lunchtime phone calls with my mother are a combination of a pleasure and a pain. It's nice to catch up with her, but my mum does like to talk, and I only get an hour for lunch.

'I was quite surprised to see just how bushy it's got, actually. I may have to trim it back.'

My mother would not know a double entendre if it ran up to her painted bright red, singing the national anthem.

I, however, chuckle to myself as I plonk my arse back down on my office chair.

'What are you laughing about, Oliver?' Mum asks me.

'Oh nothing, Mum. I'm glad the geranium is doing so well.'

'It's nice to hear you laugh, actually,' she says. 'How are you feeling at the moment?' Her voice is full of the kind of gentle hope that makes my stomach knot. I would like nothing more than to tell my mother that I am feeling hale and hearty. Enjoying life. Getting much better, thanks.

And if I could lie to my mother, I would tell her exactly that. But I have never been able to lie to my mother. She may not be able to spot a double entendre at a thousand paces, but she can sure as hell spot when I'm being economical with the truth from ten thousand.

'Eh, I'm not too bad,' I reply, deciding to stay as neutral as possible. 'Still processing what happened with Sam, and have a deadline for "Dumped Actually", but other than that . . . could be worse.'

This is more or less the truth. It's been five days since my confrontation with my ex-girlfriend. In that time I've done a lot of soul searching. Sadly, it's been conducted with a broken torch and no map, so I haven't really got any further along with it. I still have no answers.

'Oh, okay, sweetheart.'

Ouch. That sympathetic disappointment in her voice is unavoidable, isn't it?

I take a deep breath. 'I'll be fine, though, Mum. Honestly. Like you and Dad always say, *these things take time.*'

That's another cliché they like to come out with when I get dumped, along with all of the nautical ones I've previously mentioned.

'That's right, Oliver. It will all come out in the wash, you just see.'

I roll my eyes. She means well . . . she really, really does. But how can a woman who has enjoyed decades of trouble-free marriage possibly have any real advice for a broken toy like me, eh?

'I'm sure it will,' I reply, forcing a smile on to my face, to try and sound positive.

'Yes. It certainly will,' she says, matter-of-factly. 'The right girl is out there for you, Oliver. I just know it.'

'Yeah. I'm sure you're right.'

How many times have we had this little exchange in my life?
Too many times.
Way too many.
'Anyway, Mum, I'm really sorry, but I'll have to get back to work now,' I tell her. I'd like this conversation to end. I feel horrible for thinking that way, but it's the truth. Mum means well, but talking to her or Dad at times like this is frustrating and pointless.
They just don't *understand*.
'Oh, okay, sweetheart. I'll let you go and get back to it. I'll see you in a couple of weeks, anyway, won't I?'
'Yeah, of course you will. I'm really looking forward to it.' This last comes out in a flat voice, which sits well with the words themselves, and there's a very good reason for that.
It's the fortieth anniversary of my parents' wedding in a fortnight, and to celebrate they're holding a ceremony to renew their vows in the expansive garden of the rambling old house I was brought up in. They're only inviting a few people. Some of their best friends, my aunt and uncle, and me – their only offspring.
It was something I thought I'd be taking Sam to, once upon a happier time. But now I'll be going alone.
'Oh. Good,' my mother replies, knowing that I'm lying through my teeth.
I feel a pang of guilt. I should be happy for them. Hell . . . I *am* happy for them. But it's hard to muster much enthusiasm about the occasion when I'll probably be the only one there who's single. And under the age of sixty, but that part is irrelevant.
'Well, have a lovely rest of the day, son,' Mum says to me. 'Let me know if you need anything.'
'I will, Mum. Love you lots.'
'Love you too.'
I end the call and chuck my phone down on to the desk with a sigh.

If I thought my mum could give me any help, I would certainly ask her for it. But she can't help me with advice about my love life, and she sure as hell can't help me with my other big problem . . . what to write about next for 'Dumped Actually'.

Literally the only other decent prospect for a story that I have in front of me is the suggestion I try a bit of mindfulness meditation. But how interesting is that going to be, when you get right down to it?

I struggle to think of a way I can make ten minutes of heavy breathing sound fascinating to my horde of subscribers.

But I don't have much of a choice in the matter. There's simply nothing else to go on.

I construct a short but pleasant email to Lizzy Moore, asking her where her classes are, and if it's okay for me to attend. Once that is sent, I try to think of something else to do, but as I can't progress any more with 'Dumped Actually' right now, I have very little to occupy myself with. This invariably leads me back to the fruitless soul searching I've been doing so much of recently – and I pretty much spend the rest of the afternoon trapped in a haze of unwanted introspection and self-recrimination.

This time around, I decide to concentrate on how badly I handle the events in my life.

Because I do that. Every single time, it seems.

Look at how I handled the wedding proposal, and the break-up. Or the trip to the salon, and Laughlin's insistence on stripping my red-raw arse of its hair. Or the thing with the deer, or Vanity and the mask, or not telling Benedict Montifore where to go, or—

Or, or, or, or, *OR!*

My life is full of *or*s. I have more *or*s in my life than the Cambridge rowing team.

What the hell is *wrong with me?*

***

I still have no answer to this question as I rock up to Brantree Community Centre, four days later, for my first session of mindfulness with Lizzy Moore.

They have been four days of continued masochistic self-examination, so I do not look my best as I walk into the centre's largest hall and look for Lizzy. The bags under my eyes are as heavy as my feet as I make my way over to a small crowd of women.

'Excuse me, is one of you Lizzy?' I ask them politely.

From the middle of the crowd, a small, slightly plump and happy-looking brunette smiles and waves at me. 'Hello, Ollie! Thank you so much for coming!'

I try smiling back. It sort of works. 'My pleasure. I'm looking forward to seeing what all this mindfulness stuff is about.'

There's a low murmur from the rest of the women as they realise who I am. The looks I'm getting suggest I might have a fair few fans here today. I wish I was in a better state of mind to appreciate this.

'Okay, everyone,' Lizzy says to the group, 'if you want to go and roll out your mats, we'll get started soon. I'm just going to have a quick chat with Ollie.' She turns her attention back to me. 'How are you?'

For a moment, I think about the putting on of the legendary brave face, but decide against it, just because I can't really be bothered, as I don't have the energy. 'Been better, to be honest,' I say, with a wan smile.

'Oh, poor you,' Lizzy says, and touches my arm. 'I know exactly how you feel. When Alfie left, I thought the world had ended. But taking a little time to myself and doing some mindfulness really helped me. I hope it will help you too.'

'So do I.' I look at the others as they position themselves on a series of brightly coloured yoga mats. 'What do I have to do?'

'Not much at all. Pick up a mat from over there on the rack, and sit yourself down cross-legged on it anywhere you feel comfortable.

Then you just have to follow what I say.' She smiles again. 'Don't worry, though, it's all quite easy.'

For this, I am extremely grateful. Easy is all I want from my life at the moment.

I pick a spot at the back of the twelve-strong group, and sit down on my purple yoga mat, wondering what's going to happen next.

I'm expecting a lot of chanting and deep breathing. Maybe with a little light stretching to go along with it. I have done absolutely no research prior to coming to this class today, so have no actual idea what mindfulness is – only that it's some kind of new-age meditation thing that probably requires joss sticks and kaftans at some stage, to make it truly work for you.

'Hello, everyone,' Lizzy says, settling herself on to her own mat. 'Welcome to this week's class. I know a lot of you have been many times before, but we have a few fresh faces, so I'm just going to briefly explain what mindfulness is all about.'

As she does this, my entire opinion begins to change.

Mindfulness sounds a lot more sensible than I thought it would.

The idea that consciously spending more time in the present moment – rather than constantly looking back or looking forwards – can be beneficial to our mental health sounds quite reasonable.

All I seem to do is look back on my past failures, and worry about my future ones, so getting out of the habit of doing that – even for a short period of time – sounds rather fantastic to me.

I've never been one to stop and smell the roses, so to speak, so mindfulness seems like an alien concept – but I'm happy to give it a go, as what do I really have to lose?

In a soft, gentle voice, Lizzy starts to talk to the whole class, instructing us to close our eyes, breathe comfortably and try to let our minds relax by focussing on the environment around us, and letting all other thoughts and distractions fade away.

This is incredibly hard for me to do – at least at first. My mind is a maelstrom of doubt, recrimination, worry, depression and anxiety. How on earth do I even begin to let that go?

Slowly, though, as Lizzy's soft tone lulls my brain, I do start to let my thoughts dribble away to a certain extent. The more I attune myself to my immediate surroundings, the more I am able to ignore the thoughts that pass through my brain.

So much so that by the time the half-hour class has passed, I actually feel quite calm and chilled out.

This is a *revelation*.

I say as much to Lizzy as the class packs up their yoga mats.

'Great, isn't it?' she tells me. 'I hope you can see why it helped me so much with my anxiety and depression after Alfie left. The fact you've had such a good experience your first time means that mindfulness might just be the thing for you!'

I nod in happy agreement. 'I think you might be right! When's the next class?'

'I'm running another one in a couple of days, if you want to come to that too.'

'You know what? I think I will!'

And you know what? I do!

Only this time I bring a friend along . . .

'Oh God, chief. This is barking mad,' Wimsy says, with a disgusted look on his face. 'How the hell you persuaded me to come here is beyond me.'

I clap him on the back. 'Trust me, Wims. It'll be good for you. I've felt worlds better in the couple of days since the last session.'

He squints at me. 'You sure you didn't go out and get drunk after it?'

'Haven't touched a drop,' I tell him, shaking my head.

I drag Wimsy – who is decked out in a pair of my old grey jogging bottoms – into the community centre hall like a dead weight.

He may be reluctant to be a part of this, but it'll be good for him – I just know it. Also, having a friend along for the experience will add a little colour to the story I'm writing – if he lets me mention him, that is. Wimsy has been adamant that he doesn't get included in any of my 'Dumped Actually' stories so far, but I'm hoping he might change his mind, if this is a positive experience for him.

And what do you know? It absolutely is!

'Blimey, that was pretty good,' he says, after we've popped our yoga mats back. 'I thought it would be a complete waste of time, but I actually feel calm for the first time in ages. My right eye has stopped twitching entirely.'

'That's just how I felt! Unbelievable, isn't it?'

'Yeah. I'm fucking flabbergasted. I'm really glad you made me come along, Ollie.'

It's at this point Lizzy Moore comes over to say hello. 'How are you both?' she asks expectantly. She knows she's on to a good thing here, and wants to make sure everyone else feels the same way.

'Great, Lizzy, thank you again,' I tell her.

Wimsy says nothing.

Wimsy has gone bright red.

Ah.

I think there might be more than one reason why Wimsy is glad I brought him along.

'And did you get something out of it . . . er, Wimsy, was it?'

'Mm.'

'Yeah, that's his name!' I butt in, instinctively understanding what's going on here. 'He really liked the mindfulness too, didn't you, Wimsy?' No response. '*Didn't you, Wimsy?*'

'Yeah. Yeah. It was great,' he eventually says. 'You're lovely.'

It's Lizzy's turn to get a bit red in the face. 'Thank you, Wimsy. That's a very nice thing to say. I'm glad you came along, and hope you'll be back.'

Wimsy's head nods so fast it's a wonder it doesn't fall off and roll into the corner. 'Yeah, yeah. I'll be back! Don't worry about that!'

'That's fantastic,' Lizzy replies. 'Well, I'd better go and sort out the money I've taken tonight. It was nice to see you both, and even nicer that you'll both be back again.'

Lizzy bids us farewell and goes to pick up her cash tin. Wimsy watches her go like a little puppy dog.

I have to suppress a smile.

Good for him.

The guy could do with someone new in his life. He deserves a break.

So could you! So do you!

I clench my fists as I try to quell the raging of the jealousy monster. I'm trying to be positive about this whole mindfulness experience, and I do not intend to let anything ruin it.

'Do you want to go get a drink, Wims?' I ask my friend as he continues to give Lizzy the old puppy-dog eyes.

'Okay,' he replies, not looking at me.

'Good. We can talk about when we're coming back here again.' I smile. 'I'm assuming it'll be quite soon.'

It is quite soon. The next week, in fact.

Wimsy and I attend two classes that week, and a further two the next.

By the time all four have passed, I'm feeling that mindfulness was the best thing I've done since the break-up with Samantha. I'm also watching a tentative romance blossom between two people who have been as hurt as I have. It's a wonderful thing to watch, while at the same time being extremely difficult to be around.

'My brain never shuts down completely,' Wimsy tells Lizzy as we stand at the back of the hall together. The rest of the group have long since left, but neither Wimsy nor Lizzy have appeared to notice. Actually, I'm starting to think of some excuse to get out of there myself, so I can leave the two of them alone. 'The mindfulness gets it about as close to being calm as it can be,' Wimsy finishes.

'It can be hard to really relax yourself, if you're used to being tense all the time,' Lizzy says. 'Mindfulness can go a long way to help, but there are other ways to get an even calmer brain, if you need it.'

'Oh, what like?' I can't tell if Wimsy is actually interested, or just faking it to impress Lizzy.

'Have you heard of sensory deprivation?'

'Er, no. No, I ain't heard of that one.'

Lizzy's eyes light up. 'It's quite something. You're cocooned in a tank, floating in really salty water so you can't sink. You can't hear or see anything. It gives you a chance to just let go of every stimulus, and sink deep into yourself. It's the most relaxing thing I've ever done. You should give it a try.'

'Yeah, yeah. Sounds great!' Wimsy agrees.

Wimsy would agree to having his toenails pulled out, if Lizzy suggested it, I think.

'We should give that a go, shouldn't we, Ollie?' he says to me, bringing me into a conversation I really shouldn't be part of.

'What?' I say, amazed that either of them has remembered my presence.

'The sensory deprivation thingy Lizzy's on about. We should have a go at it.'

'Umm. I guess so.' I don't sound convinced, because I'm not. Sinking deep into myself isn't something I'm sure I want to do. I might not like what I find.

Wimsy's face clouds when he sees my reluctance.

He then says the one thing that's guaranteed to get me to go along with it.

'You could write about it for "Dumped Actually"!'

Bloody hell. He's right. It would make for some solid material, wouldn't it?

'Oh. Yes. That's a good point, actually,' I agree.

'I can give you the leaflet for the place I've been to,' Lizzy adds. 'After you've visited it, we could meet up, and you could let me know how it went.'

This last bit is aimed squarely at Wimsy, of course. I don't think I'll be getting a bloody invite.

Stop it, jealousy monster! Back into your cave with you!

'Fantastic!' Wimsy says, delight in his eyes for the first time since I met him on top of that car park.

Lizzy trots off to retrieve the leaflet from her rucksack. Wimsy stands next to me vibrating with excitement, while I start to wonder what I'm letting myself in for.

Lizzy returns and hands me the leaflet.

'*Floaters,*' I read. '*Sensory deprivation for rest, relaxation and self-discovery.*'

'It really is quite marvellous,' Lizzy assures me.

I flip the leaflet over to find a picture of one of the tanks (or 'pods' as the leaflet describes them). It looks like something out of a science fiction movie. Not an exciting one, though, like *Aliens*. This is more like a prop from *2001: A Space Odyssey*, which I have tried and failed to watch three times, falling asleep before the end on every occasion.

The pod is white, enormous and has a flip-up door, allowing you to see into the cool blue water inside. It looks like Pac-Man after extreme weight gain, and a bath in strong bleach.

'And this is supposed to be good for your mind as well, is it?' I ask Lizzy, none too sure.

'Absolutely! If you've enjoyed what we've been doing here, you should *love* that. It's the next step. It should get you even further down the path of healing. It certainly did for me. The sense of self-discovery I gained inside that tank was mind-blowing.'

'Sounds bleedin' fabulous!' Wimsy replies, sealing my fate. I can't very well disappoint the poor bugger now, can I?

Nope. Sensory deprivation with my new friend it shall be. And fingers crossed it does what Lizzy says it will.

Fingers also crossed that the salty water doesn't pickle my skin too much. I have no love for eating gherkins, so I don't particularly want to look like one.

***

Floaters takes up the entire ground floor of a rather grand old Georgian house. There's a chiropractic clinic on the floor above it, with a holistic therapy business on the third and final floor above that. It's like a one-stop shop for physical and mental self-improvement.

. . . or, given the prices of some of the treatments on offer across all three floors, it's a gigantic Georgian-shaped money vacuum that'll leave you penniless in seconds, and not quite convinced any of it was actually worth it.

Now Lizzy isn't around to fire his curiosity and his loins, Wimsy isn't too sure about our impending visit to a sensory deprivation tank.

'I don't like baths,' he says, looking at a large poster of one of the pods as we wait at reception to be taken through.

'It's not a bath, Wims. Unless you pour a whole box of salt in with you every time you have one.'

'It looks like a bath. A bath with a *lid*.' He looks at me disapprovingly. 'Baths should *not* have lids, Ollie.'

'Well, I can't argue with you on that one.'

I have to confess to a certain amount of apprehension myself. I'm not someone who suffers from claustrophobia, but I can't say the idea of being enclosed in a dark space sounds all that relaxing, or life affirming, to me.

But Lizzy was absolutely right about mindfulness, so I guess I'll have to trust her on this as well.

A young man in a Floaters T-shirt appears at reception and asks us whether we have a booking or not. I tell him we have, and he proceeds to empty my wallet and eat all of my money, before moving on to my clothes and my car.

That's what it feels like, at least. This sensory deprivation doesn't come cheap. I'm not sure how much I'll enjoy being deprived of my senses, but I hope it's a lot more than being deprived of one hundred and eighty pounds to lie in salt for half an hour.

The reception guy tells us where we should go to get changed into our swimming trunks, and where we should meet him down the hallway, where the pods are kept.

I had to lend Wimsy a pair of my old swimming trunks, obviously. This is how these things work. The Chinese have a proverb that states if you save someone's life, you are responsible for that life. I certainly appear to be responsible for Wimsy's wardrobe.

We both jump into our respective swimmers (mine from M&S, his sadly from Primark) in cubicles in the changing rooms and meet Mr Floaters outside the room that houses the pods.

'All ready to go, then?' he asks us as we self-consciously approach him.

'Yes?' I say, hesitantly.

Wimsy mumbles something about baths and lids.

'Great! Then let's get you set up and going.'

Mr Floaters holds the door open, and we enter the room, to be presented with the opening scene from every slow-paced science fiction movie you've ever seen – when the crew of the ship awake from hypersleep.

The sensory pods are arranged in a circle around a central bit of decking. Two of the enormous white blobs have their mouth-like lids open invitingly – in much the same way that a shark does.

Mr Floaters explains that all we have to do is lie in the pod, in the temperature-controlled salty water, and he'll do the rest. The pod lids are shut automatically, and will re-open once our allocated time has passed. After we've dried ourselves off with the towels he's going to provide for us, we can then don fluffy dressing gowns and partake in the fresh chocolate or lemon sorbet that Floaters offers in its small, but ever so lovely, relaxation room.

I am a mere thirty minutes away from chocolate sorbet. Even if this floating in a dark tank thing doesn't do it for me, then surely something cold, sweet and chocolate-flavoured will.

Somebody really needs to invent chocolate that doesn't have any calories in it. They'd destroy the entire therapy business of the United Kingdom in one fell swoop.

Wimsy looks decidedly nervous about all of this, so I step forward and climb into my tank to show him that everything will (probably) be alright.

The water is neither hot nor cold, but quite tepid. I lie down in it, and it doesn't make *me* feel hot or cold, either. I'm assuming this is the point.

The level of buoyancy my body achieves is quite amazing, though. I had to give my weight along with Wimsy's when I made the booking, and now I can see why. They have to get the salt levels just right, so you can bob about with no fear of going under.

'See, Wims? It's fine,' I call over to him.

I can feel myself relaxing already. The feeling of floating around like this is quite lovely in and of itself.

Wims peers into my tank and gives me a look of suspicion, but then he does indeed climb into his own tank and lie down.

'I feel like I'm being pickled!' he cries over the lid of his pod.

'Please relax, sir,' Mr Floaters says. 'Enjoy the experience.'

Wimsy doesn't reply, but neither does he leap back out of the pod, so I'll assume he's still willing to go along with this. If there wasn't a promised date with Lizzy to discuss the experience, though, I'm not sure he would.

Mr Floaters leaves us, and a few moments later, the lid begins to close. This forces my heart rate to climb a little, as daylight disappears gradually, until it's just a thin line, before being extinguished completely as the lid closes with a deep thunk . . . and an ominous click. I also hear a hydraulic hiss that makes me feel even more nervous.

'Bloody hell,' I say out loud. My voice is flat, dull and without echo.

I strain my ears to hear something . . . anything. But there's nothing other than the gentle lapping of the water beneath me, and my own breathing.

Oh my. How strange.

'Oh my. How strange,' I say out loud, marvelling at how odd my voice sounds in this environment. We're used to the acoustics of our voices being an almost living thing – bouncing off other objects and reverberating around in the air. Having all the energy and three-dimensionality of your voice sucked away is quite, quite bizarre.

I elect to keep quiet, and just try to relax and enjoy this experience, like Mr Floaters suggested.

This starts with realising I have tinnitus.

Not much. Not enough to impact my life in any real way, but in this closed-off environment I can definitely hear a small amount of whining coming from both ears. Too much indie rock when I was a youngster, possibly.

I try to ignore this and concentrate on some nice, even deep breathing, the way I learned in Lizzy's mindfulness class.

This calms me considerably, and I do start to feel myself loosening up a little.

Five minutes later and I'm pretty much fully relaxed. The sensory deprivation has gone from alarming to quite soothing in a remarkably short space of time. There's something about the feel of the water against your skin, the sensation of floating comfort and the lack of any external stimulus that slows your brain to a satisfying near-halt.

I can actually feel myself starting to fall asleep.

. . . and that's when the hallucinations begin.

Look, I'm not sure if they actually *are* hallucinations, or just that I've dropped off, but trust me, none of what is about to transpire feels like a dream to me. Not at all. Something profoundly *different* from dreaming happens to me in this tank, and it's going to stay with me for many years to come.

At first, the hallucinations are auditory only. My brain, obviously starved of outside stimuli, has decided to make some of its own. This begins with the sound of cheerful birdsong, for some reason.

Then I realise that I'm recalling the pleasant evening I spent in the New Forest in the tent, before BambiWanks happened.

This birdsong lasts just a few seconds before being replaced by a sweet-sounding Latin guitar.

Now I appear to be flashing back to the music played in Manucode – and I am instantly transported to a vision of Vanity's lingerie.

Great. I do not need an erection right now. I already resemble some kind of adrift sailboat in this water, I don't need to add a bloody mast.

Then the guitar music recedes, and different music begins to play . . . the sound of a sitar, gently picking out a few exotic chords.

Then, in accompaniment to the sitar, the rest of the hallucinations begin. The first is a smell – a kind of faint waft of warm vegetation. This is what I always imagined India would smell like.

Ah . . . of course.

This was my dream.

This was what I wanted to do with Samantha once we were married – take a trip to India, listen to some sitar music and ride an eleph—

'Alright there? How you going?'

Right in front of my eyes, the head of an elephant has appeared. It has a huge trunk, enormous eyes, set wide on its wrinkly grey head, and gigantic flapping ears on either side.

'Jesus Christ,' I exclaim out loud.

The elephant recoils a little bit. 'Not quite, buddy. Be bloody weird if Jesus was an elephant, right?'

'I suppose so,' I reply, in the full and absolute knowledge that I have completely lost my mind.

'You haven't lost your mind,' the elephant reassures me. 'And you don't have to speak out loud, it bangs around in this tin can like a right bugger. Just think your words, that'll do ya.'

Okay, I say, in the vaults of my brain.

'Yeah, there you go. Much better!'

Who are you? I ask the elephant.

'I'm an elephant, mate,' the elephant replies.

Yes, I'm aware of that, but who exactly are you?

'Ah, gotcha. I'm you, mate. I'm your *mind*. The underneath bit. The bit you keep suppressed, so you can go about your business up on top, so to speak.'

My mind?

'Yep. I'm your subconscious – set free from its bonds by the deprivation of the senses, to wander in the vaults of your brain, unmolested and unfettered.' The elephant nods at this. 'Here, you're quite bloody lyrical when you want to be, aren't you? Good vocabulary, and no mistake.'

Right, okay. Thank you . . . I suppose.

'No worries.'

So, why are you an elephant?

'Ah, now that's the interesting part, mate. It would appear that you've decided to let your subconscious manifest itself as both an object of your dreams and a reminder of the love you've lost.' The elephant looks at me meaningfully. 'Probably says a lot about your state of mind that, mate.'

Probably. So you're my subconscious mind, manifested as the elephant I dreamed of riding with my ex-girlfriend?

'Yep.'

Well, that makes about as much sense as the rest of my life, I guess.

'Probably.'

Can I ask just one more question at this juncture, though? I feel it's an important one.

'Go right ahead, mate.'

Why are you talking in an Australian accent?

The elephant shrugs. This should be impossible, given that it's just a floating head, but it manages it all the same. 'Search me, mate. I'm just your subconscious given metaphorical flesh, I only know what you know.'

You should be talking in an Indian accent, surely?

'I guess so. But here I am, talking like I just stepped out of an episode of *Neighbours*, for some bloody reason.'

You are. I wonder why?

'Dunno, mate.' The elephant leans in a little. 'Maybe it's because you're a bloody idiot, and your grasp of how an Indian person should sound isn't very good. You're therefore trying to avoid descending into stereotype, by replacing that accent with one more familiar to you, from years of watching low-grade, imported soap operas.'

Sounds quite likely, I have to agree. *But calling me an idiot is a bit steep.*

'Is it? Because I appear to have huge flappy ears, mate . . . and the only elephants that have huge flappy ears are African ones. You're a good four thousand miles too far to the west – in terms of your visual representation of the largest member of the pachyderm family.'

Oh, right. Fair point. I pause in reflection for a second. *But would an idiot know what a pachyderm is? Or have a vocabulary large enough to use words like unfettered and manifested?*

The elephant ponders this salient point for a moment. 'Ah, you're right, mate. Fair go, fair go. Let's just agree your grasp on the accuracies of the Indian subcontinent and its varieties of fauna aren't great, and move on, shall we?'

Agreed . . . and what are we moving on to?

'Well, bloody hell, mate. We're in here for some *self-discovery*, ain't we? Let's discover some shit!'

Okay, elephant, what exactly should we be discovering?

'Troy.'

What?

'My name's Troy, mate.'

Wasn't that a horse, not an elephant?

Troy the elephant gives me a disparaging look. 'Don't try to be clever, sport. We haven't got all day.'

Sorry. But I have to ask again . . . What should we be discovering?

This earns me another meaningful look. 'Reasons, mate. Reasons.'

For what?

'For why you keep making the decisions you do! For why you keep making the same mistakes with your life! Answers to the questions that plague you, so to speak.'

But I don't know the answers, Troy! I spit in frustration. *That's the problem!*

'Ah . . . yeah, you do. Deep down you do, mate. It's just hard to engage with them. Difficult. That's why I'm here, to help you confront things that otherwise you probably wouldn't.'

Such as?

'Well, now . . . how about your pathological need for love?'

I do not have a pathological need for love!

'Oh yes, you bloody do! You've spent your entire life searching for *the one*, haven't you? Gretchen, Yukio, Lisa, Sam . . .'

And what's wrong with that??

'Well, mate. It's made you kind of . . . *desperate*, don't you think?'

Desperate?

'Yep. And desperate is just another word for *needy*, isn't it?'

Is it?

'Yeah! A man with your extensive vocabulary knows that! And that desperation is why you went so overboard with Sam, so early. Why you scared her away.' Troy looks upward thoughtfully. 'Come to think of it, you're not just needy with women, are you?'

What do you mean?

'Look at "Dumped Actually".'

What about it?

'Well . . . you get dumped by Samantha, and what do you do? You start writing a feature all about it!'

So what? Erica wanted me to do it!

'Ah, bollocks, mate. You didn't *have* to do it! You *wanted* to do it! And it wasn't just to help you get over Samantha!'

Why, then? Why am I writing it??

'Like I say, mate. *Love.* In this case, the love you get from other people. You couldn't get that from Samantha any more, so you substituted her with about a million other folk.'

Oh God.

'That's why you've been putting yourself through all of these ridiculous bloody pursuits, sport. To keep your readers happy. To keep them *loving you.* You can't find the love you want with a woman, so your readers will just have to do in the meantime.'

That's awful – and a little weird.

'Eh, could be worse, to be honest. None of us are fuckin' perfect.'

Do you have to swear like that?

'Yes, I do have to fuckin' swear! Because it feels *good!*' The elephant narrows its eyes. 'And that's another fuckin' thing, while we're on it. You never swear. Not fuckin' properly, anyways!'

Stop it!

'No! You fuckin' drongo! Why don't you swear more?'

Because it's rude!

'Bollocks! You don't fuckin' swear more, because you don't want to fuckin' offend people! You don't want their fuckin' disapproval!'

That's not true!

But it *is*, isn't it? The elephant knows it – so *I* know it . . . deep down, anyway.

'And that's the root of your problems, mate. That pathological need for love makes you a bit . . . *soft.* Skews your perspective, so to speak. You're constantly searching for the love of your life, and it's not doing you any good, is it? Look at what happened with Sam. And it didn't just ruin your relationship with her, either. It dribbles over into every aspect of your life.'

He's right. He's bloody well *right.*

Oh, for fuck's sake.

'There you go!' Troy the elephant shouts triumphantly. 'Now you're swearin'!'

Fuckity fuck.

Hmmm. Maybe the elephant is on to something. The swearing *does* feel good.

'Fucking fucking fuck!' I say out loud into the confines of the tank.

'Yeah! Go for it, mate! Swear it up a storm!' the elephant cries, rocking its head back and forth.

'YEAH! YEAH! FUCK!' I shout. Then I take a deep breath. 'FUCK YOU, YOU CUNTS!'

The elephant recoils. 'Bloody hell, mate. Steady on!'

What??

'That word's a bit much, ain't it? No need to go that far!'

Er . . . I'm sorry? I say, instantly flaming red with shame.

'Okay, no worries. Just watch it, though. Up to now, this book has been perfectly suitable for a nice, wide audience. Let's not risk the sales figures and review scores by going too far with the bad language.'

What? Book? Sales figures? Review scores? What the hell are you on about?

Troy the elephant contrives to look extremely guilty. 'Never mind, mate. Forget I said that. Trips into the subconscious can sometimes go a little bit *too far*. Once you've hit the metaphysical, it's best to slam on the brakes and backpedal like a bastard.'

I have no idea what you're talking about.

'No, me neither,' Troy says unconvincingly. 'Maybe we should have a little break and listen to the sitar music. Calm ourselves down a bit.'

And with that, the background sitar grows a little louder, and Troy the elephant starts to bob his head about in time to the melody.

This is all extremely weird.

'You can say that again,' Troy says, continuing to bop back and forth to what is rapidly beginning to sound like a very familiar piece of music – albeit one played a lot slower, and on a sitar.

I sigh.

That's the Super Mario *theme, isn't it?*

'Yeah, course it is. Makes perfect sense, given the context.'

I might just lie here quietly for a few moments.

'I would, if I were you . . . which I am, of course.'

While the sitar *Mario* theme is a tad annoying, I am able to zone it out of my thoughts, and consider the revelation that the elephant – or my own subconscious – has just provided me with.

I have a pathological need to be in love with someone, and because I want that above all else, I've become a bit of a pushover – with everyone, not just women.

'Now you're getting it, Bruce,' Troy says, blissing out to the sitar with his eyes closed.

So how do I stop being like that?

Troy ponders this for second. 'Dunno. I guess you have to know why, before you can know how.'

I roll my eyes. *Very philosophical.*

'Elephants are philosophical creatures,' he replies.

Not very helpful ones, though.

Troy shrugs. 'Possibly not. Let's just enjoy the sitar a bit more. It'll calm you down. Have a look at this lovely pot of geraniums as well. They're very soothing – and I'm sure they're entirely unconnected to what we've been talking about.'

A pot of bright-red geraniums pops into existence in front of my eyes. It looks exactly the same as the one I bought my parents for their garden.

I look at Troy suspiciously from over the geraniums. *Is there a reason you decided to show me these geraniums, Troy?*

'Why do you ask?' the elephant replies, contriving to look innocent.

I don't know. They just feel a little too . . . symbolic for my liking. As if you're trying to tell me something . . .

'Such as?' Troy says, giving the geraniums a long sniff with his even longer trunk.

Oh, I don't know. That maybe the geraniums are meant to represent my parents in some way . . . and that they might have something to do with this pathological need for love I seem to have?

'Search me, cobber. I'm just your subconscious, remember.'

Yes. An extremely unhelpful subconscious at that! Why can't you just give me some straight answers, instead of teasing me with symbolic geraniums?

'It's straight answers you want, is it, mate?' Troy says, eyes narrowing.

Yes!

'Like . . . everything laid out in front of you with no ambiguity or confusion?'

Yes!

'None of this beating around the bush nonsense?'

That's right!

Troy smiles. 'Ah well. You should have just said so.'

Aaaargh!

The elephant takes a deep breath, widens his eyes and starts to speak. 'You see, mate, your problem is that—'

Suddenly, light streams into the pod as the hatch is opened. I see Mr Floaters peering in at me. 'Time's up!' he says with a smile.

'No! No!' I roar, thrashing around in the water. 'Close it again! Put me back in!'

Mr Floaters looks a little shocked at my outburst. 'Sorry, sir. But your thirty minutes have elapsed.'

'What?!' I cry, incredulous. 'That was *never* thirty minutes!'

'Yes, it was, I'm afraid.'

I slap one hand on to the water, splashing it everywhere. 'But he was about to tell me about the geraniums!'

Mr Floaters now looks utterly confused. 'About the what?'

'The geraniums! The elephant was about to tell me what they mean!'

'Elephant?' Mr Floaters says, wisely beginning to back away from the pod a little as I sit up straight.

'Yes! Troy the Australian elephant! He was going to talk, damn you! He was going to tell me what's wrong with me!'

'Umm. Are you having an episode?' Mr Floaters asks.

'What?'

'Are you having an *episode*, sir? Only, I've not done the training for people having episodes, yet. That's next month.'

'Episodes? What, like on Netflix?'

'No. I mean . . . you know . . . *episodes.*'

Wimsy's head appears over his shoulder. 'He means, have you gone completely barking mad, Ollie?'

I stare up at my friend for a moment, trying to think of a decent response. 'I don't think so. Though, at this stage in proceedings, I can't be one hundred per cent sure, I'll be honest with you.'

Wimsy holds out a hand. 'That probably means you're alright, then. It's the ones who don't think they're at least a bit mad who you have to look out for.'

I take his hand and pull myself up to standing. I can't help but feel bitterly disappointed to have my session in the tank interrupted at such a crucial juncture.

'What was all that about elephants and geraniums?' Wimsy asks as Mr Floaters goes to get me a towel.

'Oh . . . I don't know.' I give him a speculative look. 'Did you . . . Did you *see* anything while you were in there?'

Wimsy shakes his head slowly. 'Nope. Just a whole lot of silence, and a wee bit of snoring, I have to confess. Quite relaxing, though.' He returns the speculative look. 'Why? Did you?'

I rub a hand over my face. 'I don't know, mate. Maybe? I could have been asleep as well, I suppose.' I heave a sigh. 'It all felt so real. And I was close to something. I'm sure I was . . .'

Wimsy gives me a sympathetic look.

I must seem quite pathetic, stood there in my swimming trunks, covered in salt, and looking like I've just had something very valuable stolen away from me.

He pats me on the shoulder. 'Cheer up, Ollie. You were probably just close to farting. I did that quite a lot in there too.'

I let out a chuckle and climb out of the pod. 'So you enjoyed it, then?' I ask him as I take the towel from Mr Floaters.

Wimsy grins. It's the happiest I think I've ever seen him. 'Yeah. It was fabulous. I kept thinking about Lizzy. And I didn't think about Penny, Mr Sparkles or the long one in Phuket *once*.' He says this like it's some kind of miracle.

'Good for you,' I tell him.

Wimsy suddenly looks very shy. 'I think . . . I think I'm going to ask her out. Lizzy, I mean.'

'Okay,' I say, smiling.

'Yeah. That's what I'm going to do. Definitely. I made my mind up while I was in that tank.' He thinks for a moment. 'It was peaceful, you know? It let me . . . let me see things for the way they could be, instead of worrying about the way things were . . . if that makes any sense.'

'Yeah, I think it does,' I tell him, with a wry grin.

Well, there you have it.

The flotation tank may have done nothing for me, other than show me how little I know about elephant taxonomy and the symbolic nature of geraniums, but at least Wimsy has come out of the experience well.

I'm no closer to a better understanding of how my mind works – thanks to Mr Floaters and his innate sense of bad timing – but it looks like Wimsy has taken a big step forward, and that makes the experience worth it for me as well, I guess.

I just wish . . . I just wish I could look *forward*, the way Wimsy spoke about.

I want to think about the way things could be, instead of worrying about the way they were, as well. But I just feel completely unable to do that – because I have this unanswered question hanging over me, about why I have such a pathological need to find love and be in a relationship.

It's so incredibly *frustrating*.

There's nothing else for it. I'm just going to have to go and eat my own bodyweight in chocolate sorbet. And God help Mr Floaters if he gets between me and that spoon. He's already ruined one sweet revelation for me today, I'll be damned if he's going to ruin another!

And who knows . . . perhaps I'll fall into a diabetic coma, and Troy can come back to finish his bloody sentence.

INTERLUDE

From: Carla Moreau (CarlaMoreau19@outlook.
com)

Dear Ollie,

Thanks very much. I'm sat here with my make-up
running down my face.

That last meeting with you and Sam was heart-
breaking – and wonderful at the same time.

I've been enjoying 'Dumped Actually' so much. It's
made me laugh and laugh. I wasn't also expecting
it to make me cry, though!

I wish I could give you the answers you're looking
for, but my divorce from my husband didn't happen because one of us was needy. It happened
because one of us didn't need the other one
enough.

And now I feel like crying again, so I think I'll move on!

The only thing that really helped me when I got divorced was that I had lots of friends and family to lean on for support. If you can do that as well, you should. My mum was a rock for me. Without her I would probably have fallen apart completely.

So my advice to you would be, if you have loved ones in your life that you can go and be with – do it! Friends, family, it doesn't matter. As long as you have some moral support from the people you are closest to, you can get through this, Ollie, I promise you.

The very best of luck, and I look forward to reading about what you get up to next!

Very best of wishes and love,
Carla

***

From: Skeez (SkeezyFlipper360@bohemia.co.uk)

Yo Olsberth! How r u doin??

I was like you once, dude – all miz and no smiles, until I changed my life by seeing how RADICAL the world is!

I got off my ass & lived more, loved more & risked more. It was the most amazing thing I've ever done.

I felt like the walking dead when Shelly upped and left me for that dweebus Nolan, but I just woke up one day & knew I had to get high to feel better!

You ever done a parachute jump? You should, dude! It opens your mind, man. It opens everything inside you. Shows you how your world could be.

I had an ephipanany on my way down that first time. Like, saw the future without Shelly, and saw that it might not be that bad, if I just lived life on the edge.

And I never looked back since, cuz. I been jumping and riding and singing and diving ever since, and never, ever felt better in my whole life!

Serious to the max – give it a go. Throw yourself into your new life, by throwing yourself out of the plane!

Bestest and fastest,
Skeez

***

From: Laurel Pearce (Pearce.Laurel@hotmail.com)

Ollie,

What do we do with you, eh?

In the past few months, I think I've felt more sympathy for a man I've never met than anyone who I actually know!

I've also never been as *frustrated* with someone, either.

I want to give you a hug, and a big smack at the same time.

In each chapter of 'Dumped Actually', I've willed you on to a better understanding of who you are, and have inwardly cheered when it looks like you've made a breakthrough.

But then, things seem to either backslide, or just come to a grinding halt, and I want to pull my hair out on your behalf!

I never intended to get in touch like this, because I know you've had so many people email you. One more voice probably wouldn't do any good! But eventually, I just had to say something to you. I'm slightly afraid that you'll just keep trying all of these weird, outlandish and possibly soul-destroying antics, until I end up reading your obituary.

So – to hopefully help put a stop to all of that, I'm going to tell you the real secret to getting over a lost love. It's the one you don't want to hear, and the one that most people will steer clear of saying, but in my experience it's always been the only one that's ever worked.

And it's quite simply this: find someone else to love.

It's the easiest and hardest thing to do, isn't it? But that doesn't make it any less true.

And the sad thing is it might take *years*. Everyone wants a quick fix to the problems in their life, but there's just no such thing when you're mending a broken heart. It takes time, patience and the love of another person to truly get you back to where you want to be.

The pay-off is that the love you find after the love you've lost is usually the best you'll ever have – because you can't really know the joy of love until you've properly felt its pain first. Not in my experience, anyway. And I doubt you'll find many who will disagree.

So, that's my advice, I'm afraid. It's probably not what you want to hear, but there it is.

No matter how long it takes, the only way to get over a broken heart is with patience, and the knowledge that there is someone else out there for you who's even better than the one who's just gone. When you find her, you'll feel a whole lot better.

Love and best wishes, Laurel xx

CHAPTER TEN

Vows

I have become obsessed with geraniums.

And not in a healthy way.

I have never before shared my parents' joint love of gardening, so have until this point in my life never given plants – potted or otherwise – any attention whatsoever.

But now I have become obsessed with geraniums.

Or at least what geraniums might represent.

My subconscious certainly isn't letting on. And I have no intention of ever going anywhere near a sensory deprivation tank again to make it talk.

I've always had a . . . let's call it a *healthy internal dialogue* with myself, but I wasn't aware just how loud that dialogue is until the experience I had a fortnight ago at Floaters.

My subconscious is clearly trying to tell me something. About geraniums. And about my parents.

I feel like the answer is on the tip of my tongue but, as yet, I've not been able to get it off the tip and into the outside world. I remain confused, and unsure of how to proceed.

I've closed the door on my relationship with Sam, but the door on Ollie remains firmly wide open, and flapping about in the wind. I need answers. I need guidance. I need to speak to the people who know me best.

Just as well, then, that I will be seeing my parents today for their fortieth wedding anniversary vow renewal, to be held in that garden I ran around in so happily during my childhood. While I am there, I hope to get a chance to pin them down for a conversation that might give me some answers.

Like Carla Moreau says, connecting with your loved ones is a great way to get over heartbreak, and I really should take the time to speak to my mother and father about it all properly. Face to face.

They've never been all that great about giving me advice after a break-up, but maybe they could shed some light over what my stupid subconscious was trying to tell me. If nothing else, I'll get a crash course in the proper care of geraniums.

My parents are both intelligent, well-respected people, who have done very well in their lives, so they must be able to offer me some kind of advice about how to better understand myself. After all, they know me better than anyone else. They should have insights into the way my mind works that nobody else can provide.

And also, there will be cake.

Everybody enjoys cake.

Even if I can't unlock the secret of the geraniums (which sounds like the dullest idea for an Indiana Jones movie ever conceived) then at least I'll go home full of chocolate sponge.

With this positive frame of mind, I drive up to Mum and Dad's place – to watch them reaffirm their love for one another after forty years of blissful marriage.

The house my parents live in, and the one I grew up in, is *enormous*. One of those 'Arts and Crafts' jobs that were so popular at the start of the twentieth century. They got it for a song back in the early 80s and have never looked back since. It's probably worth a bloody fortune now. It should be, given that it has views over the Solent and a garden you could lose a squadron of Royal Marines in.

I almost feel like an interloper – coming here in my bargain-basement Asda suit. I'm probably far too common to be seen in this area. It's a wonder an alarm didn't go off the minute I drove on to Mum and Dad's street in my 59-plate Fiesta.

Mind you, it's not like they're posh themselves. Both were born to working-class families at a time when that could actively damage your prospects in life. They met at a bus stop. Dad was off to his job as a bookkeeper's apprentice, and Mum was going to hers at the post office. Both of them were eighteen years old, and both of them maintain it was love at first sight. It took Dad three attempts to ask Mum out as they waited for the same bus, but when he did she said yes immediately, and they have never been apart since.

Married at nineteen and living in the lovely house I'm currently driving up to shortly thereafter (thanks to a little help from my maternal grandfather – who knew what stocks and shares were before anybody else in his street), they lived a blessed life. In fact, the only real shadow cast over their marriage was the difficulty they had falling pregnant. But even that issue was solved in 1986 when Mum got knocked up with yours truly.

Mum and Dad have had a wonderful life together, so it's no wonder they want to mark the occasion of their marriage with this ceremony today.

It's not going to be overblown. Mum and Dad don't do overblown. If you're looking for people who enjoy a lavish and gaudy lifestyle, you've come to the wrong place.

You can see that's the case when I pull my Fiesta up next to Dad's thirty-year-old BMW – which he has lovingly cared for all these years. It looks brand new compared to my bloody car.

And when we get inside, you'll see that the house's interior hasn't been changed in years either, but still looks like it was put together yesterday.

When Mum answers the door, she looks equally like she was put together yesterday. I've obviously caught her in a very happy and upbeat mood. Which is no surprise, given what I'm here for today.

'Hello, sweetheart!' she says, giving me a huge hug.

'Careful, Mum! You'll wrinkle your dress,' I reply, as she squeezes the life out of me. I haven't seen her for a few weeks, but you'd think it was a few years, given the strength of the hug.

'Oh nonsense. It'll be perfectly fine. It has been every other time I've worn it.' She pats the front of the cream dress almost affectionately. It doesn't appear to have suffered any creasing. My suit might be a different matter, though.

'Leonard! Your son and heir has arrived!' Mum calls back through the house's expansive hallway.

With a cheesy grin on his face, my father appears from the kitchen, also bedecked in a suit. This is the same suit he's had for twenty years – and it looks as pristine as the car does.

'Oliver! About time you got here, my boy. Everything's just about ready, and I really want to get going before the vicar keels over.'

'Leonard! Don't say such a thing!' Mum says in mock horror.

'Daphne, the man is three hundred and seventeen years old. I have no doubt he feels as close to Jesus as he says he does, because he knew him personally.'

'Leonard!' Mum shrieks. 'That's awful!'

Dad wraps his arms around her. 'I know. But you love me anyway, don't you?' He leans in and starts to kiss her theatrically on the neck.

This is my father ninety-seven per cent of the time. A man unafraid to tell a bad joke – and openly show his love for his wife.

Mum giggles and pushes him away. 'Stop it! We have to get on!'

Dad rolls his eyes. 'That's what I've been trying to tell you. Vicar Simpkins has one foot in the grave. I'd like to get these vows renewed before he plants the other one in there too.' Dad grabs me by one arm. 'Come on, son! We have to hurry before this vow renewal turns into a funeral!'

I allow my father to drag me along the hallway, through the kitchen and out into the largest garden I've ever been in.

It's the reason my parents bought this house in the first place. They fell in love with it almost as quickly as they fell in love with each other. Encircling the house, the garden is getting on for an acre in size, and is landscaped to within an inch of its life. A large circular grass lawn is ringed by exquisitely maintained flowerbeds, containing rose bushes, lavender, chrysanthemums, the legendary geraniums – and a whole heap of other plants I don't know the name of. They're very colourful and pretty in the sun, though, that's one thing I'm sure about.

At the rear of the garden, they've allowed Mother Nature to have free rein, and there are some gorgeous wildflowers back there, nestling among the trees, through which you can see the sea beyond. I built many a fort and treehouse down there. There's still some evidence of their existence if you look hard enough, and don't mind poking around the undergrowth for old planks of wood and a few rusty nails.

Today, a gazebo has been set up at the back of the lawn. In front of this are several rows of chairs, each one of them occupied by Mum and Dad's friends. I also see my Aunt Jean and Uncle Harry – who I will probably have to speak to at some point, whether I like it or not. Jean is Mum's sister, and has been jealous of her for sixty years. Any conversation I have with them usually consists of her telling me how much they enjoy spending all the money they have. I could tell them that this wouldn't make Mum or Dad jealous in the slightest, given that they've never cared one jot about being rich. Jean's never realised that she's jealous of Mum just because Mum is *happy*. I fear if she did, it might kill her.

My own anxieties are confirmed when I see that I am indeed the only person here without a partner. I will have to sit next to an empty seat throughout the ceremony.

Speaking of which, I'd better get my arse parked on that seat, because that vicar really does look like he's about to die and fall over into the begonias.

I sit down in the chair in the back row as Mum and Dad step under the gazebo together. I try very hard to concentrate on them, and not the empty chair beside me.

The vicar, who has a very strong and clear voice for such a frail man, opens proceedings with a little speech. It's the usual 'we are gathered here today' gumph that we've all seen and heard a thousand times. Even Mum and Dad look a little impatient. Neither of them are religious, but they are of a generation who value the customs of the land – even if those customs go on a little too long and sound quite dry.

Eventually, the vicar reaches the end of his spiel, and we get to the important bit.

Mum and Dad told me they were creating their own vows for today, and you're about to get a good insight into how I have the skills to be a writer.

It's Mum who starts. And I want you to bear in mind that *none of this is written down anywhere.*

'Leonard . . . I cannot imagine a life without you. These forty years have been everything I hoped they'd be when I first said my vows at our wedding. You are kind. You are gracious. You are constant.' A few of the ladies in front of me are already reaching for their tissues. 'You are my rock. My guiding star. My life is only filled with light because you shine next to me.' Jesus. I'm starting to fill up now. 'I have been by your side for forty years, and I will be there for all the years to come, and beyond. I love you, my Leonard. I love you with all of my heart.'

I wipe the tears away with my hand and begin to wish I'd brought a handkerchief with me.

Now it's Dad's turn – and, if anything, he's even more eloquent than Mum.

'Dear Daphne. I tried to come up with the right words to tell you how much I love you. But they would not come. Because there are no words to express how I feel about you. Not even God himself could utter them, because my love for you goes beyond even Him.' Where Mum goes for the simple sentiment, Dad goes more for the theatrical. 'Without you I would be an ocean without land, a voice without a soul, a plant without soil.' Oh. That's very nice. Getting a mention of gardening in. That'll please Mum.

Sure enough, I can see her starting to cry now too.

'I would renew my vow of love to you every day like this, if I could,' Dad continues. 'But I would struggle to find the words every day. So instead, I will show you how much I love you by my actions, by doing everything I can to make you feel safe, loved and happy in the rest of our lives together.'

Oh Christ.

He said all that from his heart. Not a cue card in sight.

For a moment, I feel my breath being taken away. The scale of it all makes me light-headed. How much love can there be between these two people, that they can speak like that so easily, so openly, so from the heart?

What must it be like to be that in love? To be that perfect for one other? To have found the right person to share your entire life with?

It's something I want so, so much for myself . . . but the harder I try to find it, the more elusive it becomes.

Through tears that are just as much about my own misery as they are about my parents' happiness, I glance over at the geranium I bought that day in the garden centre, after my confrontation with Sam. It really is very bushy.

And while I'm staring at it, something clicks in my head.

Something *fundamental.*

Something unbearably *true.*

This is what I want. *This* is what I'm chasing. This is what I've been desperate for all of my life. The kind of effortless and towering love that my parents have for each other.

I pushed so hard at my relationship with Sam because I was trying to recreate what I see in front of me right now. The perfect romance.

My parents have given me nothing but love, care and affection my entire life – but they've also provided me with an example of what love can be, that I can never hope to match. No matter how hard I try.

I am pathologically addicted to finding the love of my life, because that's what my mother and father did all those years ago.

And it's *ruining me.*

My hands start to shake, and I can feel my breath coming in short, sharp gasps. The rest of the ceremony is blocked out as I sit there, looking at my parents, but seeing absolutely nothing.

This is the revelation that Troy the imaginary elephant was trying to force upon me. This is what the bloody geraniums were all about.

And I didn't need to even speak to my mother and father to realise it. I just had to hear them speak to each other – in words of love that were as wonderful as they were awful. Wonderful because that's the way they feel about each other, and awful because they are words *I* may never get to say or hear.

I just about manage to compose myself through the rest of proceedings. It's not like I'm the only one blubbing, anyway. Just about everyone has been reduced to tears by the vows my parents have just exchanged. I'm probably the only one whose tears are as much about their own pain as they are about happiness for Mum and Dad's love for one another, though.

I give Mum and Dad the biggest hug imaginable when the ceremony is over, and the vicar has gratefully gone to sit down in the shade. Of course, I don't tell them about the disturbing revelation I've just had about myself, and them. That'd just ruin their special day completely.

I don't need to force them into a potentially uncomfortable conversation any more. It appears the conversation I had with myself in that bloody tank was all I really needed. Sitting next to the geraniums, watching my parents, was the final extra push required to get me to face up to the truth.

When they suggest I spend the night in my old room, I immediately agree.

I feel comprehensively drained of all energy by the time Mum and Dad are saying goodbye to the rest of the guests, and can think of nothing more pleasant than spending the night in the room I spent my childhood in. It was always a comfy bed back then, and I'm sure it's just as comfy now.

'Are you okay, sweetheart?' Mum says to me as the three of us sit in front of the TV later that evening. I'm supposed to be watching *Escape to the Country* with them both, but am in fact just staring ahead into space, still mulling over the epiphany I had earlier.

'What?' I reply, startled out of my reverie. 'Oh. Yes. I'm fine, Mum. Just a little tired.'

'Are you sure? You look like you have something on your mind.'

I open my mouth. Then close it again.

For the briefest of moments, I feel like telling them both everything. But I stop myself, because I don't want to ruin what has been a very pleasant day for them.

Besides what exactly would I say?

I feel miserable as sin, because you have the perfect marriage, and I've ruined my own relationships trying to emulate it?

I think that there must be something wrong with me, because I can't achieve what you two have had all of your lives, with no effort?

Oh yes. That'd go down really well, wouldn't it?

'I'm just tired, Mum,' I eventually say. 'I think I might go up to bed.'

'Okay, sweetheart,' she replies, her brow creased with concern.

I stand up and walk over to the door. 'It really was a wonderful ceremony,' I tell them.

'And the vicar didn't die even once!' Dad says with a snort.

'Leonard!' Mum exclaims in mild shock.

I smile at them both and take my leave, trudging up the stairs with a heavy heart.

Lying in my childhood bed (which is indeed still comfortable, if a little small for me, now I'm in my thirties), I stare up at the ceiling for what feels like hours, turning everything over in my head.

And the central questions I keep coming back to are . . . Why can't I have what my parents have? Why do I keep getting dumped? What's wrong with me?

Eventually, I fall into a fitful sleep. In it, I dream of golf balls and geraniums. Of Wendy houses and baby deer. Of rollercoasters and car parks.

But most of all, I dream of Sam, riding an elephant off into the distance . . . without me.

I am woken the next morning by the sounds of banging.

And raised voices.

I've woken up in this house to the first sound many times. Dad likes to attempt DIY every now and again, when enough time has passed for him to forget that he's not very good at it. He may have green fingers, but he definitely doesn't have an eye for a spirit level or hammer.

I have never woken up to the second noise, though.

Raised voices downstairs can mean only one thing – something dreadful has happened. Mum and Dad are two of the most placid and laid-back people on earth, so there must be some kind of emergency!

I leap out of bed and throw my clothes on in what feels like a split second. I then hurry out of my bedroom, across the landing and down the broad flight of stairs.

'Mum! Dad!' I holler, fear and panic in my voice. Something awful must be happening!

I storm towards the kitchen, fearing that I'm about to see some sort of hideous accident. Maybe Mum has put her hand in the blender, or maybe Dad has somehow managed to impale himself on a bread knife.

A whole series of dreadful images shuttle across my brain as I rush down the hallway. I can still hear Mum and Dad's raised voices, but I'm not paying much attention to what they're actually saying, such is the sense of impending dread that has overcome me.

'Mum! Dad! Are you okay?' I wail as I speed through the kitchen door, expecting to see blood everywhere.

However, instead of finding my parents locked in a death struggle with a pair of maniacal burglars, I find them stood in front of the hob, with a boiled egg between them. I can tell the egg is boiled, because there's a pot of bubbling water on the front hob, and steam rising from the egg itself.

It isn't even a gigantic boiled egg, imbued with murderous sentience, and about to kill the two most important people in my life. It's just a regular old boiled egg, sat on the spoon that Dad is holding in front of him.

Mum has her hands placed firmly on her hips and a look of fury on her face. Dad also looks like he's about to bust a blood vessel.

What the hell is going on here?

What could that boiled egg have possibly done to incur such wrath from my parents?

I mean, boiled eggs are possibly the most harmless thing on the planet. They're even more harmless than an unboiled egg, which at least has the potential to give you food poisoning if not cooked properly. A boiled egg, on the other hand, has had any danger comprehensively removed by the boiling process. Its only capacity to cause any real harm has been taken away from it. About the only way you could now make the boiled egg dangerous is to throw it, but unless it's a *hard*-boiled egg, then it couldn't do much damage anyway, could it? And my father likes a soft-boiled egg, so we can safely rule out its effectiveness as a ballistic weapon.

No.

I have no idea why I've developed this sudden obsession with the lethality or otherwise of your average boiled egg, either.

Maybe it's got something to do with the fact that both of my parents look extremely angry – and I'm having trouble processing it, as I've never seen it before.

'Good morning, Oliver,' Mum says, still looking angry as all hell and back.

'Hello, son,' Dad intones, the boiled egg quivering on the spoon a little.

Why do they both look so *mad*?

'What's the matter?' I ask them. 'Has the boiled egg done something?'

'What?' Mum and Dad say in perfect unison.

I point at the boiled egg. 'The boiled egg. Has it done something to make you both angry?'

This is how alien it is to see my parents looking angry around one another. I am perfectly willing to accept that a non-sentient, softly boiled egg is the cause of their anger, rather than anything else. The concept of them being angry at each other is completely impossible. It just doesn't happen.

No. It *must be* the boiled egg.

Mum and Dad seem to forget their towering rage for a moment and both stare down at the boiled egg as if it's about to leap at one of their throats. They then both turn back and look at me, mirroring the same expression of confusion as they do so.

'It's a boiled egg, son,' Dad says. 'It can't make anybody angry.'

'It could if you threw it at them,' I reply, knowing full well that I've now dragged my father into my boiled egg obsession.

'Are you feeling alright, Oliver?' Mum asks.

'Um. . . no. I heard you both shouting. I thought something was really wrong.'

Mum then glares at Dad. 'Something *is* really wrong, son! And I'm sorry we woke you up because of it!'

'Is it the boiled egg?' I ask.

What the hell is wrong with me? I need to get off the boiled egg talk and fast, before my nearest and dearest have me committed.

'It's got nothing to do with my ruddy boiled egg, son!' Dad snaps, and drops the offending article on to the counter top, where it breaks, allowing the soft yolk to run out.

You see? No ballistic integrity at all. The egg would just break open, and all you'd do is cover your assailant in runny egg yo—

'Your father is being intolerable again, Oliver!'

Dad gasps. '*I'm* being intolerable??'

Mum wags a finger at him. 'Yes, Leonard! Completely intolerable!'

'I . . . I . . . Er . . .' I stammer.

What the hell is this?

What in God's name is going on?

Mum and Dad don't argue! Mum and Dad *never* argue!

Dad thumps his hand down on the counter. 'Oh, for God's sake Daphne. We needed a new pergola, and that one was fifty per cent off. You *know* we need a new one!'

'Yes, Leonard, but I thought we'd agreed to wait until we'd picked out the right clematis, so we'd know what colour pergola to get!'

'I know that. But this was a bargain. We can choose the clematis to go around the pergola instead!'

'But I don't want to do it that way, you insufferable man!'

'And I don't want to waste money on a more expensive pergola, when this one will do the job very well, for half the price!'

'Oh bloody hell, Leonard! We could have afforded the full-price one without a problem!'

'Yes, but why spend more than you need to?'

'You'll just have to paint it, to match whatever clematis I choose.'

'Oh right! It's whatever clematis *you choose*, now, is it?'

'Yes, Leonard! You choose the pergola without consulting me! So I get to choose the clematis without consulting y—'

'STOP!'

Mum and Dad both cry out in shock and immediately look at me.

'PLEASE STOP!' I shriek, tears coursing down my cheeks.

This isn't Mum and Dad.

This isn't what Mum and Dad *do*.

They don't argue. They don't fight. They don't talk to each other like this.

What is happening? Why are they *doing* this?

Why can't I stop bloody crying???

'Oliver! Oh, Oliver!' Mum says, all the anger gone from her voice. She rushes over to me and gives me a hug. 'What's wrong, son? Tell me.'

Dad also comes over, the look of anger on his face replaced with worry. 'Whatever is the matter, my boy?'

I point at them both as Mum stands back a bit. 'You two. Arguing like that. Talking to each other like that. What's wrong? You were so happy yesterday! What the hell is wrong?'

Mum and Dad look to one another briefly in confusion, before returning their gazes to me.

'Why . . . nothing's wrong, Oliver,' Mum says softly. 'Your Dad and I were just having a disagreement about the pergola.'

'That's right,' Dad interjects. 'Nothing to worry about.'

'But . . . But I've never heard you speak to one another like that,' I insist. 'There must be something wrong with you. You've *never* spoken to one another like that!' I wipe my eyes. 'Are you . . . Are you getting a *divorce*? Was yesterday just a sham to keep everyone thinking your marriage was okay?'

'Oh my God!' Mum exclaims in horror.

'Of course not, Oliver!' Dad blurts out. 'Why would you think such a thing?'

'Because you were *arguing*.' I say this like it's the most bizarre and dreadful thing in the world – which I guess it is, from my perspective.

'So?'

'You and Mum *never* argue. You . . . You have the perfect marriage, Dad.' I look at him, misery writ large across my face. 'You have the thing I can never have.'

Mum looks aghast, before quickly staring at her husband, who appears equally shocked.

'I think we should sit down and have a chat,' Mum suggests, pulling out one of the kitchen chairs beside us. 'Why don't you sit on this, Oliver? I'll make us all a nice cup of tea, and you can talk to us.'

Mum looks quite distressed. And no wonder. This is the first time I've expressed my feelings quite so openly with them. It must be something of a shock.

While Mum busies herself making the tea, Dad offers me a wad of kitchen roll. 'Here you go, son. There's no need to cry. I'm sure we can get to the bottom of whatever it is that's getting you down.'

I look up at him. 'I don't know, Dad. I'm really not in a good place . . .'

We sit in silence for a few minutes while Mum pours the tea, Dad's hand gently resting on my arm. I dab away the tears from my eyes and blow my nose.

I am such a bloody mess.

'Now,' Mum says, plonking the tea in front of me and sitting herself down in one of the other chairs, 'why don't you tell us what's going through your mind, son?'

I take a deep breath, and start to talk.

It barely takes me five minutes to tell them what the problem is.

That's the way with the 'big stuff'. It's rarely that complicated or hard to describe, once you allow yourself to do it. It often goes that when we're finally ready to be honest about how we feel, it never takes that long to get it off our chests. We think the big things are complicated and difficult to explain, because we're afraid of them. Afraid of facing, and expressing, the unvarnished truth. Anything that scary must be hard to explain, right?

But within those five minutes, I neatly manage to outline everything that's going through my head, from the shock of seeing Mum and Dad argue, to the knowledge that I've spent my life chasing the kind of relationship they have with each other. A relationship that's been undermined completely by the argument I've just seen them have. Hence all the tears.

'You . . . You think we *never argue*?' Dad asks me, a little stunned.

'Yes.' I nod my head. 'You've never argued. I've never seen you raise your voices to each other once. That's why it was such a shock to see you doing it now.'

'Oh, Oliver. Your father and I snap at each other all the time,' Mum says.

Dad nods. 'Oh yes. We've had some right barnstormers.'

'But I've never seen you . . . never heard you . . .'

'Of *course* you haven't, sweetheart,' Mum tells me, hand squeezing mine. 'We've always tried to keep it away from you. You're our son, and we love you. We don't want you to see us *arguing*.'

I blink three times in quick succession, staring at her. 'You argue *all of the time?*'

I am utterly incredulous.

'Of course we do!' Dad exclaims. 'Every couple does, Oliver. It's just the way of things.'

I shake my head again, adamant. 'No. You're not like other couples. You're . . . You're *perfect.*'

Dad actually lets out a loud bray of laughter, while Mum puts a hand over her mouth.

'There's no such thing as perfect, my boy!' Dad says. 'And just as well. Perfect sounds bloody boring to me!'

'Leonard,' Mum chides, before leaning forward in her chair towards me. 'Is that what you've always believed, Ollie? That me and your dad have some sort of perfect marriage . . . with no problems?'

'Yes! Absolutely! And I realised yesterday that I keep screwing things up with the women in my life because I've been trying to emulate you. Trying to emulate your relationship. Because . . . Because it's *perfect.*'

Mum puts her hand over mine. 'Sweetheart, *nothing* is perfect. No relationship is perfect. There's just no such thing.'

No such thing.

No. Such. Thing.

Oh God.

The universe makes another one of those fundamental shifts as I let this sink in. It's going to have to stop making them soon, otherwise I'm going to fall off the bastard.

I've been chasing an impossibility.

I've been hankering after a falsehood.

I've been wasting my time on a thing *that can never be.*

I heave the longest, loudest and deepest sigh I have ever let out of my body, and slump in the chair. It feels like someone has let the air out of me.

Some vast and invisible weight is being lifted from my shoulders as I sit there staring at my mother's concerned face.

Everything slots into place in my mind – for the first time in my life.

I have idealised the notion of romance, because I idealised the way I saw my parents.

I have lived with this dream of the perfect relationship that was so strong, it forced me into making terrible decisions . . . and into losing the girl of my dreams.

I have been nothing short of a bloody fool.

'Oh dear. We're so sorry, son,' Dad says, looking pretty damn miserable himself now. 'We always tried to protect you from any problems we might have had . . . but maybe we went a little too far with it.'

Mum nods in agreement.

Both of them look guilty.

That's *horrifying*.

'No! No!' I say, sitting up straight again. 'You mustn't blame yourselves at all! You gave me everything I needed when I was a child. You loved me, cared for me, and always did the right thing by me. None of this is your fault. It's all down to me. Because . . . Because I didn't want to see. You understand? Because . . . I didn't . . . I didn't want to *grow up*.'

Oh boy.

There it is.

There's the answer.

I have lived my entire adult life with a *child's* idea of what romance is, and what it should be. I have walked around with this idealistic vision in my head – born of what I thought my parents' relationship was.

Watching all of those bloody romantic comedies probably didn't help, either. They would have just reinforced the fantasy I had in my head. Maybe I should have watched more action movies, after all.

I have simply not allowed myself to grow up. To accept that no relationship is perfect. That they all have their own problems.

And it took an obviously inconsequential argument about a pergola to realise that.

I say all of this to my parents.

They sit in silence digesting everything, before Dad lets out an explosive breath. 'Blimey. I never realised that's how you felt.'

'Nor did I,' Mum agrees. 'We made things very difficult for you.'

I shake my head again. 'No, Mum. I made things very difficult for *myself*.' I square my shoulders a little. 'And that's the truth. I've been acting like a child for too long when it comes to the women in my life. When it comes to my relationships. And that needs to change. If I'm ever going to find the right woman, I have to grow up. I have to see being in love for what it really is.'

'And what is that?' Mum asks, curiosity in her voice now.

I think for a moment. 'Imperfect. Frustrating. Difficult.' Sam's face flashes through my mind, followed by Gretchen's, Yukio's and Lisa's. 'And *wonderful*,' I say with an exhausted smile.

Mum also smiles, and once again squeezes my hand. 'I'm very proud of you, son,' she says softly.

I feel my dad's hand on my shoulder. 'Me too, my boy.'

We sit there for a moment together in warm communion, before Dad eventually breaks the silence. 'Just . . . Just try not to get a boner in front of any more baby deer, there's a good boy.'

'Leonard!' Mum roars in shock.

We carried on talking, the three of us, for hours that day.

Not as two parents and a child, but as three adults. Probably for the first time.

And that is what was important – that I began to see my parents for who they actually are. Two flawed, but wonderful human beings, who have had their ups and downs in life, just like everybody else. By doing that I can accept that their relationship is not perfect, that it's not the dream marriage I thought it was. That should give me more realistic expectations of what I can achieve. Which can only be a good thing.

And as we talked, I started to feel better. *Much* better, in fact.

I never realised how much pressure I had been putting on myself to achieve this impossible dream of the perfect relationship. Understanding that there's no such thing has immediately alleviated almost all of that pressure. I feel like I've had a boil lanced.

Okay, there is still a lingering regret inside me as well. Regret that I lost Sam because of my unrealistic expectations. Regret that I've spent so much of my life looking at love from the wrong angle. Regret that I tried to force things with Sam, even though I had no idea if we were actually compatible as human beings. How could you after only three months? And the worst part of that lingering regret is that I will never know how things could have gone with her if I'd been more laid back and realistic about the whole thing.

But it does feel *small* now, somehow – all that regret. Like an afterthought. Like something I know I'll be able to leave behind me as I move forward.

And funnily enough, I feel like I have a newfound sense of *strength* inside me.

Chasing an impossible dream all of this time has made me weak. It's made me needy. It's made me *desperate*.

But no more. Not from this day forward.

I am not going to chase that dream any more. Instead, I am going to face reality head on. I'm going to live in the real world, and I'm going to bloody well *enjoy it*. Because you can never really enjoy a fantasy . . . or a dream. You might as well try to hug smoke.

By the time I left Mum and Dad's house that afternoon I felt like I was walking on air.

To finally have a real and proper understanding of yourself is a *wonderful* thing. To gain knowledge of what actually makes you tick is a gift that not many people receive in their lives. I should count myself lucky.

I have spent months lost in a fog of confusion and self-doubt – ever since that fateful day at Thorn Manor. But now, for the first time in a long time, I have a clear head.

Which gives me a spring in my step.

And now I need to do something . . .

Something *big*.

Something *huge*.

Something that I can only do now that the weight has been lifted from me. I feel a huge surge of energy coursing through me almost permanently at the moment. I'm like a cat on a hot tin roof.

And I need some sort of *release*. Some sort of grand gesture – to myself, and to everyone else, to show that Ollie Sweet has started a new chapter of his life. A better chapter.

One with more exciting words in it.

And I think I have just the thing I can use to show all of this, sat back at the Actual Life offices, waiting for me, in my email inbox . . .

CHAPTER ELEVEN

Everything is Going to Be Fine

No. No. Stop it.

Seriously, stop it. It's going to be absolutely *fine*.

I have to do this.

I *want* to do this.

I'm going to be perfectly safe. The company I found on Google is a well-respected skydive outfit that operates from an ex-RAF airfield. They have many, many five-star reviews on TripAdvisor AND Trustpilot. The guy who runs the company is an ex-paratrooper himself.

It all sounds legitimate, safe and expertly run. I've done my research. I will be *fine*.

So, are you going to come and watch me throw myself out of a functioning plane, or not?

***

The crowd that turns up at Harriston Airfield on a cool September morning is quite a bit larger than I thought it would be.

There's about a thousand people here.

A *thousand*.

And all of them are standing around shivering, because I thought it would be a nice idea to ask the readers of 'Dumped Actually' if they'd like the chance to watch me do something totally out of character.

. . . but not at all risky. I will be *fine*. Absolutely fine.

You might argue that a thousand people isn't all that big a crowd, given how popular I've been telling you 'Dumped Actually' is all this time, but when I say I only put the invitation out *yesterday morning*, would that change your perspective?

It was a spur-of-the-moment decision, obviously. I'd already published the story about the visit to my parents' house a few days earlier and wasn't planning on writing about the parachute jump until after the fact – but then I impulsively told Erica I'd like to invite people along to watch me do it, figuring it'd make for a good bit of publicity, and some more flavour for the story.

Strange, isn't it?

Me – Oliver Sweet – being *impulsive*.

It's like finding out that Joseph Stalin ran an animal welfare sanctuary, or that Nigel Farage was once nice to a foreign person.

Completely out of character.

But that's how I've been feeling since I came away from Mum and Dad's house – *impulsive*. And maybe even a little reckless in the bargain.

That spring that I've had in my step has thankfully not gone away since that day.

It's amazing what a bit of perspective can do for your mental outlook on the world. I feel like I've turned a very large and very long corner in my life.

So now I'm fairly buzzing with anticipation of what life holds for me in the future. And I'm also buzzing with a lot of pent-up energy that needs to be released. Released in a grand and overambitious way, to signify a change in Ollie Sweet's outlook on life.

Hence why I'm now walking towards a twin-prop aeroplane, with 'REACH FOR THE SKY' written down the side of it in exciting, jazzy blue lettering.

It's also why I'm wearing a black helmet, a small radio headset and a bright-yellow jumpsuit, with a parachute on my back that is getting heavier by the second.

No.

No.

Stop it.

I said it'll be *fine*, and I meant it. I've had two full days of instruction with Ted the ex-paratrooper, and am feeling confident that I know what to do once we get airborne.

Ted is a very good instructor, and he'll be with me the entire way down, just in case I start doing anything too Oliver Sweetish on the way to the ground.

Also, it's not like I'll be going the whole hog and doing a skydive from fifteen thousand feet. That, my friends, is something you take a long time to build up to.

I'll be doing a static-line parachute jump from five thousand feet – which is more than enough for me, thanks very much.

The eyes of a thousand people are upon me as I make my way over to the plane. Among them are Erica, Wimsy, his new girlfriend Lizzy, Vanity, Laughlin McPurty, Skeez – the guy who suggested I do this parachute jump in the first place – and both of my parents. I don't think I've ever seen my father as proud of me as he is now. My mother looks worried. But she has no reason to be.

And no.

Neither do you.

Everything is going to be *fine*.

'All set, then, Ollie?' Ted asks me as I clamber into the open side doorway of the plane – which wouldn't be able to fit more than a dozen people in it, if it was set up for passenger flights.

Ted is square of jaw, square of head and square of outlook. Everything about him screams solid and dependable. It's this that persuaded me to go through with the jump, once the initial rush had worn off. If he hadn't exuded such an air of competence and enthusiasm about the whole damn thing, I would have probably bottled it by now. But Ted has been there – over the course of two hastily arranged days – to keep my courage from faltering too much.

I'm slightly annoyed I'm not gay, to be honest. Ted would make a wonderful husband.

'Yep!' I say to the husband material with a grin. 'I'm good to go!'

Just *look* at the thumbs-up I'm giving, would you?

Look how proud and erect it is!

Not a trace of nerves. Not a bit of shake. It's the thumbs-up of a man who is confident he's made the right decision – and knows that chucking himself out of this plane today will mark a new and exciting chapter of his life. A leaf will be turned over here at this airfield. Of that you can be sure.

Onwards and upwards!

Fifteen minutes later, my arse is trying to take bites out of the side of the plane.

I'm *terrified*.

I'm *scared* to *death*.

You were absolutely right – this was a stupid, stupid idea.

Everything is resolutely *not* going to be fine.

I got vertigo just leaning out over the side of a car park, what the hell made me think I could come all the way up here, without being consumed by an ocean of extreme terror?

Look how small everything is!

Look! Look at that bloody field! It looks like a postage stamp!

And I'm going to throw myself at it, am I?

What the bloody hell was I *thinking*?

My arse is now attempting to affix itself like a limpet to the part of the plane bulkhead that it hasn't already eaten.

If it wasn't for the bright-yellow jumpsuit, it would probably succeed. You wouldn't be able to prise me away. I'd become half man, half barnacle.

It's one thing to feel calm and confident about a parachute jump when you're on the ground – it's quite another when you're five thousand feet in the air. When you're five thousand feet in the air, all logic is thrown to the same wind that's buffeting the wings of the plane like an angry elephant.

Fuck Ted and his square head.

It's his fault I'm up here – about to evacuate the contents of my bowels as I contemplate the horror that is to come.

'How are you doing?' Ted the bastard asks me, probably sensing that I've gone from considering him husband material to wanting to rip his face off for making me come up here.

'I'm shitting a fucking brick, Ted. How are you doing?'

Ted laughs. Even his laugh sounds square, and ever so upright. You could probably lay the foundations of a house on top of it.

'You'll be absolutely fine,' he tells me, echoing my own thought process, when I was still on terra firma, and not in firm terror.

I nod. 'Yes, I know I will, Ted, because I'm not fucking jumping!'

He pats me on the shoulder. 'Yes, you are! You'll love it!'

This time I shake my head. 'No, Ted. I will not *love* it. I don't mean to be disparaging about your line of work – but you're *mental*. And everyone else who does this is mental. *I* was mental for thinking I could do it too!'

Ted doesn't seem offended by this. In fact, he just laughs again. I get the impression I'm not the first person to start cursing him and everything he stands for when they're on the brink of throwing themselves out of his twin-prop.

He looks at a large and fiendishly complicated watch on his arm. 'Come on, Ollie! It's time to do this!'

'No.'

'Yes!'

'No.'

'Yes!'

'No, Ted. No. No. *Bad* Ted. Bad Ted!'

Ted doesn't reply, but starts to gently push me towards the plane exit, which has just been pulled wide open by one of his assistants. Did I say assistants? I meant evil minions.

'Fuck off, Ted!' I wail. 'I can't do this, Ted! I *won't* do this, Ted!'

Hark at me, eh? A while back I couldn't say no to a camp Scotsman with a waxing strip, and here I am telling a square-jawed paratrooper called Ted to fuck off.

Progress, people. *Progress.*

Ted stops pushing me. 'Look, Ollie. I can't make you do this. It's your decision.'

'Yes, Ted! It is! I'm glad you've seen the light! Now, tell me where the nearest big, thick seatbelt is, please. I wish to strap myself in until we reach the ground.'

'But Ollie . . . I've read your stories on Actual Life. I know what kind of guy you are. I know what you've been through,' Ted says, ever so earnestly. 'And doing this thing . . . this one thing . . . I think it really will be a great way for you to move on from Samantha once and for all . . . and move on from all the neuroses and doubts that have been holding you back your entire life.'

I'm gobsmacked.

Then I waggle a pointy finger at Ted. 'Now, look here, you. You're just supposed to be the square-jawed ex-paratrooper who wants to throw me out of a plane, not a source of emotional strength in times of severe adversity! That's not your bloody job!'

Ted nods sagely. 'You get to know a lot about people when they come up here, and the door is wide open, Ollie. Trust me on that.'

Oh, for crying out loud. Profound wisdom at five thousand feet is just about the most unbearable thing I think I've ever experienced.

But Ted the square-jawed ex-paratrooper (and now wise life guru, it appears) has hit the nail on the bloody head, hasn't he?

This is more than just a parachute jump – it's a symbolic turning of the page.

If I don't go through with it, can I really move past the things that have been holding me back? Can I really get over Sam, and all the other heartbreaks I've had, and find a better way to live my life? If I don't chuck myself out of that wide-open door, will I ever be the man I want to be?

The logical and right answer to this question is – *of course I bloody well can.*

The ability to jump out of a plane at five thousand feet has absolutely no bearing on one's capacity to live a more fulfilled and happy life. Anyone who thinks otherwise is bleedin' crackers.

So, why am I now shuffling towards the wide-open door, with my heart in my throat?

If I could answer that question, I could probably unlock the secrets of the universe.

As I reach the open door, I look down on the patchwork of quaint English countryside, and the fear skyrockets again.

Turn around, you galumphing great cretin. This isn't worth it!

Yes, it is!

No, it isn't! You have nothing to prove!

Yes, I do!

To who? All those people down there? To Ted with the square jaw? Do you really think doing this idiotic jump will make a blind bit of difference? This isn't a bloody movie. Especially not one directed by Richard Curtis.

There isn't a happy ending waiting for you out there! Who are you doing this for?!

Me! I'm doing it for me! Not for any of them, not for anybody else . . . just me!

Why?

Because . . . Because I want to do something that doesn't have a bloody *why*, that's why!

'Er, Ollie? Are you okay?' Ted shouts at me. 'Only you've started babbling incomprehensibly to yourself!'

'Yeah . . . I know! I'm just trying to work up a bit of courage!'

'Oh, okay. Only you looked like you were having some sort of mental breakdown!'

I give Ted a long, hard look. 'Story of my life, mate,' I tell him as he clips the line that runs from the back of my chute pack to the one that's fastened to the interior of the plane's fuselage. Once I do jump, that line will make sure my parachute springs open as soon as I'm out.

'You ready?' Ted shouts again. 'We're over the jump zone!'

'I'm not sure! Should I say something? Or maybe pray a little?'

'Are you religious?'

'No, but it probably can't hurt, can it?'

Ted shrugs unhelpfully.

I stare out at the wide blue sky and green fields below, trying to think of something meaningful to say to myself. Surely, this is a moment that deserves a meaningful speech, after all that I've been through. A heartfelt plea to whatever god may be watching, possibly. Something that sums up all of my wishes and desires from this point forward. Something profound. Something elegant. Something *memorable*.

. . .

Er . . .

. . .

Um . . .

. . .

'Ollie! It's time to jump!' Ted wails at me.

'Yes! Yes! I know!'

. . .

Ah . . .

. . .

Ah, to hell with it.

'I just want an easy fucking life!' I scream, and chuck myself out of the plane.

My most humble apologies for not coming up with something more profound or life changing. You know . . . the kind of thing you can take away into your day-to-day life, and tell all of your friends about smugly when they ask why you've got that smile on your face.

Unfortunately, I'm wearing a bright-yellow jumpsuit that makes me look like an ambulatory banana, I enjoy masturbating in front of wild animals, am unintentionally racist when attempting an Italian accent, and like to have conversations with imaginary antipodean elephants.

Am I really the person you want to be getting profound or life-changing advice from?

Go buy a motivational poster. Or get drunk.

Or get drunk and *then* look at a motivational poster. Probably one with a nice big mountain on it.

'Aaaaaarrrrrgggh!' I screech as I leave the plane at an extreme rate of knots.

My mind goes blank as gravity starts to do its terrible and inexorable job.

I feel the parachute pack yank backwards as the line goes taut for a moment, before the chute is unfurled in a glorious blossom of life-saving silky green material.

My breath is taken from me as the air fills the parachute, and my descent towards the patchwork fields below is arrested from a terminal velocity to something much more gentle, and survivable.

This gives my brain a chance to regain its faculties, which I suppose must be a good thing.

Wisely deciding that I am still highly discombobulated by the jump, it goes into autopilot for me, remembering everything Ted told me to do, during those two long, hard days of instruction.

I have hold of the control lines before I even realise what I'm doing. These things are pretty vital, given that without them I'd have no control over the parachute at all, and would probably float off over the English Channel.

They're pretty simple to operate, thankfully. A tug on one sends you to the left, a tug on the other sends you right. Both together slows you down. Simple.

'How are you doing?' Ted's voice crackles at me through the headset, which I'd forgotten all about until this moment.

'Jesus!' I scream in shock.

'No, it's just Ted,' he replies.

Frankly, I'll take the definitely corporeal Ted over the possibly non-existent Jesus any day of the week, given the circumstances.

I look up to my left and see Ted descending at roughly the same speed as me, in his jet-black jumpsuit and charcoal-grey parachute. He looks about 247 per cent cooler than me. I am in a bright-yellow jumpsuit, and my parachute is equally bright green, so I look like something that's just escaped from the Mardi Gras.

'Sorry,' I reply, sheepishly. 'I'm fine, thanks.'

'Good. Control lines okay? You've got control of the parachute, like we practised?'

'Yes,' I tell him. 'It's all coming back to me.'

'Excellent stuff. Well, we'll start to turn ourselves towards the landing zone, then. Can you see it?'

I look down . . . and down . . . to see the airfield below us, with the large red circle that I'm supposed to aim for clearly visible on the grass. 'Yeah. I see it.'

'Good. How are you feeling?'

Oh blimey.

How *am* I feeling? I hadn't given it much thought, until Ted asked me the question.

I guess . . . I guess I feel *calm*.

Which is ridiculous.

I should not feel calm. I should feel on the verge of a heart attack. I have just thrown myself out of a plane, and the only thing between me and certain death is a few yards of thin parachute material. Panic should have set in long ago.

But you know what? I actually feel quite *relaxed*. There's something very soothing about drifting through the sky on a crisp, sunny September morning. I didn't expect to feel like this at all.

I tell Ted as much.

'Yep. Not surprised,' he says. 'People think this is all about the rush of the jump . . . but that's only part of it. Floating along like this, just you and the wind – that's as big a part of the fun for me.'

I see Ted swing his parachute away from me somewhat. 'I tell you what, Ollie. I'll leave you alone for a bit. You look like you've got everything under control, so I'll let you enjoy the peace and quiet. I'll speak to you when we get on the ground. Just talk if you get into any problems, though.'

'Okay, Ted. Thanks very much.'

What a guy.

Seriously, why am I not gay?

I watch Ted pull away from me to a distance of about a hundred feet.

Then I spend the next minute or so doing something that does not come easily to me – absolutely nothing.

My brain goes back into autopilot, steering me in the right direction over the landing zone, in a series of gentle, falling loops – leaving the rest of me to do very little, other than look out at the green countryside below, and blue sky above.

Later, there will be time for reflection. Later, I will think long and hard about how I felt during the parachute jump – but for now, there's nothing. No internal monologues, no external anxieties. Just Ollie Sweet and his parachute, descending towards the earth at a speed that shouldn't break anything once he reaches it.

It's quite fabulous.

It's a real pity it only lasts a few brief minutes. I could stay up here all day. I have no idea why birds are so bloody bad tempered all the time. This is immensely relaxing.

Ted comes back on the mic again, asking me if I'm prepared for the landing.

'Yes, I'm ready,' I tell him as I watch the ground coming closer and closer.

My voice is steady, and there's a calm confidence about it that sounds quite alien to me. It also sounds *marvellous*, though. Something quite profound appears to have occurred in these few minutes in the sky. And though I will spend quite a lot of time in the near future thinking about what that profound thing was . . . I'll never come up with a satisfactory answer.

Some things just aren't meant to be examined and fretted over until they make sense. Some things are just meant to happen. Some things are just meant to be.

It's high time I learned that, and accepted it, for that matter.

The ground is getting very close now. So close that I can see the faces of the expectant crowd again, all watching the last few moments of my descent, with a mixture of delight and apprehension. I can see Erica standing slightly forward of everyone else, her hand shielding her eyes as she watches me descend.

This is the hardest bit of the jump, and the part Ted spent the most time teaching me in our training sessions. Landing a solo parachute isn't something even experienced skydivers take lightly.

As I get within a few feet of the ground, I pull down hard on the control lines, which arrests the speed of the parachute to a near walking pace. Now I'm drifting towards the ground, more or less right towards the centre of the red circle.

As I do this, I bring my legs together, slightly bent, and cross my arms over my chest. My feet hit the grass at a comfortable speed, and I immediately bend my knees even more, and shift my body weight so I collapse into a half roll, which prevents any injury occurring.

The landing is pretty much *perfect*.

Time to be smug!

I stand up as the crowd starts to cheer and clap my landing.

I feel a fist pump is appropriate at this juncture. I've never really felt that I've done anything in my life that could justify a fist pump before, but surely making your first successful parachute jump qualifies, doesn't it?

I don't really care. I'm doing a fist pump, anyway.

At this point I should be gathering in my chute, but I'm too damn busy being smug and pumping my fist like I'm doing an emergency tyre change.

Smug – I think you'll find – is an emotional state that never gets you anywhere good in life.

Because I'm being smug, fist pumping, and also waving at the crowd, I am not noticing that my parachute is beginning to fill with air again as the breeze catches it. This makes it billow out, and fly right over my head, in the direction of the crowd.

In a split second I go from smug, fist-pumping champion of parachutes, to stumbling idiot, being dragged along by thirty square feet of bright-green material.

'Ollie!' Ted exclaims from his own perfect landing position a few yards away. 'Pull the cutaway!'

The cutaway is the handle you yank when you want to release your parachute in an emergency – for occasions such as this one.

I scrabble at the handle on the right-hand side of my chest, desperately trying to pull it before the parachute launches me into the air again.

Luckily, the wind isn't quite strong enough to do that, but it is more than strong enough to propel the parachute at the crowd, with me right behind it.

And who's standing at the head of crowd? Poor old Erica.

This is how Ollie Sweet's life functions.

If he's going to be propelled towards a crowd of people, he *is* going to head straight at the worst person possible.

Crashing into Wimsy wouldn't be much of a problem. Nor would hitting my father, who is still a strong and capable man, even at his age. Hell, even whacking a complete stranger is something I could probably get away with – if I didn't cause any major injury, that is.

But no, I have to make a beeline straight for the person who pays my wages, don't I? Literally the last person I want to crash into.

The drifting parachute pushes me inexorably towards Erica, who has gone wide-eyed as she realises what's about to happen.

Luckily for both of us, I do manage to yank the cutaway handle down just in time, and the parachute flies up higher into the air, no doubt happy to be free of my dead weight.

Sadly, I am still being propelled forward by the unhelpful forces of inertia, so cannot stop myself from tumbling into Erica, face first.

I'm not going all that fast, though, so what could have been an immediate trip to casualty, instead becomes an awkward pratfall – sending us both to the ground, with me flopping on top of her. I throw both of my arms out to cushion the blow as we hit the grass together.

For a few moments we just stare into each other's wide-open eyes, both in disbelief that neither of us has been hurt.

'Hi Ollie,' Erica eventually says to me in a breathless tone as the parachute floats down on top of us, having lost the balloon of air that sent me hurtling towards her in the first place.

'Hello,' I reply in a shaky voice. 'Fancy meeting you here.'

The parachute now settles over us completely, blocking our view of the crowd – who are now surrounding us, probably quite concerned for our welfare.

Erica and I look at each other for another couple of moments, both trying to process what's just happened, and more to the point, what's currently *happening*.

Because something is definitely happening, let me tell you that. I'm finding it extremely hard to stop looking into those deep green eyes of hers.

I can feel a spark of electricity moving between us . . . though that may just be static from the parachute silk.

Then Erica's phone starts to ring, breaking the tension.

'I'd . . . I'd better get that,' she says as I continue to stare down at her, my breath coming in short gasps.

'Okay,' I say, still not moving. Being this close to Erica is making my heart beat faster than it did when I jumped out of the plane, to be honest.

'Hello,' she says into her phone, still staring right into my eyes. From the periphery of my vision, I can see people grabbing at the parachute silk to pull it off.

Erica listens for a few moments to the person on the other end of the phone, before her face darkens considerably. 'He's doing *what?*' she spits in the phone. 'Today? Without me there?!'

'What's going on?' I ask her as Ted pulls off the chute material.

Erica looks livid. 'The bastard's making a play, Ollie. He's trying to screw me completely!'

And with that, she pushes me off, and swiftly climbs back to her feet. There are a few grass stains on her grey pantsuit, but other than that, I don't appear to have done her any harm. They don't come much tougher than Erica Hilton.

I get up as well, yanking the last of the parachute from off one shoulder. 'Who are you talking about, Erica?'

'Benedict! That son of a bitch has called an extraordinary general meeting of the ForeTech board of directors today!'

'Jesus! Why?' This is a stupid question. There's a very obvious reason why.

'Because he knows I'm *here*, Ollie! He's going to try and convince the rest of the eleven that they should shut Actual Life down once and for all, and I won't be there to stop it!'

'But why would he?' I implore. 'Everything's going so well!'

To underline this, I gesture at the crowd that surrounds us. If I can pull a thousand random strangers along to a parachute jump on a September morning, with only twenty-four hours' notice, things must be alright, *surely?*

Erica shakes her head. 'None of this matters, Ollie. He wants Actual Life to go under, no matter what we do. And even though you've done such a good job in the past few months, Benedict will have something up his bloody sleeve to ruin us. I know he will!' She fishes in her jacket pocket, pulling out her car keys. 'Look, I have to go. I have to stop this. I'll see you later.'

'I'm coming with you,' I tell her.

Oh my.

Did you hear that?

There was a *commanding* tone to my voice there. Yes. Very definitely.

I sounded confident back up in the air a few minutes ago, and was happy with that. I never thought for one moment I could ever actually do *commanding*!

'No. I can handle this, Ollie,' Erica replies. 'You stay here with everyone. They'll want to talk to you about the jump, and you need to speak to them for the story. Get the colour.'

I clench my jaw. 'Fuck the story,' I reply, in a deep, resonant tone.

Okay, this is starting to make me a bit light-headed now. I'd better stop, before I faint.

Erica looks taken aback. Then she blinks a couple of times. 'Alright, Ollie. Come with me, then. If I drive fast enough, we should be able to reach the city in less than an hour. Prendergast says the meeting begins at twelve. We might make it in time.'

'Right. Sounds good to me. Who the hell's Prendergast?'

'Alan Prendergast. One of the other members of the board, and about the only one I trust. Come on! We have to go!'

Erica turns and starts to run towards her grey BMW, which is parked a good hundred yards away from where we're standing. I take off after her.

'Sorry, folks! Something very important has come up!' I shout at the crowd as I rush by.

They all look pretty stunned. They came to see a parachute jump, but they've also got an impromptu bit of street theatre (or *grass* theatre, if we're being accurate) in the bargain.

Sadly, they're not going to get to see the ending of this particular show, because it's going to take place in a high-rise office block, up in the city. Shame, really, it promises to be a barnstormer. I'd better make sure I do a good write-up of it, whatever happens.

'Ollie! Ollie!' Ted calls after me as I hurry to keep up with Erica. 'I need my jumpsuit back!'

Oh bugger. I'd forgotten about this stupid thing.

I whip off the helmet and throw it at him. 'Here you go! I'll bring the suit back later, I promise!'

'Er . . . okay!' he shouts, a little unsure of himself.

Now, that's got to be something worthy of note. In a hectic situation where two men are involved, and one is unsure of himself – for the first time ever, it's not bloody *me*!

I have purpose! I have drive! I have determination!

. . . I have to get this stupid yellow jumpsuit off as soon as I get in the car. There's no way I want to face Benedict Montifore looking like I've just been imported in a fruit crate from the Caribbean.

Erica is already in the driver's seat and firing up the engine as I throw the passenger door open and climb in. I'm being so manly right now, it's quite breathtaking. I would offer to drive, but I don't know the way, and have a habit of stalling when I'm in a rush.

'You ready?' she says to me, hands gripped firmly on the wheel.

'Let's fucking rock it!' I shout back at her – and pump my fist.

Good grief.

I could have just said 'yes' and had done with it, but I just had to try and be cool, didn't I?

Erica looks at me in a way that tells me I am being far from cool – what with the idiotic pronouncement that just came from my lips, and the bright-yellow jumpsuit I'm still wearing – and guns the accelerator.

I am thrown back into the seat as we hurtle out of the airfield – and towards a confrontation that we've all known has been coming for quite some time now, if we've been paying attention, and haven't got distracted by all the bloody fist pumping.

CHAPTER TWELVE

IT'S JUST MEANT TO BE

I thrust my genitals towards Erica as we speed up the motorway off-ramp.

'Ollie! What the hell are you doing?' she exclaims.

'Trying to get this stupid jumpsuit off!' I explain to her, bucking my hips again as I attempt to slide the suit underneath my buttocks. The damn thing is not cooperating with me at all, and it's taking a supreme effort to get the suit off without ripping my clothes underneath.

This might have something to do with the fact that Erica is driving like Nigel Mansell, throwing the BMW around like we're taking a tricky corner at Monaco.

'Well, hurry up! I'll crash the car if you keep thrusting your crotch at me like that!'

'Understood,' I tell her, before I let a huge grunt out as the suit finally slides over my arse, and forms a puddle of yellow material at my feet.

'How does Benedict expect to convince the board of directors that they should go along with him?' I ask. 'Actual Life is doing so well. Didn't you say we were nearly back in profit?'

'Yes. And that means he's found something to fuck us over with that we don't know about. Something he thinks is convincing enough to turn everyone against us. All he needs to do is get a majority of seven from the thirteen members of the board including himself and we're dead in the water. And with me not there, he won't have to worry about my vote.'

'Oh fuck.'

'Precisely.'

'But that Prendergast chap wouldn't vote against you, would he? You said you trusted him?'

'I do. But he's the only one I know will stand by me. The rest . . . Benedict can persuade them to do what he wants. He's done it before.'

Erica makes another sharp turn, and we're on the dual carriageway, headed right towards the financial district, where ForeTech's offices are situated.

I'm assuming that's where we're going, anyway. I've never actually been to ForeTech before. I'm far too low on the food chain to get an invite.

As Erica speeds us towards it, I start to feel a bloom of fear in my chest. Now I've had a moment to think about what we're actually about to do, the gravity of it all has hit me. We're heading towards a confrontation that could very well result in the loss of my job and the end of 'Dumped Actually' – not to mention everyone else's job at the website.

'What are our chances?' I ask Erica as the BMW leaves the dual carriageway and starts to wend its way around streets that are fast becoming surrounded by high-rise office blocks.

Erica looks at me darkly, before returning her attention to the road.

Gulp.

I lapse back into silence as Erica drives through increasingly empty roads, at increasingly unsafe speeds. I'm too caught up in my fear of losing my job to be afraid of the speed she's going at, though.

Her red hair – always so impossibly expressive – is now a raging fire. Her emerald-green eyes are blazing as well. I don't think I've ever seen Erica look this angry or determined before.

It's a completely inappropriate thing to think, given the circumstances, but she's frankly never looked more beautiful.

My mind casts back to an hour ago at the airfield, when we were staring into each other's eyes. Was there something actually . . . *there*?

Another sharp turn to the left brings me back to my senses, and the BMW is now careening towards one high-rise office block in particular. It's enormous, with a blue tinge to the glass that wraps around its entire structure. It looks more or less exactly the same as most of the others do, frankly. I'm glad Erica knows where she's going, because I'm completely lost in this sea of corporate architecture. If this is the kind of place that breeds men like Benedict Montifore, I'd rather be nowhere near it.

Speaking of whom, I still have an unanswered question burning at the back of my mind. One that's been there ever since I first spoke to Erica about Benedict's plans for us.

'Why is he doing this, Erica? Why would a successful businessman want to destroy a part of his portfolio that's doing well? It makes no financial sense!'

'This isn't about money,' Erica replies as we charge around the side of the blue high-rise, and towards a ramp leading into its depths.

'Then what is it about?'

Erica ignores me, and slams on the brakes as the BMW comes to a large gate. This immediately starts to swing open, having detected Erica's number plate.

'Erica!' I say in a sharp tone as we drive into a vast underground car park.

'It doesn't matter, Ollie. I've told you before, Benedict is my problem, not yours.'

In times past, I would have just meekly accepted this. I would have let Erica keep her secrets, and followed her into battle, hoping that she could see us through without my help.

Not now, though.

Not after everything I've been through.

If I'm going to go up to this meeting and fight for my livelihood, I want to know exactly what I'm up against. I want to know why I'm in this stupid situation in the first place, otherwise I won't know how to get out.

In trying to understand why Sam dumped me, I learned that to find the right answers, you really need to know how to ask the right questions first. You have to know *why*, to know *how*, just like Troy the Elephant said.

And I'm not going to go a step further until I know why Benedict is doing this to us.

Erica slams the BMW into a parking space with her name written on a plaque on the wall in front of it. She turns the ignition off and goes to release her seatbelt. She can't do this, however, because my hand is over the release button.

'What are you doing?' she shouts at me. 'We have to get up there!'

'Why, Erica?' I say, staring at her. 'Why is Benedict doing this?'

'Oh fuck, Ollie! It doesn't matter! Let me go!'

'It matters to *me*!' I exclaim, my voice strong and powerful. This scares me a little again, but I know I need to stick with it. It's important I get the answers I need.

Erica is quite taken aback by this – not for the first time today. If I keep acting like this, I'm likely to give her neck ache. But she can see the determination in my eyes, and slumps in her seat. I've never seen Erica slump before. It's a very odd thing to witness.

'When Benedict bought me out, I thought it was the greatest thing that had ever happened to me,' she explains. 'I was suddenly rich, successful and on the board of a powerful company.' She smiles ruefully.

'I let it go to my head a bit. Benedict was all smiles and compliments back then, of course. I thought it was because he valued me as a business partner.' Erica shakes her head. 'I was very stupid for thinking that. What Benedict Montifore wanted was to get in my knickers.'

'Oh, for the love of God,' I say, everything falling into place.

'He wined and dined me. He made me think he was genuinely interested in my ideas for the company going forward. He made me think he saw me as an equal, you know? Someone whose opinion he valued.' Erica's eyes turn flinty. 'And then he tried to seduce me right up there' – she points upwards – 'on the boardroom table.'

'Fucking hell.'

'I wanted none of it, of course. Benedict was a man I wanted to do business with, not get into bed with. I tried to push him away . . . and he wouldn't take no for an answer.'

'God.'

'I had to knee him in the groin to get away from him that night. If I hadn't, or if he'd been a little less drunk . . .'

Erica tails off. She doesn't need to go any further.

I don't think I've ever been so instantly filled with rage in my life. 'So, let me get this fucking right,' I say to Erica in a flat voice. 'This bastard is willing to destroy the lives of everyone at Actual Life, including mine, because you didn't want to have sex with him.'

Erica nods. 'That's about the size of it.' She then says something that absolutely makes my heart want to explode. 'I'm so sorry, Ollie.'

This *dumbfounds* me. That Erica feels the need to apologise to me for something that the gold-plated arsehole has done is just so, so *awful*.

I take hold of Erica's hand and shift in the seat to look her squarely in the eyes. 'You have nothing to apologise for. Nothing at all.'

'Thank you,' she replies, squeezing my hand.

I squeeze it back. 'Let's go up there and ruin his fucking day, shall we?' I suggest.

Erica smiles fiercely. That awful apologetic look on her face is thankfully gone. The real Erica is back, and I couldn't be happier about that.

I'm not happy when we arrive on the twelfth floor of the building and are told by the ForeTech receptionist that I can't go into the meeting.

'Why not?' I snap, giving him the stink eye.

'The EGM is strictly for board members only,' he tells me. 'Mr Montifore was very specific about that.'

'Yes, he bloody would be,' Erica says, looking at the smoked-glass double doors in front of us with a grim expression on her face. We can just about see the outlines of several bodies in the boardroom beyond. Most are sitting down, but one is on his feet, gesticulating wildly.

'But I have to be allowed in,' I insist, leaning over the desk.

The receptionist – who certainly doesn't need this kind of grief in his life – sits back in his chair. 'I will call security if you don't settle down, sir,' he tells me, hand straying to the telephone on his desk.

Erica puts her arm across me and gently pulls me back. 'Ollie, it's okay.'

'No, it isn't!' I protest.

'Honestly, it is. I can go in there on my own, don't worry.'

I gasp in frustration. 'But I don't want you to be alone!'

Erica rummages in her jacket pocket and pulls out her mobile phone. 'Call me.'

'What?'

'Call me on my phone. You might not be able to come in, but you can at least listen to what goes on in there.'

We both look at the receptionist to see if he has any problem with that. He returns the gaze for a moment, before shrugging his shoulders. 'He never said anything to me about phones.'

'Right. It's better than nothing, I suppose,' I say, pulling out my own phone and dialling Erica's number.

She gives my arm a squeeze and smiles briefly, before walking past the receptionist's desk and towards those smoked-glass double doors.

I immediately go and sit on a chair beside the receptionist's desk and hold my phone up to my ear. I stare out at the semi-full office floor as I do this. Most of the staff at ForeTech are getting on with their work, but a few keep throwing glances over at me and the boardroom. They know something of importance is happening in there today. It's probably testament to the way Benedict Montifore runs things that most of them look scared to death. I want to go over and tell them not to worry – it's not their jobs that hang in the balance today . . . it's mine.

'Good afternoon, gentlemen!' I hear Erica say through the phone. 'I'm so sorry I'm late.' The sarcasm in her voice is palpable. God knows what shade of red her hair has gone.

'Delighted to have you here!' the voice of an old man says. I have to assume this is Alan Prendergast. He sounds genuinely pleased that Erica has made it.

'Glad you could join us,' Benedict Montifore says. There's no mistaking the venom in his voice. 'I was just explaining to the board how you and your lackey, Mr Sweet, have lied to all of us.'

I sit bolt upright in the chair.

'*Lied* to you?' Erica exclaims.

'Oh yes, Erica. I was just telling our esteemed board members how you and Mr Sweet have been fabricating subscriber numbers and website hits for that "Dumped Actually" thing of his. It's all very sad and very shameful, Erica.'

I jump out of the chair and start to pace up and down angrily.

'We have done no such thing!' Erica says, probably speaking directly to the other board members. 'The success of "Dumped Actually" is there for all to see!'

'Ha!' Benedict interrupts. 'Fine words, Erica, but these gentlemen are not going to be hoodwinked by your falsehoods.' I suppose Benedict is now addressing the board members as well.

Argh! This is so *frustrating*! I need to be in there with her, not out here, wearing a hole in the bloody carpet!

Benedict then starts a speech that is designed to paint Erica and me in the worst light possible. He talks about how we've consistently falsified the popularity of 'Dumped Actually'. He tells the board members that we've faked all of the emails that have been coming in, and that all the things I've been doing for the feature have been completely made up.

He even produces some pieces of paper as evidence. These have no doubt been cooked up somewhere by one of his lackeys, to back up the accusations he's throwing at us.

Benedict tells the board that we've conducted all this deceitful activity just to save our own jobs; never mind the damage this might do to the reputation of Actual Life, and – more importantly – the parent company, ForeTech.

He has absolutely no *real* proof of any of this, of course – but my God does he sound convincing.

Benedict has not a shred of proper evidence for any of his claims, but he obviously believes he doesn't need it. He thinks he can just bluff his way through to a vote on the continued existence of Actual Life with his speech and a few bits of paper, knowing that the board will probably acquiesce to his wishes.

I have a horrible feeling he might be bloody right. *I'm* half convinced he's telling the truth from out here, and I'm the one whose reputation he's destroying.

Erica is trying as hard as she can to argue against Benedict, but I don't think it's working. She was caught wrong-footed by him today and has had no time to prepare a defence. Benedict has probably been planning this for weeks, and knows precisely what to say, and how to say it. He's appealing to the reputations of the men sat around that table – going right to the heart of what makes them tick.

Do they want to be associated with liars and charlatans? That's his plan of attack. Make them think that associating with us will lead to their own reputations being irrevocably tarred.

Of course, the irony here is that he's the biggest liar of all!

I clench my phone so hard in my hand that I'm in danger of breaking the screen.

How is this *fair*? How is this allowed to happen? How can one man – more full of shit than a sewage works – be allowed to destroy Actual Life, with nothing more than words and falsified documents?

But that's clearly the way this is going to go. I can tell that, even though I can only hear what's going on. Erica is losing this fight. Her words sound like they are falling on deaf ears. These old farts are quite prepared to accept Benedict's version of the story, given that he's managed to terrify them with the prospect of being connected to such deceitful bastards as Erica and I are being made out to be. The vote will go ahead, we will lose . . . and I will have to stand out here and listen as my life is taken away from me.

Because that's what 'Dumped Actually' is. That's what Erica is, for that matter.

My life.

Both have seen me through the heartache of Sam's loss, and both have helped me understand myself better, and grow as a person. Without them, I'd still be mourning the end of yet another relationship and hiding in the dark somewhere . . . rather than jumping out of a plane and finally seeing the light.

I would also not have changed the relationship I have with my parents for the better, because I wouldn't have known there was anything that *needed* changing. I'd still be looking at them on a pedestal, rather than as the lovely human beings they actually are.

Without Erica, without Actual Life, without 'Dumped Actually', where exactly would I be?

For the briefest of moments, I flash back to being on top of that car park and leaning out over the edge, with tears in my eyes and very dark thoughts in my heart. This time, though, in my mind's eye, I don't push back. Instead, I lean out more, past the point of no return, and I—

'Fuck this,' I say under my breath, turning to face the smoked-glass double doors, with my head up and my shoulders square.

The receptionist – who has clearly been watching me all this time – rises from his seat. 'You're not allowed to go in there!' he barks at me.

I glare at him.

For a moment, it seems like he's going to say something else, but the look in my eyes is all he needs to know that he's far better off just sitting back down again.

As he does, I look at the double doors and take a deep breath.

I've been going through a lot of doors recently. And I've mostly done it kicking and screaming – and probably crying.

Everything in my life has been difficult. Painful. *Challenging*, you might say. I've had to face many things that brought me grief, and I've been reluctant to do so on every single occasion.

Not this time, though.

This time, I've never wanted to do anything more in my life.

I start towards the smoked-glass doors, just as I see a load of arms shoot into the air beyond them. The vote has started.

With one hand thrust out, I stride at the doors, hitting them dead centre. They both fly open, and I walk into the boardroom like I own the fucking place.

'Stop!' I roar as I take in the room for the first time. A long oak table, covered in sheets of paper, full of charts, numbers and lists, is surrounded on three sides by a series of cookie-cutter old white men in dark suits. I think I recognise a few from Sheldon Brook.

Erica is stood off to the left-hand side of the room, looking sick to her stomach, and Benedict Montifore is at the head of the oak table, staring down on his board with barely concealed glee as they make their decision about the future of Actual Life – having been convinced by the gold-plated arsehole's lies.

I see at least nine arms in the air. More than enough to seal my fate.

Benedict immediately straightens when he sees me, with a look of unbridled rage on his face. 'Get out! This has nothing to do with you!'

I return his look of rage with 1000 per cent interest. 'Oh, fuck off, Benedict,' I tell him, earning me a few gasps from some of the board members.

Erica looks like she's just seen her cute puppy turn into a wolverine.

'You're not allowed in here!' Benedict roars, moving towards me, spittle flying from his mouth.

Usually, people move out of his way when he comes at them like this.

Not today, though.

I stand my ground.

But as Benedict comes at me, I feel one leg start to shake. He really is quite a big man. Far bigger and stronger than me, without a doubt.

I shouldn't be doing this. I shouldn't be here. Benedict is *right*. It's just better for me to let all of this happen, and to try to pick up the pieces afterwar—

Then I see Erica's apologetic, hurt expression again, from our conversation back in the car, and my leg stops shaking instantly.

Come on, then, you son of a bitch. Come and test your worth against mine.

As he gets within two feet of me, Benedict's expression changes. This is not a man who is used to people standing up to him. He doesn't know how to deal with it.

Is that . . . Is that *doubt* in his eyes? Maybe even a little . . . *fear?*

'I said, you have to get out!' he tells me again, his voice actually cracking a little.

'I don't think so,' I reply. 'I've listened to you lie about me from out there, and there's no way I'm going to let you get away with it. These fine gentlemen are going to hear my side of the story.'

'No!' Benedict retorts. 'You know what you've done! I've told them all!'

'You've told them all lies and bullshit,' I say, taking a step forward. This causes Benedict to take a step *back* . . . and something fundamental realigns itself in the universe.

'I'd like to hear what he has to say,' one of the board members says.

I turn and nod. 'Thank you, Mr Prendergast,' I say, hazarding a guess. He responds with a warm smile.

'Yes. Let Ollie speak!' Erica adds, moving forward herself to stand at my side. 'He's been as slandered as I have today. He deserves the right to reply!'

The raised hands of the board members all go down again slowly, and they stare at Benedict. A few of them look chagrined in the extreme. Those are probably the ones loyal to Benedict, no matter what happens. The rest are looking at him with a mixture of concern and suspicion, though.

He stares right back at them for a moment, before wiping his jacket sleeve across his face to remove the thin film of spittle from his mouth. 'Go on, then, you little bastard. Say your piece. None of them will believe you over me.'

I smile at him. It's a broad, *dangerous* smile. One I both love and hate at the same time. 'We'll see, Benny. We'll just see.'

Oh, he *hates* being called Benny. Just look! How fantastic!

I gaze at the board members and draw myself up to my full height. It's still quite painful to do this, as my spine really isn't used to it. 'Gentlemen, you've been told a lot of lies here today, just so Benedict can convince you to liquidate Actual Life. He's tried to tell you that *we're* lying about the website's popularity, and that things aren't going as well as they appear to be. And . . . to tell the truth . . . I can understand why you'd believe him. After all, he is the CEO of this company, and has made you all an *awful* lot of money over the years.'

The board all nod in a self-satisfied way when I say this. God, what a bunch of old monsters. Only Prendergast has the decency to look a bit shamefaced.

'But lying to you he is, whether you like it or not. Actual Life *is* doing better. It *is* making money again, and it *does* have many more subscribers. Benedict here doesn't want to get rid of it because he thinks it's unprofitable, or because Erica and I are going to ruin your reputations with our skulduggery.' I look at Benedict again, this time with a loathing I no longer care to suppress. 'He's doing it because he tried to force Erica to have sex with him on this very table, and she turned him down.'

Gasps. Loud gasps from the board.

'Ollie!' Erica exclaims.

'Lies!' Benedict screams. 'I never did anything of the sort!'

'Yes, you bloody did!' Erica shouts back at him.

'No, I didn't! You lying bitch!'

I move forward again, pinning Benedict against the edge of the oak table, forcing him to lean back over it. 'Not nice when someone makes accusations against you with no proof, is it, Benedict?'

'I'll kill you, Sweet,' he says in a low voice.

'No, you won't, honey,' I reply, dismissively. 'I've got the measure of you, Benedict. I know what kind of man you are.' I lean into him even more. 'You know what kind of man I am?'

He doesn't answer, but just glares at me defiantly.

'I'm a man who likes to *write*,' I say. 'And I do a pretty good job of it. And despite what you've claimed here today, people *do* like what I write. They like it *a lot*. And they *listen* to me, Benedict. They believe what I have to say. Thousands of them. *Hundreds* of thousands. They believe me, because I've been honest with them about myself. About the things I've done wrong. About the things I've learned. About my *experiences.*'

Benedict's eyes widen. I think he's starting to get the point.

'And all of this would make a *fine* last story for "Dumped Actually", wouldn't it, Benedict? Just think about how all those thousands of people would *love* to hear about what's gone on here today . . . about all the things you've said . . . about all the things you've accused us of.'

If I lean in any closer to the man, I'm going to have to either kiss him or headbutt him.

'And then, I could tell them all about what you tried to do to Erica on this table. And what she did to you. How she fought you off. How she *rejected* you. Yeah . . . I bet they'd be *really* interested in hearing all about that.'

Somewhere, deep down inside of me, Troy the Elephant is beating the shit out of that demon.

'And think about what that would do to the reputation of this company. If all of this came out in one final glorious chapter in the story of "Dumped Actually". And I write *fast*, Benedict. I bet I could have the story out there by the end of the day . . .'

Benedict tries to straighten up. I don't let him.

'Go ahead! Write what you want!' he spits. 'I'll sue the shit out of you! How dare you think you can come here and threaten me like this! How dare you *talk* to me like this!'

My eyes flick up over his shoulder, and stare directly at the board of directors. 'Oh, I wasn't talking to *you*, Benedict.'

The faces of eleven terrified old men stare right back at me.

I will take the look of horrified realisation on Benedict Montifore's face to my grave – along with every other momentous occasion that I've found myself a part of on this strange journey.

These old men know exactly what kind of damage a story about all of this could do to their reputations. The very same reputations that Benedict tried to play on to get them to vote his way.

I don't really need to say anything else. When you turn the tables on someone, it's vitally important you get out of there before they get a chance to rotate them back.

I straighten up and move away from Benedict swiftly. 'So, gentlemen, I think I've taken up more than enough of your time for one day. I'll allow you to take your vote without any further hindrance from me.' Then I give them all a very meaningful look. 'I'll be down in the car . . . waiting for the result.' The smile I give them doesn't touch my eyes. 'And thinking about what my next – or maybe final – story might be.'

I swivel on the ball of my foot and start towards the door. As I do, I catch sight of the look on Erica's face as she watches me go. Her mouth is agape.

I give her a little wink and march out of the boardroom, with that shark's smile still on my face.

Once I step into the lift that'll take me back down to the car park, though, the strength goes out of my legs completely. I managed to keep the pretense up for long enough, but now I'm on my own, and don't have to perform for anyone any more, reality is reasserting itself.

My hands start to shake uncontrollably, and I can feel my heart hammering out of my chest.

What the hell did I just do?

You took a stand, mate. And it was glorious!

Maybe so, but I'm now in severe danger of having an accident in my underpants.

The lift reaches the lower ground floor, and I emerge from it on wobbly legs. I make it back to the BMW and am incredibly grateful to find that Erica forgot to lock it in the rush to get upstairs. I collapse into the passenger seat and take several deep breaths.

All the techniques I learned at Lizzy Moore's mindfulness classes come back to me, and within ten minutes or so I have control of my body back.

I look up again as I hear the lift *bing* open and see Erica hurrying over to the car.

I climb out as she reaches it and go to meet her behind it. There's a hectic look on her face, and her hair has gone the deepest shade of red I think I've ever seen.

'They've . . . They've voted,' she says breathlessly.

'And?'

She shakes her head in disbelief. 'Nine to three against closing down Actual Life!' she cries with joy, and throws her arms around me. 'You did it, Ollie! You did it!'

'*We* did it,' I reply, my head buried in the wealth of her auburn hair.

Erica moves her head away, but doesn't release me from her embrace. 'I've never seen anything like that. I've never seen anyone stand up to Benedict like that.'

'You did,' I tell her. 'You stopped him on that boardroom table.'

'Well, maybe. But I've never shouted him down like that. I've never turned the tables on him like that, either.' She smiles at me. 'Who are you, and what have you done with Oliver Sweet?'

I smile back. 'Still me, I assure you. I nearly crapped my pants once I got out of there.'

Erica laughs.

And then she kisses me.

It's a strong kiss, full of a passion and desire I had no idea was there.

I respond in kind, because let's face it, I feel exactly the same way about her.

So . . .

Here it is, then.

A moment that has been coming down the tracks for a long time now, I think. A moment that anyone with a good handle on these things would have seen coming from at least two chapters of 'Dumped Actually' ago.

Erica is the right woman for me. And I'm pretty sure I'm the right man for her. I didn't realise it until this kiss, but I know I'm *right*. She probably feels the same way too. This kiss is certainly telling me as much.

Our relationship has been founded on mutual trust, respect and a strong friendship. One that not even someone as forceful and powerful as Benedict Montifore could undermine.

Without Erica, I doubt I would have been able to grow as much as I have done. Without her, there would be no version of Ollie Sweet who could do what he just did.

Of course I should be with her. *Of course* we should be together.

It just feels right, doesn't it?

It's just meant to be.

I stop kissing Erica, and gently push her away.

She looks confused. 'Ollie? I'm sorry. I thought . . . I thought you wanted this.'

I nod, tears forming in the corners of my eyes. 'I do, Erica. I truly do.' I take her hand. 'You're an amazing person. I would love to be with you . . . and for the first time in my life, I actually believe I *deserve* to be with someone like you.'

She's crying a little too, now. Her eyes glimmer with a light that I could fall into for a thousand years. 'So *be with me*, Ollie,' she says, her hand tightening on mine. 'Will you do that?'

I look into her eyes – a thousand possibilities, a thousand futures hanging in the balance of the words I say next.

'No.' I close my eyes. 'I can't, Erica. Not now.'

'Why?' The look of rejection in her eyes is unbearable.

'Because I'm not ready, Erica. I'm not . . . I'm not *there yet.*' I let go of her hand and step away. 'So much has changed for me . . . but I know I'm not done changing yet. Do you understand?'

Erica nods slowly, tears coursing down her cheeks.

'I would love to be with you more than anything – but if I do it now . . . if I do it too soon . . . it won't be right. It won't be right for you. And it won't be right for *me.*'

Erica breathes a deep sigh. 'I understand,' she says.

Well, of course she does. This is Erica Hilton we're talking about.

'I just need more time,' I explain. 'I'm on the right path, but it's one I have to be on *alone.* At least for now.'

I'm hating myself for saying all of this, but I equally know that what I'm saying is absolutely *correct.* If I can't be happy on my own, there's no way I can be happy with anyone else. I have to stand upright by myself, so I don't need to lean on someone else.

I say as much to Erica.

'Yeah. I get it,' she tells me, regretfully.

'I have to know I can be confident with myself, before I can be confident alongside someone like you,' I say, wiping the tears from my eyes.

Erica shakes her head and touches my cheek with a gentle hand. 'Such a shame. I don't think I've ever met a man like you before.'

'Likewise.'

Her eyebrows crease.

'I mean . . . I mean I've never met a woman like you!' I blurt out. 'I don't think you're a man, or anything. You're quite clearly a woman. I mean, look at you!' I don't quite point at Erica's breasts by way of demonstration, but I'm not far away from it.

And with this ridiculously awkward exchange, the spell is broken, and Oliver Sweet is back to his usual self. Which, for the first time, I don't think is such a bad thing.

Erica laughs. 'You are something else, Ollie.'

I smile ruefully. 'I know. There's not much I can do about it.'

She takes my hand again and looks deep into my eyes. 'I'm not going to wait for you, Ollie. I'm not that kind of woman.'

'Oh, I know that, Erica!' I reply, with a grin.

'But when you feel ready, and if I'm still available . . .'

She leaves it hanging there – an unspoken promise.

'Great. I'll remember that,' I tell her.

She lets go of my hand again, for the last time, and fishes out her car keys. 'And now, I think you and I need to go back to the office and tell everyone that they still have a job.'

I laugh. 'Sounds like a plan to me.' I think for a moment. 'And I have another story to write for "Dumped Actually" after we've done that. One about *doorways*.'

Erica gives me a puzzled look.

That's okay, though. She'll understand what I mean . . . once she reads all about it.

AFTERLUDE

'Hello, Troy,' I say to the elephant as he sniffs at my T-shirt.

'His name is not Troy, sir,' Manish says to me, with a puzzled expression on his face. 'His name is Sundar.'

I give the conservation officer a small grin. 'I know, Manish. He just reminds me of . . . another elephant called Troy that I once met.'

Manish looks perplexed by this. 'Troy is not a good name for an elephant, sir.'

'No. I know it's not,' I reply, looking out over the lush rainforest of Uttar Pradesh in northern India, where this elephant sanctuary is based.

I've been in the country for three days now.

It's been a whirlwind of interesting smells, loud noises and friendly locals. All of which I could spend six years writing about, and never truly capture the sheer cacophonous beauty of it all.

It's been a month since I kissed Erica Hilton and helped to save Actual Life. A month that has gone by in a flash of productivity and continued personal growth.

You'd be forgiven for thinking that things might have been a bit awkward between Erica and me, given what had happened in that car park, but you'd be wrong – thankfully.

Erica and I have more or less slipped back into the relationship we had before that climactic day. She's the boss, and I do what she says — most of the time, anyway.

But there is something else there, now.

An *understanding*, if you will. An unspoken agreement between us that there could be something more than just friendship, if things turn out well.

And, in a funny way, that tacit promise has actually brought us closer as friends. Given us a further bond to add to the strong ones that were already there.

Whether our friendship will have a chance to blossom into anything else is not for me to know right now. But it's not something I intend to dwell on. I've done far too much dwelling in my lifetime. The time for dwelling has most definitely *ceased*.

Mum and Dad drove me to the airport last week. Mum cried a little as I said goodbye to her at the gate, and Dad gave me a big hug. I almost couldn't bring myself to leave them.

I went to mindfulness class again with Wimsy. It's something I intend to keep doing for as long as I need to. He's still in the fledgling stages of his relationship with Lizzy, so I'm more than happy to provide a little moral support, while he works the whole thing out for himself. They look very nice together, though. In fact, they look like they were made for each other.

But they're taking it very slowly – and who can blame them? They're two people who have known the pain of a lost love – and finding a new one can be a difficult and slow process. I think they'll make it, though. I've seen the way they look at each other.

It's the same way I look at Erica these days.

But!

All of that is in the future . . .

One possible future, anyway.

Who knows what will happen?

Not me, certainly.

I've given up trying to predict what lies ahead for me.

I've also given up trying to understand the past.

What's done is done, and what will be . . . just *will be*. It'll happen, whether I spend time worrying about it or not.

I don't know if I will end up with Erica – or if I'll end up with anyone else for that matter.

But right now, I really *don't care*.

Does that sound strange to you? Does it sound a little cold?

It's not meant to. I can assure you my feelings for Erica are real, as I'm sure hers are for me.

But if there's one thing I've learned since that day at Thorn Manor – other than the fact you can't force a happy ending – it's that I can't spend my time caring so much about what other people feel. Or what other people think.

Not for the minute, anyway.

Not at this stage in my life.

Because right now, I have to think of *myself*. I have to think of Ollie Sweet, first and foremost. It's still hard to do, but I'm getting more and more used to it.

Because that's the only way I can make myself happy. That's the only way I can *love* myself.

(Not like that, don't be so disgusting.)

And then maybe, just maybe, when I've learned to love and accept who I am . . . I'll be ready to love someone else. *Properly*, for the first time.

And, hopefully, she'll have deep green eyes and red hair that seems to have a life of its own.

But we will see.

We will just have to *wait* and *see*.

Right at this moment, though, Sundar the elephant is kneeling down to allow me to climb on to his back. He looks relatively happy about this, I think. I am pretty light and inoffensive, when you get right down to it.

I clamber up on to Sundar's back and gaze out once again at the lush rainforest in front of me. Then I reach into my pocket and pull out my iPhone. When I pop the earbuds into my ears, the gentle sound of a sitar fills them.

Yes.

This is *perfect*.

This is just what I dreamed about.

And sometimes – at the right time – dreams need to be lived out on your own.

I pat Sundar's big grey head and smile.

'Off we go, my friend,' I say. 'Let's see what the future holds.'

ACKNOWLEDGMENTS

As ever, writing a book requires a lot of support from the people around you. They might not actually be there when you're tapping away feverishly on the keyboard, but without them, I can honestly say none of the stories I've written would ever see the light of day.

So, thanks – as ever – to my wife, Gemma. Every time I've been dumped in my life, it was entirely worth it, because it eventually led to her.

Thanks to my mother, Judy, and my sister, Sharon, for their support. And to all of my close friends as well . . . you know who you are.

More thanks go to everyone at Amazon Publishing, and to my agent, Jon, for continuing to have faith in these silly little stories that I insist on writing.

And finally, as ever, there's you . . . the person good enough to buy and read this novel. Without you, there really is no point in doing any of this. If you ever dumped me, I don't know what I'd do.

ABOUT THE AUTHOR

Photo © 2017 Chloe Waters

Nick Spalding is the bestselling author of twelve novels, two novellas and two memoirs. Nick worked in media and marketing for most of his life before turning his energy to his genre-spanning humorous writing. He lives in the south of England with his wife.